PENGUIN BOOKS

THE FINISHER

RuNyx is a *New York Times*, *USA Today* and international bestselling author of romance. Her stories range across subgenres from dark contemporary to gothic to historical to fantasy and more, and are currently being translated into over 10 languages.

Her pen name has a very special meaning to her. When she's not writing, she's reading, traveling, meditating, daydreaming, and most of all, procrastinating.

THE FINISHER

RuNyx

PENGUIN BOOKS

PENGUIN BOOKS

UK | USA | Canada | Ireland | Australia
India | New Zealand | South Africa

Penguin Books is part of the Penguin Random House group of companies
whose addresses can be found at global.penguinrandomhouse.com

Penguin Random House UK,
One Embassy Gardens, 8 Viaduct Gardens, London SW11 7BW

penguin.co.uk
global.penguinrandomhouse.com

Published in Penguin Books 2026
001

Copyright © RuNyx, 2025

The moral right of the author has been asserted

Penguin Random House values and supports copyright. Copyright fuels creativity, encourages diverse voices, promotes freedom of expression and supports a vibrant culture. Thank you for purchasing an authorised edition of this book and for respecting intellectual property laws by not reproducing, scanning or distributing any part of it by any means without permission. You are supporting authors and enabling Penguin Random House to continue to publish books for everyone. No part of this book may be used or reproduced in any manner for the purpose of training artificial intelligence technologies or systems. In accordance with Article 4(3) of the DSM Directive 2019/790, Penguin Random House expressly reserves this work from the text and data mining exception.

Set in 9.92/14.06pt Adobe Caslon Pro
Typeset by Six Red Marbles UK, Thetford, Norfolk

Printed and bound in Great Britain by Clays Ltd, Elcograf S.p.A.

The authorised representative in the EEA is Penguin Random House Ireland,
Morrison Chambers, 32 Nassau Street, Dublin D02 YH68

A CIP catalogue record for this book is available from the British Library

ISBN: 978–1–911–74638–6

Penguin Random House is committed to a sustainable future
for our business, our readers and our planet. This book is
made from Forest Stewardship Council® certified paper.

To everyone who ever made a cocoon of their blanket, and never wanted to leave the bed. This is for you. There is a rainbow beyond the gray. Just wait for the clouds to part.

Author's Note

This is the fourth book in the Dark Verse series. Although the book deals with a new couple, there are characters and events from the previous books that heavily influence the plot in this. Reading the series in order (The Predator, The Reaper, The Emperor) is recommended for the best reading experience. This is NOT a standalone.

Please note that this book has a happy-for-now and not a settled epilogue. The reason for that is the timeline. Alpha and Zephyr's big epilogue falls after the final book in the series, and for that reason, it will be included in a novella released after the series is complete.

If you have read the previous books, this one will get darker.

This book includes graphic violence, foul language, and sexual content recommended only for 18+.

I also want to list a few trigger warnings of the darker themes. This book contains scenes of character death, murder, arson, torture, solicitation and sex work, depressive episodes, post-traumatic stress disorder, human trafficking and mentions of human slavery, mentions of violence against a minor, mentions of sexual assault of adults and minors, mentions of illegal dogfights.

If reading about any of these is in any way detrimental to your mental health, I sincerely urge you to pause.

If you continue with the book, I hope you enjoy the journey.

Thank you.

Book Playlist

Scars - Boy Epic
Scars - Tove Lo
Scars - I Prevail
Believer - Imagine Dragons
Be Mine - Ofenbach
Bad Things - Jace Everett
Friction - Imagine Dragons
Fisherman - The Peach Kings
Beat the Devil's Tattoo - Black Rebel Motorcycle Club
Looking At Me - Sabrina Carpenter
Glowing in the Dark - The Girl and The Dreamcatcher
High - Whethan ft. Dua Lipa
I Love Rock N Roll - Joan Jett & The Blackhearts
Teeth - 5 Seconds of Summer
Bom Bidi Bom - Nick Jons ft. Nicki Minaj
My Oh My - Camila Cabello
Glow - Ella Henderson
Capital Letters - Hailee Steinfield
Love is a Bitch - Two Feet
Give 'em Hell - Everybody Loves an Outlaw
On My Way - Alan Walker

THE FINISHER

Push - Royal Deluxe
Pray For Me - The Weeknd ft. Kendrick Lamar
Pray - JRY ft. RuthAnne
Rockabye - Clean Bandit ft. Sean Paul
Skin to Bone - Linkin Park
Soldier - Samantha Jade
The Wolf - The Spencer Lee Band
Making Love on the Mountain - The Woodlands
Side to Side - Ariana Grande
Full Playlist On Spotify

PROLOGUE

It was his third murder that week.

His fiftieth in total, over the course of years. This one was special, something he would celebrate later.

The woman's body lay torn open in the dingy alley, her heels askew, her lipstick smudged, her eyes vacant.

He loved that look in their eyes, the unseeing gaze up at an open sky they would never fly in because he was their god in their last moments. They called him the *Fortis Finisher*. He preferred 'Lord of Death', but nobody really called him that. They would someday though, when all the murders got connected to him and the corrupt cops stopped sleeping.

Smoke seeped out from the crack between the buildings in tendrils, a light bulb flickered somewhere, and the butcher? He wiped his knife on a torn part of her skirt, the blood soaking into the white fabric as a souvenir he would stash with the rest of them. He was still high on the kill, on the chase, on her desecrated body nude to the elements. The incoming rain would wash away all evidence, the cops would never give a shit about another whore gone missing, and the one man who owned the city would go down for it, framed for the crimes.

And the butcher—he would then be the entire city's god.

It was the *perfect* plan.

A movement in the shadows at the end of the street had him stilling. He squinted, trying to see what had shifted the thick air, and saw a silhouette leaning against the wall. The same silhouette he had been seeing at every kill for the last two weeks.

A sound pierced the silence. A lighter flicked open. A flame, barely showing a hand, before being extinguished.

The same.

Fear was not an emotion he was familiar with, but watching the silhouette in the dark, uncaring, unmoving, observing him, stalking him for two weeks, a frisson went down his spine.

No, it couldn't be the myth.

He said that to himself every time. A myth to many, a truth to some who never lived to tell the tale, the name everyone deep in the underworld knew to be wary of. Was that him? No, no way. The man wasn't real. It was possibly just a homeless guy who had seen everything and was scared to come out, or maybe even an undercover cop. Nothing else.

"Get lost before I cut you open," the butcher called out, glad his voice didn't have the tremor he felt.

No sound. No movement. Nothing but eyes watching him quietly.

It scared him, emasculated him, and he didn't like that. He, who had terrorized and killed over fifty women, felt fear watching a silhouette in the shadows because of a fucking underworld myth.

Sirens sounded somewhere in the city, far away at this time of the night. A nightclub down the block pounded the music as its door opened and closed.

And he just heard his own breathing, angry at being afraid, angry at feeling hunted.

He took a step back.

The silhouette didn't move; just kept watching him.

Just a scared homeless guy, that was all.

He pocketed his knife and backed out of the alley, slowly checking to see no one else saw him, and began to sprint away from the crime scene. But just before he turned off the block, paranoid, he looked back at the mouth of the alley like he did every time.

And like each time, a man in dark clothes stood in the shadows, leaning against the wall, playing with a lighter, and watching him run like a coward into the night.

The Shadow Man, a bigger monster than him, was real.

PART 1

THE CRUST

*"Love looks not with the eyes, but with the mind,
And therefore is winged Cupid painted blind."*

-William Shakespeare

EIGHTEEN YEARS AGO

ZEPHYR, 10

Broken bones hurt.

Zephyr struggled to lie still, alone in the general hospital room. The nice nurse had just made her mama and papa leave her behind. They promised to come back in the morning, but they had to get home to take care of her new sister, Zenith. Zephyr called her Zen. She was five, and really pretty and quiet, but she loved playing with Zephyr, and Zephyr loved her already.

She wanted to go home.

She sniffled, wiping her nose with her hand. It was cold, and her sides hurt.

"Why's a pretty girl like you crying?"

The older woman's voice from the bed across from hers made Zephyr look up with her red eyes. *There hadn't been any beds in the children's area of the hospital*, the nurse had told her parents. So, she'd put her in with an older lady for the two nights. She looked really thin and sick.

"I want"—Zephyr hiccupped—"to go home."

"You will, sweetheart." The lady smiled at her. She looked like she was her mama's age, maybe a bit older. "Your parents will take you tomorrow."

Zephyr nodded. Yes, she just had to stay two nights. "Will your parents take you too?"

The woman's smile turned sad. "No, I'm not going home, although my son wants to take me."

"Then why don't you go with him?" Zephyr leaned to the side, her little mind distracted by the older lady with the tubes in her hands.

The lady laughed, but her voice broke. "I don't have much time in this world, sweetie. I'm just sad I'll be leaving him behind with no one to care about him."

That was a concept Zephyr could not understand. Everyone had family, didn't they? She had so many uncles and aunts and cousins she barely remembered all their names. "He has no one else?"

The woman shook her head sadly.

Her heart broke. Everyone should have a family.

Zephyr jumped down from the bed, her side hurting a bit, and wobbled over to the older woman, extending her pinkie out. "I can be there for him. I promise. What's his name?"

The woman laughed again, a tear trailing down her face, and hooked her rough pinkie with Zephyr's. "You're a sweet child."

Zephyr nodded. She liked being sweet. "His name?" she asked, stuck on the boy who didn't have a family.

"Alessandro. Alessandro Villanova. Alpha."

CHAPTER 1

ZEPHYR, PRESENT DAY

He was cheating on her.

Zephyr was a hundred percent—all right, maybe not a hundred, she tended to overexaggerate things in her own head, perhaps ninety percent—sure that opening the door of the seedy little dungeon hole he'd led her to, for a fight of all things, would reveal him with some bimbo. Or maybe she wouldn't be a bimbo. Maybe she would be some incredibly nice but naive girl who fell for his handsome looks and witty charm without realizing he was in a relationship with a curvaceous hairstylist. A curvaceous hairstylist he'd told numerous times that she needed to lose some of the curves and she'd be *'so fucking sexy, babe'*. The curvaceous hairstylist, aka her, aka Zephyr de la Vega, aka the biggest idiot on the planet to ever imagine there could be a future with him when she wasn't in love. But god, she'd been tired of being single at twenty-eight, with everyone telling her she should be with someone.

And though she didn't love him, she *was* in a relationship, and she had her pride, which was exactly why she stood outside the door; dread, anger, and certainty pooling in the pit of her stomach.

You're sexy, you're beautiful, you're a goddess, she kept chanting, her belief in her own words slightly lesser compared to the morning when she'd woken up with a good life, in a mostly-okay relationship with the perfect guy. The perfect guy who, she was sure, was railing someone behind the door.

"Oh, yes," a feminine wail from inside made the wince on her face tighten, her hand gripping the dirty-looking handle that made her want to scrub it clean.

"And now, the finisher is in the cage!"

The crowd roared from the arena beyond the dingy corridor she was in. It smelled like something had died in there, and something probably had. She couldn't be sure. Her boyfriend had traveled to the industrial district for this shady fight, and she'd followed him, only to be lost in the crowd with two scary-looking bouncer-type dudes who'd looked at her suspiciously. She wasn't surprised, though. In her colorful floral dress reminiscent of spring, she was as out of place in the dungeon hole as an elephant at an airport. Wait, did elephants even go to airports? How did they transfer them overseas in case of emergencies, though? Maybe they—

Focus, Zee.

She took a deep breath, halting the internal rambling. She did that a lot, ramble that was. Word vomit was a common affliction where she was concerned, especially when her nerves were taut. And they were very, very taut as she stood in the corridor she'd found her boyfriend walking into. Because if she found what she knew she was going to find, she'd be single again. Moreover, it would also strain things with her parents because her mother already considered him a son-in-law, though her father was pretty *'meh'* about him.

Gritting her teeth, calling on her nerves to calm down, she tugged on the handle, only to open the door a few inches to see a man's bare ass pumping into a woman against the dirty wall. The fact that she was more concerned about the woman's hygiene than the fact that she recognized that butt was a bit revelationary.

So this was what being cheated upon felt like.

Huh.

Kind of anti-climactic, if she was being honest.

Zephyr had always wondered in the back of her mind, seeing it in movies or reading it in books, the cliché of the woman finding her lover's infidelity or the bride being jilted at the altar, and she'd always wondered if the tears had been because of the hurt, the humiliation, the anger, or the loss of that idea of perfection. Maybe it was all of them. She couldn't exactly pinpoint.

Weirdly, as she watched the very nice ass pump away, she only felt a sense of *'I told you so'* within herself. Had a part of her always known he was scum underneath the pretty? Had she written it off as her own insecurities rearing their head? Perhaps. And though, surprisingly, she wasn't as hurt as she'd thought she would be, she was pissed, getting more so with each oblivious pump. And being pissed was not a good look on her, especially because she did irrational shit in the heat of the moment.

She locked her jaw, trying to contain her anger, but with each thrust, she remembered each little way he'd made her feel inadequate, made her feel just a bit less. Every 'don't eat that', every targeted comment about thigh gaps being sexy while jokingly telling her she'd never get one, every exasperated sigh about her quirky hair colors whenever she changed them. She'd been with him for over two years, and now looking back, all she saw was a bunch of gaslighting and good, old dickery. And the fact that she'd always prided herself on being a good lover, his penis falling in another woman's vagina was a hit to that belief, more than she wanted to admit.

She wanted to feel adequate. She wanted to feel beautiful. She wanted to feel desirable.

The last man who'd made her feel all those things—

Don't think about him.

She wanted to feel anything but what she was feeling as she watched the man she'd been thinking of settling down with. And she wanted to make him feel like shit. Yeah, she was petty like that. God, she was an idiot. But at least she was an idiot who'd dodged a bullet. Stepping back from the door, Zephyr looked at the dirty handle, unsure what she was going to do exactly.

"Alpha! Alpha! Alpha!"

The chanting of the crowd drew her attention, suddenly making her heart stop, taking her entire focus away from the scene toward the arena.

Alpha?

Did they say *Alpha?*

No, it couldn't be.

She looked at the door leading to the arena, her palms clammy, her heart pounding. It was an unusual name, and she'd only known of one man who'd used it. He'd been a fighter too, but it couldn't be him. That was almost a decade ago...

Unnerved, her cheating boyfriend forgotten by the stronger memory elicited by that name, she followed the noise of the spectators and exited the foul-smelling corridor to a slightly better-smelling sort of open space. It smelled like places that had never seen the sunlight did—slightly dank, slightly musty, slightly sweaty. It wasn't a place for a girl like her—one from a nice family, dressed in a bright floral dress, with hair she'd dyed pink recently because her mother was certain something good was going to happen to her soon.

'Just a feeling, baby,' her mama had told her affectionately.

She'd been waiting for that good thing. Was this it? Was it him, back again? It couldn't be. God, she was a *gigantic* idiot.

Watching the spectacle in front of her, she tried to see for herself if it was *her* Alpha before she had to deal with real life.

The fight was probably illegal, which was most likely why it was in such a dungeon-like space in the industrial district, better known as the creepy no-go zone of the city. This was the part of the city kids who wanted to play scary games came to. Mostly, it was just famous for seedy criminal activities. She just hoped no one got raided because the prison wasn't on her bucket list.

The dungeon, if it could be called that, was huge and dark and not like any basement she'd ever seen. The walls were solid rock and the ceiling super high, with some huge lights that would honestly be painful to look at directly. The central space was a caged-off ring and the crowd of mostly men and a few women surrounded the cage, with some bouncer-type scary men against the walls, keeping an eye on everyone.

"Break his arm, Alpha!" the guy immediately to her right yelled loud enough to wake the dead.

"Spray his fucking blooooood!"

"Knock him out and I'll suck your dick, you beast!" That came from a particularly enthusiastic lady somewhere in the room. Zephyr cringed. As long as it wasn't *her* Alpha, the lady could suck whatever she wanted. She'd always been irrationally possessive of him.

A violent crash of a body hitting the metal of the cage broke her thoughts, drawing her eyes toward the main event.

Her eyebrows hit her hairline.

A shirtless man, no, a shirtless *giant* had another smaller guy (who would've been huge on his own, but looked tiny in comparison) pinned against the cage from the back. She could see what the lady had been talking about. A beast, indeed. He had the smaller guy's arm twisted behind him at an awkward angle, the other holding him down like a dog. But it wasn't just the fight that had Zephyr's attention.

It was his eyes, or rather his one eye. He wore an honest-to-god eye patch over his right eye, his left glimmering a light color she couldn't really make out from afar. Eye patches, in her head, were things pirates wore to look badass, as they raided ships and claimed maidens in historical romances. In this day and age, people usually just put in a fake prosthetic eye if they needed. The fact that this veritable giant wore an eye patch to a fight with an opponent of seemingly good vision . . . *damn*.

But he looked nothing like the boy from her fateful memories.

"Fuck him up gooooood!!!"

Jesus, the guy next to her was really, really bloodthirsty.

"I want him so bad!" another woman's voice said from somewhere. "Can you believe he's not fucking anyone for over a year now? I've tried to hit him up so many times."

"Girl, he scares the living shit out of me. No way I'm going near that."

"Just imagine the sex, though. I've heard he makes you praise the lord."

Zephyr listened to the conversation intently, trying to place if this was him.

She tried not to let the crowd jostle her smaller frame as she watched the fight from the back, her mind occupied for the moment, the weight on her chest heavy.

The beast stepped back from the smaller guy, setting him free, putting his entire frame in her line of sight to her for the first time. A long scar went down from his hairline, under his eye patch, down to the corner of his mouth, permanently pulling it down in a scary frown on one side. A million more scars littered his torso with some tattoos over a million muscles she didn't know a human could possess. And for such a large man, he moved with a fluidity that belied him.

Raw, brutal strength—that's what he was.

Alpha, that's what the crowd had called him, and she could see why. The more she watched him, the more fascinated she became, the more the urge to confirm his identity seeped into her pores.

Shortie turned to him, swinging his arm out, his fist aimed at the black patch, and Zephyr could feel her breath locking in her throat, suddenly invested in not wanting the beast to get hurt. Before she could blink, in a move that she wouldn't have thought he could have caught with his limited peripheral vision, he blocked Shortie and delivered a sharp uppercut on his side, possibly breaking a rib with the force behind it.

Oof.

Shortie gripped his side and howled as the crowd went crazy. Yeah, that would've hurt.

Just as she winced in sympathy, as Shortie stayed bent on the cage floor, this Alpha cracked his neck and looked out at the crowd for the first time. She saw that singular gaze glance over the gathering and pause on her. It was probably her shock of pink hair that caught his eye or her dress. She didn't know, and she didn't really think.

She *couldn't* think.

It was the same heaviness. There had always been something... *intense* about being looked at by him. Something so heavy she could feel it weighing down on her chest, escalating her heartbeats, making her palms clammy. A bead of sweat rolled down her neck into her cleavage, and dear lord, she remembered what it had been like being looked at by him with both his eyes.

It felt like him.

Tears burned her eyes.

So fucking long.

It lasted for a few seconds before he turned to his opponent again.

"Zee? What the hell are you doing here?"

The words made her eyes flutter shut for a second as reality crashed back on her. She'd hoped for a little more time before the confrontation. For all her outgoing, exuberant personality, confrontations were something she could never get herself to handle. She hated them. And whenever the need arose for one, she avoided them completely. This wasn't how she would've imagined it. She would've gone home and sent him a break-up text.

Now, there was a confrontation to be had and she had no interest in it, her entire attention on the man in the cage. Blowing out a breath, she slowly turned around to face the man she'd be making her ex in three seconds.

"We're done, Alec," she told him, taking in his very handsome profile. He was hot, there was no denying it, and he knew it too.

She saw his dark brows slash down as they did when he was about to mansplain something to her. "What do you mean?"

"Meaning you can go fuck yourself or fuck another girl like the one in the back. We're finished."

"Zee—"

She held her hand up. "Save it."

The crowd went wild at something happening in the cage, and Zephyr felt her emotions crash all over the place. She didn't want to deal with Alec, but he knew he was caught and he couldn't talk himself out of it, which meant he was going to go on the offensive. In moments, a predictable sneer curled his lips, and Zephyr braced herself.

"It's too late, Zee," he reminded her, as though she needed it. "You'll be twenty-nine in a month, and your grandmother's fund will be frozen out if you don't marry me. I was going to propose to you on your birthday. One fuck isn't worth all that."

Her throat tightened even as rage infused her veins. Yes, her grandmother's fund. Her lovely grandmother had never married and regretted it her entire life, so she'd made sure that her granddaughter wouldn't make the same mistake and find herself a life partner. She'd left some old family heirlooms with a clause that Zephyr had to be married by her twenty-ninth birthday to access them.

Now, Zephyr was pretty non-mercenary, and didn't care enough for the money to get married. But the family heirlooms had been in her father's line for over five generations, and the sneaky old lady had known her mother would rather get her married at gunpoint than let something so valuable to their heritage go to charity. Alec had been a catch. She was a middle-class girl, and he was a good-looking man, came from money, and had influence in the city. She loved her parents and they loved her, and she couldn't deny that seeing Alec's profile had made them feel more satisfied about their relationship. Eventual access to her grandmother's fund was a side benefit. It was probably the only reason she'd considered settling down with him.

"And let's face it, Zee," Alec continued with a soft, almost placating smile that would've looked good had she not wanted to punch it off his face. "You won't get a better offer. You're not a beauty like your sister. Finding a rich, powerful husband like me is a rare opportunity for you."

The audacity of this man truly galled her. Forget asking for forgiveness, there wasn't an ounce of remorse or shame on his face. And like a true narcissist, he'd turned it around on her and her so-called inadequacy, and tried to make her feel insecure using her own sister. That was possibly the stupidest thing he'd tried to do. Her sister was her best friend, her outside beauty not even half of her inside. She loved Zen and was proud of her every damn day. Trying to drive a wedge between them was idiotic.

A loud bell rang from the back and she turned to see the fight end, the beast clearly the winner as he walked to a corner of the room to talk to some bald guy. She looked at his back, marred and tangled with scars, and wondered what had happened to him.

Turning to face her ex for one last time, she stepped closer and patted his chest.

"We're done, Alec," she declared as the crowd slowly headed to the opposite side of the room. "I'd marry anyone but you."

He chuckled. "You're crazy."

Zephyr smiled. Finally, something he'd said right. "I am. I was also the best you had. Now go and fuck everyone you want. I know I will."

Before he could say another word, she turned on her heel, her target locked on a massive back now covered in a black t-shirt, the fabric stretched tautly across it. As she cut through the crowd, she knew Alec was watching her, and as she headed in the direction she was heading in, she could feel the eyes of the others fall upon her.

And none of it mattered, because if this was *him,* if she'd found him after ten years . . .

She had to know. She needed to know. Fuck everyone else.

She was almost three feet from the beast and the guy he was speaking with when she saw the muscles in his back stiffen, his neck turning to sear her with one golden eye.

Liquid, molten gold.

Gold that had once seared her veins.

Him.

Her step faltered for a split second.

He was larger now, more intimidating, and not just because of his massive size. It was the way the ugly scar slashed from his hairline, over his missing eye, across his cheek, and down to the corner of his lips, disappearing under his short beard. It was the way he was wearing a leather patch over his eye and still sensed someone in his personal space before they announced themselves. It was the way he held more power in that singular gaze than most people did in their entire bodies. He hadn't lost that with his right eye.

His face showed nothing, no recognition. Was it because of the hair? She'd kept it blonde back then, and she'd definitely gained some curves in the time in between. But had she really become that unrecognizable? She was completely out of her depth, but she'd already jumped off-board, and hell if she wasn't going to swim.

Inhaling with purpose, she closed the distance between them even as he watched her like a hawk, and jumped.

His hands instinctively caught her as she wrapped her legs around his waist, her hands gripping his shoulders. He was solid, immovable, and holding her up with an ease she'd never, ever experienced again in the last decade.

Without giving him a moment to ask anything, she slanted her face and kissed him, her lips trembling with emotion.

He stiffened, his grip on her waist tightening slightly as he pulled back a bit, something akin to curiosity emanating from him. She didn't know what his sex life was like, but she doubted he had random girls climbing his frame and planting one on him. Or maybe he did.

"Please," she whispered in the space between their mouths, knowing it was that girl inside her who had kissed a wild boy speaking. She needed to believe for herself that this was him, feel it in her bones, feel it in their kiss.

His golden gaze considered her for a small second before suddenly he shifted her, holding her up with only one arm under her ass, the other hand still wrapped in tape, fisting her hair and pulling her neck back in a move that was sheer *power*.

Raw, unadulterated power.

Zephyr didn't know what she'd expected, but this hadn't been it. Not the way he'd taken control, not the way her heart began to pound a frantic beat in a response to it, not the way her core clenched. It was as though the tug on her scalp and his taped hand around her hair had found something primitive deep inside her and poked it into a strange awareness.

He'd not done that before.

His mouth came closer to hers, and she waited, unable to move her neck and close the distance. In essence, she was immobilized and it did something to her. Up close, she could make out the slight sheen of sweat over his bronzed skin, the depth of his scar tissue, the intricate detailing on his eye patch. It was fancier than she'd expected, some kind of leather. She wondered what it felt like to touch. Lord, she was crazy. She'd just seen this man pummel another, and there she was on him, like an orangutan with its favorite tree.

"What's a little rainbow like you doing in a shithole like this?" he murmured as he inhaled the side of her neck, so softly she felt his words more than heard them. She knew she had a colorful personality, but she'd never been called a rainbow before, and the way he said it was nice, really nice.

But it also told her something—he didn't recognize her.

Nothing.

Something akin to hurt and disappointment crashed over her. What did she expect, though? He had clearly lived through a lot, and it had been ten years.

"It's a long story," she told him softly, swallowing the turmoil of emotions inside her.

He didn't move, just observed her.

Zephyr closed her eyes in mortification. The last hour had been one hit to her heart after another. She should probably just go home and have a good cry.

She began to move her legs, and his grip on her hair tightened, freezing her in place.

She could feel the heat emanating from his body. He smelled like the wilderness, like what she imagined the dark depths of the wild forest beyond the city smelled like—sweat, wood, musk, and something unknown. With her eyes closed, she could imagine him in another time, another place, hunting in the wild, coming to his cave and fucking his woman raw. That was the word. Raw. She'd never smelled anyone so raw. Most boys during her teens had drowned themselves in body sprays that advertised women falling on them if they used it, and Alec always put on cologne that probably cost more than what she earned in a month. Alpha had always smelled like he looked. *Raw.*

Before she could think another thought, he angled her head with his grip and slashed his mouth upon hers.

Her heartbeat fractured.

Coffee.

Mint.

Him.

His taste exploded on her tongue, his mouth moving over hers expertly, tongue gliding along with hers in a way that made her thighs tighten around his torso in memory.

He could kiss. Like really, really kiss. He always could.

She felt the scar tissue on the side of his mouth press into hers, the sensation not unpleasant but one she was unfamiliar with, his short beard creating subtle friction that really did something for her. She'd never have thought she'd be into facial hair, but damn ...

She wrapped her arms around his neck, unconsciously pressing her body as close as she could to his, her hips grinding over his solid muscles without thought, rubbing her in a way that was decadent.

It wasn't a kiss; it was an *experience*, and she felt like a virgin having her first with him again. New sensations coursed through her body, the promise of something dark and delicious and depraved on the horizon that had everything feminine in her unfurl and open and accept his pillaging of her being. It was a kiss, both new and familiar, like a melody she'd heard long ago and never forgot. And her core knew; he would fuck now like he kissed, and god she wanted to know what that would be like. Would he hold her down and slam her into the bed? Would he pull her hair back and devour her mouth as he plunged inside her? Would he mark her skin with his teeth?

A shiver coursed down her body, her nipples tightening to hard points against his chest.

A romantic at heart, she'd always believed in love at the first meeting. Her parents had been a love-at-first-meeting couple. One of her colleagues was a love-at-first-meeting couple. Even her grandparents on her dad's side had been a couple like that. And she'd found that with him a long time ago, and kissing him kindled it back to life—the emotions, the attraction, the longing, and the pain. *Oh, the sweet, bitter pain.*

He was her love at first meeting. And she didn't know who he was now, but he was *hers*. He'd always been hers.

A few whistles rent the air, someone catcalled, and she blinked her eyes open, looking at the man who had tilted her world on its axis again. Suddenly remembering they weren't alone, Zephyr pulled back and looked at him, her breasts heaving, flushed against his chest.

His mouth was wet and slightly pink from her gloss, and he seemed unbothered as he watched her.

She wiggled down back to her own feet, tilting her neck back, because lord, the man was blessed by the vertical gods and she was not. His height seemed to be the only recognizable trait from the old him—the bulk, the scars, the injuries, and the danger were all new.

He didn't recognize her, so she needed to begin again. "Thanks."

The unscarred side of his lip twitched a bit, his golden eye going behind her. "You with him?" he asked. His voice was ... more masculine than she remembered. She really didn't know how else to put it. The baritone was deeper, the tenor was graver, the sound a little huskier. It was a voice she could imagine commanding a room of people, a voice she could imagine whispering dirty things to a lover, a voice of dark leather and wild power.

She turned around to see who he was referring to, finding Alec fuming in the crowd. She'd forgotten about him.

"No." Her refusal was loud, more high-pitched than she'd wanted. Her nose got warm as she got a bit flustered.

The bald guy from earlier came up from the side, watching the two of them with slight amusement. "That was . . . interesting."

Alpha ignored his comment. "Hector will drop you home safely." Hector, the bald guy, gave her a grin.

Alpha's hand, still taped, came up to her chin, holding her in place, his single-eyed gaze intense before he dropped a lingering kiss on her lips. "You kiss good, rainbow."

Something in the cavity of her chest shriveled at his lack of recognition, while something else bloomed with the sheer joy of finding him again.

Zephyr shook it off and let her lips curl into a smile. "You too, sexy."

She felt his amusement at that. With a chuck under her chin, he strode away from the arena, leaving her standing behind as he had ten years ago, waiting for him to turn around and come back to her again.

Her first love, the one she never recovered from. Love, the kind she could give everything and replenish yet again to give more, the kind that snuck in under the radar, and one day, it was there, mixed into the cement of her foundations. Love that went so deep into the bones it changed the course of being.

He had been that love.

He was back.

And he remembered nothing.

She was *screwed.*

CHAPTER 2

ZEPHYR

"Shit, Zee. What now?"

Zephyr glanced at Zenith seated in front of the mirror, oiling her dark, long hair. Zenith—who was five years younger than Zephyr—was what everyone called a stunner. She had a naturally petite, modelesque figure that everyone in their social circle appreciated, soulful eyes that made men line up the streets, and mannerisms that would put a queen to shame. But appearances were deceptive. Zephyr knew she was also the girl who had tried to kill herself when she was younger for reasons unknown, the girl who fought some kind of demons in her mind every day, the girl who had immersed herself in social justice and working for a nonprofit organization—Survivors of Los Fortis—that dealt with victims of assault and abuse and rehabilitated them. If there were angels on earth, her sister was one of them.

Zephyr volunteered with her on the weekends, styling and cutting the hair of the ladies at the SLF center. People always underestimated the power getting a makeover could have on one's psyche. She had seen women shed tears after a haircut, women with harsh, traumatic pasts shedding their grief, their histories, their conditioning after cutting their hair, if only for a moment. It empowered them, made them feel like a newer version of themselves who didn't have to let their pasts dictate their futures for a second, and while it wasn't a big contribution in the grand scheme of things, Zephyr loved that first emotional catharsis they had immediately afterward.

She pulled her sunflower earrings out of her lobes and dumped them on the dresser in her room as Zen watched her with curious eyes. Zephyr had spent the last few minutes updating her sister as they both went about their nightly rituals.

"I don't know," she answered, walking over to the single, large window in her room, the white gossamer-thin drapes flying inward with the wind. Her room was a reflection of who she felt she was inside—colorful and chaotic, with pretty printed sheets on a queen-sized bed, white painted walls with a plethora of photos, indoor plants sprucing up the corners, and knick-knacks from everywhere scattered haphazardly all around.

Rainbow.

He'd called her a rainbow. Once upon a time, he'd called her sunshine, back when her hair had been blonde. She liked rainbow better. Looking around, she realized her room reflected that name. Her sister's room was the opposite, all organized and minimalistic and done in pastels.

They both rented an apartment in the city, at walking distance from both her salon and the SLF center. Their parents lived in the suburbs where they'd grown up, where her father still worked at the same accounting agency he'd been working at for thirty years. Daily commute for work had become both expensive and troublesome when she'd started at the salon, so Zephyr had moved out soon after, her sister following once she'd finished her graduation.

Flopping down on her bed, Zephyr started putting lotion on her arms, while Zen massaged her own scalp with her fingers, the routine comforting for both of them after a long day.

"I can't believe he doesn't remember you." Her sister rubbed the strands. "By the way, you need to tell Mama about Alec. She needs to stop planning your wedding in her head with the toad." Zen had always been anti-Alec.

Zephyr snorted. "Fat chance of that. She wants me 'happy and married and rich', with a son-in-law she can boast about to the ladies at the club."

"Also true."

They stayed silent for a while, contemplating. Zephyr knew there was no way she was going to go through with the relationship with Alec now, but she didn't know how to shield her parents from the fallout. Knowing Alec, she knew he would take a rejection as a hit to his pride, possibly making her mother lose the social status she'd gained by association. For Zephyr, he would probably have her name smeared all over the city. She wouldn't be surprised if he came after Zen's reputation too, especially knowing she was adopted into the family. It wasn't looking good. She had a wonderful life, a great family, and though her mother could be very influenced by what others said sometimes, she was a great mother.

"Forget Alec for a second." Zen's voice broke through her musings. "I still can't believe you saw Alpha, *your* Alpha, after so long. I mean, what are the odds that you'd follow Alec and find your lost love? I thought he'd left town. You really saw him?"

Zephyr flushed slightly, the kiss fresh in her memory. It did seem insane in retrospect.

"Saw him. Jumped and kissed him, and then he kissed me. The

way he fisted my hair ..." She trailed off as she fanned her face dramatically.

Zen fanned herself too, grinning. "He sounds sexier. And Alec really saw that?"

"Alec and at least fifty other random strangers."

"Damn. What's he like now?" Zen asked, a mildly dreamy look on her face. That was the one thing they both had in common—they were both hopeless romantics, Zephyr a bit more hardcore and Zen a bit softer, but hopeless romantics nonetheless. Moreover, Zen was the only other soul who knew about Alpha.

"Huge," Zephyr recalled, her heartbeats escalating at the memory. "Solid. He just held me with one arm the entire time. Can you imagine?"

"The toad would never!" Zen giggled, tightening her hair in a bun. "Is it still there? The spark?"

Yeah, it was there all right. "It was more intense. I don't know if that's because we've both matured now, but it's ... there. I know he felt it."

"Tell me more. Let me live vicariously through you."

Zephyr finished putting the lotion on. "He's really scarred now. I can't even imagine what he must've gone through to get them all. He was handsome, but now, he's ... wild. Dangerous. Someone you don't want to mess with. He's also got an eye patch."

Zen stilled, her arms up in her hair. "Eye patch?"

"I swear I'm not making that up." Zephyr chuckled, capping the bottle of lotion and setting it on her nightstand. "He looked like a pirate, except hotter and cleaner and smelled divine. Though I don't know what pirates smelled like—possibly the sea, also can you imagine the—"

"Did you just say scarred and eye-patched?"

"—stench on board with all the—"

"Zee."

"—men not washing for—"

Zen stood from the chair in an abrupt movement and came to her. "Zee, focus!" she snapped her fingers, and Zephyr halted her rambling, frowning at the seriousness on her sister's face.

"There's only one man in the city I know about who wears an eye patch, and I sure as hell hope it's not him because he's . . ." Zen bit her lip, her brown eyes troubled. "He's dangerous."

Zephyr felt her brows furrow. "Wait, what are you talking about?"

Her sister tugged at the long sleeves of her nightgown, one she wore to bed like an old lady. Zephyr knew it made her feel secure. "A guy with the eye patch owns the SLF building. And Trident Towers. And half of the city. He's some big hotshot in real estate on the face of it. I never got his name, but there's a rumor he's heavily involved in the underworld, and I kinda believe it. You don't get all this without being powerful, and that kind of power in this city—"

"—is dangerous," Zephyr completed, letting it sink in, wondering if he was the same guy her sister was talking about, and if so, why the hell would a man, who owned half the city, fight barefisted in a shady basement illegally? It made zero sense.

"You never heard his name?" Zephyr asked.

Her sister shook her head. "I don't think anyone has heard of him in normal lives, per se. I only know about the eye patch thing because one of the girls at SLF told me about him. She was an employee of his, I think? Anyway, her father beat her up and the eye patch man sent her to SLF. She was there for a while, you might remember her. Jasmine?"

An image of a woman with the left side of her face swollen, a tattoo forcefully branded on the line of her jaw, popped into her mind. "I gave her a chic bob. She sobbed afterward. I remember."

"Yeah." Her sister's eyes were somber. "She told me a bit about the eye patch guy. Said he gave girls from the streets ... security. And if some girls came through looking for it, I should definitely mention that and give them a number to contact. But I don't know if it's your Alpha."

The silence continued for a bit as they both mulled over the news.

Was he the same man? Was he involved in the underworld? If he was, should she even consider trying to pursue anything? She'd always been a good girl. She paid her taxes on time, she helped old ladies cross the street, and she followed the law. And while Alpha had never had much regard for the law and his sense of morality had always been skewed, being involved in the underworld was an entirely different ballgame. If the eye patch man and Alpha were the same, should she even try to contact him again and involve herself in the midst of it?

Zephyr remembered the lack of recognition she'd seen in his gaze, and it didn't hurt as much now that she was not overly emotional. But now that she'd found him, she was already itching to go see him again, to find out who he had become, understand his in-between, get his excuses. She wanted the stories of his scars, the workings of his mind, the intensity of his eye.

She wanted him, even if he was the underworld man.

And if he didn't remember her, she needed to offer him something valuable, something that would make him give them the time to fall in love again.

The seed of an idea blossomed in her mind—an insane but enlivening idea.

"You said he owned the Trident Towers, right?" Zephyr voiced, the idea solidifying in her brain. She was crazy. Trident Towers were one of the most expensive office complexes in central Los Fortis.

"Oh, no." Zen pointed at Zephyr's face. "I know that face. Whatever you're cooking in your head, don't."

Zephyr blinked innocently. Her sister groaned. "You'll get yourself in deep trouble."

She waited.

"Ugh," Zen huffed. "Yes. Just don't get yourself killed."

"That's a low bar."

Her sister threw a pillow at her head before walking toward her door. "Knowing you..."

Rolling her eyes, Zephyr poked her tongue out as her sister left, the wheels in her brain turning.

Quickly opening her laptop, she spent the next hour diligently searching for the public records of ownership for Trident Towers and SLF, needing to confirm if the eye patch man and Alpha were the one and the same. It was all registered to one address.

AV Security
28th floor, Tower A,
Trident Towers, Zero Avenue
Los Fortis - LF001A

AV.

Alessandro Villanova.

It was him.

He'd never told her the name, but she knew. It was him.

Zephyr stared at the address, torn about what to do. If she pursued it, she could change the course of their lives. It would be better if she let it go.

She shut the laptop.

Yeah, she'd let it go.

She didn't let it go.

Zephyr worked as one of the prime hairstylists at Leisure

Locks, one of the premium salons three blocks down from the city center and Trident Towers.

Trident Towers were a set of three tall skyscrapers in the middle of the city, in what Zephyr called the 'bougie' part of the town. At this time of the morning, it was busy. The roads were heavy with traffic, the pavements were full of purposeful pedestrians, the flurry of activities between corporate suits and carefree artists lively. Tower A had offices for multinational corporations, affluent law firms, and powerful investors. It was the money-making tower.

Tower B housed apartments for those who could afford the vista view on the top half, and a luxury hotel on the lower. It was the money-taking tower. And Tower C, the shortest of the three, was basically an overpriced mall with everything from bars and restaurants to high-end fashion boutiques and grocery stores. It was the money-raking tower.

For the last two weeks, she had taken a longer route back to her apartment, walking by Tower A before going home, scoping it out. And in two weeks, she'd learned two things.

One, AV Security employed a shit ton of hot, muscular men.

Two, Alpha never exited or entered the building from the front entrance.

In fact, in all of two weeks, she'd only seen him thrice and that too when he'd been walking to the back of the tower after getting out of a huge dark SUV she couldn't see the name of. Two weeks of research, and a lot of conversations with her sister and SLF employees had made one thing clear—he was definitely some underworld baddie, infamous for providing the best security and pissing important people off.

He was dangerous. And she wanted him more for it, like the sucker she was.

Zephyr stood outside Tower A, nervous.

She was absolutely mental. But this was the only way forward that she could see.

Taking a deep breath, she walked with purpose toward the entrance, giving the guards a huge smile. "AV Security, please."

The guards nodded and she entered, taken aback by the massive foyer from the gates to the elevators, with a reception desk on one side with two women, a waiting area with plush chairs on the other side, and cameras on every wall. In her black dress, the one with tiny magenta flowers that were only visible in the correct lighting, she stood watching everyone, and still felt out of place. Her hair was now dyed a deep burgundy, and cut with bangs that fell on her forehead, her dress was a little too swishy, and no, she didn't fit in. Just standing in that foyer made her feel like she didn't belong. But she had to do this, for them and the future she knew they deserved. Even though she didn't know if the boss version of him would give her the same attention the fighter version of him had. She hoped he did.

Clutching the straps of her small pink bag, Zephyr stood at the entrance like an idiot, gathering all her courage.

"Excuse me, miss!"

The voice from the side distracted her, and she looked to see one of the pretty receptionists smiling pleasantly at her, the phone in her hand. She was probably going to ask her to leave.

"Yes?" Zephyr plastered a smile on her face.

"Are you Miss Rainbow?"

Miss Rainbow? Zephyr blinked, confused, before realization dawned. She looked up at the camera pointed at the entrance. He had seen her. And damn if she didn't love that.

"Yes, I am."

"Mr. Villanova is expecting you."

A slight smirk pulled at her lips, and she blew a kiss at the camera.

Mr. Villanova. So proper.

Nodding, she headed to the elevators with some other people going up, and pressed 28th with slightly clammy hands.

Until the 22nd, she was relatively calm.

On the 23rd, her stomach started to flutter.

24th, she remembered the ease with which he'd hauled her up.

25th, she remembered his taped hand fisting her hair, and her body flushed slightly. Pressing herself against the elevator wall, she watched the two other men get off on the 26th floor.

27th, she reminded herself of why she was there. For him. She was there for him. Her mama always said her stubbornness would bite her in the ass, and she was probably right. But destiny had brought him back to her, and she'd be damned if she let that go. They deserved this chance, and he couldn't fight for them, so she would.

She hung her bag on her forearm, keeping it steady, pushed up her oversized sunglasses on her hair, adjusted her silver septum ring, and gave herself a once-over in the mirror. Her dress fit perfectly and fluttered at her knee, her cleavage tastefully exposed, and her legs elongated in heels. She looked hot, and she was banking that he thought so too.

The doors opened on the 28th floor, and Zephyr blinked in surprise. It looked nothing like what she'd been expecting.

A long brown teakwood table in the shape of a log stood in the reception area, *AV Security* engraved on it. Tall, muscular men wearing black t-shirts they could bust out of and jeans milled about, some sipping coffee in the kitchenette to the left, some just lounging in a sitting area with windows that overlooked the city, one man even wearing spectacles and reading a book in one corner. Three women, dressed in high heels and short dresses, walked out of a room with Hector, the bald guy who'd dropped her home the other night.

What was this place?

"Can I help you?" A masculine voice from the side had her looking at another tall guy, his skin a deep olive-brown, his hair cropped close to his head almost in a military style. Watching his posture, she wouldn't be surprised if he had in fact served.

This was some seriously hot men marketplace. She almost wanted to sneakily take pictures for Zen.

"I'm here to see ... Alpha?" It came out more as a question than a statement.

The hottie frowned, his dark eyes assessing her clinically. "Alpha doesn't meet with potential clients. You'll have to register with us first. If you're interested in security, I can help you out. I'm Victor." He extended his hand.

Before she could take it, a large palm slid around her waist in a move so proprietary, Zephyr was taken aback. She looked up to see her beast at her side, his eye steady on the other guy. "She's with me," he declared in a voice that had her thighs clenching slightly.

Chatter stopped.

It meant something, his words. She didn't know what, but the activity in the common area came to a halt. All the hot guys she'd been ogling were now looking at the man next to her, something like surprise and confusion in the air. Even the guy who'd been reading was looking at them curiously, as she stood with a man more than twice her size.

Damn.

It was hot.

And she was wet.

Without another word to anyone, he tugged her along to the door at the end of the open space, and she followed quickly, taking two steps for his one to not fall behind, the heat of his palm burning through her dress to her skin. Though he needed to learn how to walk slower, jeez. They entered the office, and he shut the door behind them, walking to the large mahogany desk, leaning against it.

"Rainbow."

"Zephyr, or Zee if you prefer," she corrected, leaning against the door he'd left her at, introducing herself for the first time as she watched for any flare of recognition. Her name wasn't that usual either. Her mother had a thing for weird names, so she doubted he'd met many Zephyrs. But there was nothing, no sign he'd heard it before.

All right, then. Mission blank slate commencing.

Zephyr accepted that, and moved on. First things first, she needed to ogle him properly in the sunlight, see everything she had missed that night.

He wore a black t-shirt and jeans like the men outside, not what she would've expected from a guy in Tower A, who owned half the city, or an underworld lord people were scared to talk about.

He simply waited, letting her check him out at her leisure as her eyes roved over his massive frame, coming to rest on his scar.

"You look intimidating," she told him, finally locking her gaze with his singular eye. "Not that I'm scared. I wouldn't have jumped you if I was." Shit, the way he was looking at her was getting to her. "That's why I'm here. Not to be kissed again, although I wouldn't mind that." *Abort, abort, abort.* "It was a very nice kiss. Probably the best kiss I've had. I'm digressing. Sorry, I'm a little nervous."

His eyebrow above the eye went up, but he stayed silent, which made her even more nervous. "I talk sometimes when I'm nervous," she muttered to herself, shaking her head. "I just—"

She pushed her bangs to the side as he tilted his head. "What were you doing with Alec Reyes?"

Her hand paused on her bangs as she frowned at him. "You know him?"

The man contemplated her. "Our paths have crossed." Vague.

"He was my boyfriend until that night," she informed him.

"What happened that night?"

You happened.

"His dick fell into someone's vagina. Repeatedly."

"Ah." *Ah.* What was that *'ah'?*

She didn't voice that thought, though.

He straightened from the desk suddenly and went to sit behind it in the large chair, the room seeming more spacious with him seated. "So, how can I help you, Zephyr?"

She loved the way he said her name. *Zey-furr.* She'd purr if she were a cat at the way he said it. Probably go into heat too and rub all over him.

Not the time.

Swallowing, she crossed her arms over her chest to hide her nipples, noticing the way his eye dropped to her cleavage before coming back to her face. Good. He was attracted to her. That was important.

"I . . ." she hesitated, not even sure how to voice it.

He waited patiently.

And then she blurted out the words that had been on the tip of her brain for two weeks.

"Marry me."

Silence.

She'd surprised him. She could see that on his half-scowling face. He sat back in his chair, his single eye intense on her. "Excuse me?"

This would be the tough part, convincing him that it was nothing but a marriage of convenience, a *quid pro quo* scheme. But she'd come prepared.

Taking a deep breath, she walked over to the chair in front of his desk and took a seat, earnestly trying to make it make sense. She had the whole plan, had practiced it on Zen that morning, much to her sister's exasperation. Desperate times and all.

"Okay . . ." *There goes nothing.* "My grandmother, bless her soul, was batshit crazy. She had these old family relics and heirlooms that have been in our family for multiple generations, and she left it all to me, on the condition that I'm married by my twenty-ninth birthday, which is in two weeks. Don't ask me why, I still haven't figured it out. They're important to my family, and I want to pass them on to my kids too someday, which was why I was ready to settle down with Alec. But Alec is ... controlling. He will never accept that I rejected him, and he'll try to interfere so I can't find someone else in time however he can. I wasn't in love with him, even though I did try. But ..." She paused, trying to rein her emotions back in as she talked to him, his presence alone wreaking havoc inside her.

"Go on," he prompted, his large arms resting on the arms of his chair, his golden eye sharp on her.

Zephyr exhaled heavily. "That night, I felt a connection to you. Then I found out who you were and you're probably the only guy in the city who can make Alec shit his pants, pardon my language. And then I got the idea that I could kill two birds with one stone. Believe it or not, I don't go around proposing to random strangers. I know you don't know me, but I'm a great person to have around. So ... will you marry me? Only for like six months? My grandmother's will would be executed by then, and Alec would have gone down a peg, and then we can go our ways. And it won't be too bad. I mean, we have really hot chemistry and I'm a nice person and you seem like a solid guy and I just want to—"

"Breathe."

Zephyr paused, inhaled and told herself to calm down. She was talking a mile a minute, but she was nervous. This was a risk. If he said yes, she would have a great story to tell their grandkids. If he said no, she didn't know what she would do. Her grandmother's will, while important, was more of an excuse now; her primary goal with this venture was him.

THE FINISHER

Zephyr leaned forward as she pleaded with him. "Please."

Alpha watched her for a few minutes, contemplating something before he finally spoke. "And why would I agree?"

Zephyr felt her heart triple in its beat. "Because I've heard you haven't been with a woman in a while, Mr. Villanova. And you'd have me, and I'm fantastic in bed if I say so myself. I also have something of yours. And for six months of your life, I'll return the secret back to you." She leaned forward earnestly. "Be my husband, and I'm yours. You have nothing to lose, and so much to gain. I'll happily be your friend, your lover, your wife, whatever you need."

She could see he was intrigued.

"I'll sign a prenup," she continued, making it clear she didn't want his assets, at least not the financial ones. "At the end of six months when we part ways, I'll take nothing."

He tapped the top of the chair with his fingers, a scar on the back of his hand going up his arm. "So you know something about me, and if I marry you, I'll get the secret and get you?"

Zephyr kept her eyes steady on him even as her fingers gripped her dress.

"Yes."

CHAPTER 3

ZEPHYR

There was something very still about him as he considered the offer. He watched her unerringly with that one golden eye, his head tilted to the left, the sunlight streaming from the large windows casting a glow on his beautiful, scarred face.

"You're not telling me the whole truth," he spoke finally, and her heartbeat faltered.

No, she wasn't.

She wasn't telling him his secrets—that she'd known so much about him since before she'd seen him for the first time. She wasn't telling him that he'd been her first kiss, that she still remembered the way the metal from the fence he'd pushed her into had dug into her back where she'd had grooves for a week. She wasn't telling him that she'd loved him as a young man and she wanted to love him again as a grown one.

She just didn't understand how she'd become such a fleeting

memory to him. She knew it sounded like she'd been a stalker, but she hadn't. She just . . . loved the only way she knew how to—completely, utterly, without any shame. It had begun when she'd broken her ribs climbing the tree in her backyard at ten. She'd been admitted to the hospital for a week, and because the children's ward had been full, they'd temporarily put her in the adult ward with a kind older woman.

The woman had been dying, but she'd spoken to Zephyr. She'd asked about her, her family, and played a wordy game with her. She'd talked about her son, what a strong boy he was, how he was such a good person but she was sad to be leaving him alone. He would have no one after she was gone, and Zephyr, heartbroken for a boy she'd not known, had promised her that she would be there for him. The older woman, Adriana, had smiled lovingly and made her pinkie promise. She had died in her sleep that night.

The next morning, Zephyr had seen a tall, lean thirteen-year-old boy in a torn shirt throw a chair through the ward window, his golden eyes red from crying, the pain in his body something she'd felt in hers in that moment.

Alessandro Villanova had loved his mother to the point the nurses had to sedate him to ease his pained howls.

And Zephyr, even after leaving the hospital that day, never forgot about him. That had only been the beginning of them, one he didn't know about.

She didn't tell him any of that as she watched that amber eye, the shade so light she'd always called it gold in her head. His beautiful eyes, damaged, leaving him partially blinded, with a leather strap covering it up.

"Does it bother you?" he asked softly, and she knew he was talking about his eye patch. She was surprised at the question. Was he insecure about that? Maybe he wasn't. Maybe it was just curiosity.

"Not at all," she answered honestly. As long as he was okay, it didn't bother her. But she did wonder when it had happened, how it had happened, and how he had recovered from it.

"Then tell me what you're hiding."

And have him run her off like a lunatic? Oh, no.

"All in good time." She smiled softly at him, the joy in her heart visceral at finding him again. "Just know I'm not a liar. Every word I told you is the truth."

"I'm not a good man," he informed her. "In my line of work, I have enemies. As interesting as your proposition is, you have no idea about the world any wife of mine would be stepping into."

"I know. You're an underworld hotshot and all that. You have more real estate than any one man should, you take people off the streets and employ them in shady ventures, you have a circuit of sex workers around you for some reason." He tensed at her recital of the facts. "It's not hard to dig up that you're deep in some dark places, which makes you dangerous, which makes you powerful, and while I might not know the finer details, I know all that."

"Then you should be running the other way."

She stayed seated.

He leaned back in his chair. "This is ... unexpected. Why me in particular?" he asked her point-blank. "A girl like you can have her pick of men to marry. There must be another reason."

"Maybe we're meant to be." She winked. "Maybe your kiss blew me away."

The unscarred side of his mouth twitched. "I haven't been with a woman in a long time, Zephyr," he warned her quietly. "Be careful of the ways you offer yourself to me. They don't call me the beast for nothing."

That was exactly who she wanted. "You're a twisted beast. I'm a twisted beauty. We're totally meant to be, handsome. It's written in the fairytales."

He didn't react to the lightness in her tone, just observed her for a while longer, and she let him see her sincerity. She let him take in her dyed hair, her round, soft face, the dimple she got in her cheek when she smiled, the silver in her nose, and her pretty boring light brown eyes.

"All right, I'll play."

He tapped his fingers on the desk again. Zephyr watched the back of his hand with more focus, a long scar from the joint of his middle finger disappearing under his t-shirt, black ink wrapping around the line like rose vines with thorns but no blooms. *Interesting choice.* She wondered if he had more ink around his scars. She wanted to explore every little inch of them.

"So, a marriage for six months before we go our separate ways?"

"Yes."

"And I get you during the duration as I want? *However I want?*"

Her breath hitched. "Yes."

"So, what you're saying is"—he leaned forward—"that I can round the desk right now and spread your pussy while my men can hear you scream outside?"

Zephyr felt her thighs clench. *Damn.* "Yes."

"And let's say, I strip you naked right here, right now, and press you against the window for the whole city to see while I pound you into the glass, you wouldn't object?"

Oh, dear lord, have mercy, she was getting hot. "No," she breathed.

"And if I tell you to suck me off under the table like my personal little slut while I talk to one of my men, you would?" he asked her, almost daringly, either trying to scare her or thinking she was bluffing and calling her out on it.

Zephyr quietly stood up and dropped her bag on the carpeted floor, rounding the desk casually as he watched her.

She dropped to her knees between his legs and looked up at him. He appeared larger, like a true pirate overlord of the olden times.

"Talk to your man," she called him on his bluff.

They stared at each other for a long, tense moment; her ready and willing to blow his mind, him trying to understand why a girl he didn't know would go to such drastic lengths to marry him. He had no idea.

His hand went to his belt buckle.

She pulled her hair to one side.

He unzipped his jeans, watching her.

She settled her ass on her heels, watching him.

For long, tense moments, they stayed that way, waiting for the other to blink.

Suddenly, he leaned forward, gripping her chin with his rough fingers. He held her in place, one side of his mouth turning up in a smile that should have been scary, but to her was a victory.

"You're playing with the beast, little rainbow." His grip on her chin tightened. "I bite."

She exposed her neck, keeping their gazes locked. "I was hoping you would," she whispered.

"Fuck."

The space between their faces tingled, the air heavy with anticipation as she closed her eyes and waited for him to close the distance; his breaths on her face, his scent in her nose, his touch on her skin.

The breath came closer, and her lips parted, her body supple, open, needy for his affection.

His fingers tightened on her chin once.

Then, he let her go.

Zephyr blinked her eyes open, the first thing in her line of sight a sizeable bulge under his unbuttoned jeans. Her mouth salivated as she locked eyes with him.

"Are you tempted?" she asked, her voice a breathless whisper.

He didn't reply, just buttoned himself, adjusting his dick to accommodate, and stood up.

Zephyr exhaled, collecting herself. Satisfied, but slightly disappointed, she held his thigh for support, deliberately placing her hand close to his bulge, and eased herself back to her feet. She was straightening her dress when suddenly his hand was in her hair, his fist pulling her head back, and his mouth a hair's breadth away from hers. It would have been intimidating for someone who'd not seen the bones beneath his beast, who'd not know the tenderness with which he treated something he loved. It would have intimidated anyone, but Zephyr stayed fluid, keeping herself open to whatever he wanted to find inside her.

His gaze lingered on her for a moment, puzzled as though he was trying to figure her out, before he murmured, his words brushing her lips, "I will scar you."

"I might want it," she replied, puzzling him even more, passing whatever tests he kept throwing her way.

Letting her go, he walked stiffly to the door and opened it, clearly indicating for her to leave him to figure it out.

"I'll think about it."

That was the best she could've hoped for, frankly much better than what she'd expected from the meeting. Had she been in his place, she would've thrown out the idiotic scheme in five seconds flat. He definitely had a lot more patience.

She nodded and picked up her bag as he stood by the door, waiting for her to walk through. Aware of the many curious eyes on them from the outside, she placed a hand on his shoulder, went up on her tiptoes and gave him a kiss at the corner of his lip, right on the scar that pulled it down.

"I'll wait, sexy."

With a wink, she left.

One of the guys in the open seating area coughed into his coffee mug and the door slammed shut in response.

Zephyr strolled past the men to the elevator, with a little pep in her step.

CHAPTER 4

ALPHA

"Jasmine is here, boss," Hector announced from the door to his office, and Alpha nodded to let her in, leaning back in his chair.

Jasmine, one of his newest sentinels and one of his best informers, entered the office with a serious look on her attractive face. He'd found her two years ago on the street outside one of his clubs, unconscious, after getting beaten up by her father who'd been pimping her out, and he'd dropped her off at SLF to recover. She'd come to him afterward, wanting to work for him, and he'd taken her up. She was street smart, foxy, and had a non-threatening air about her, all of which made her the perfect set of eyes anywhere he wanted them.

"Boss," she said in the way of greeting, taking a seat in the chair Zephyr had left. "There's been another kill."

Fuck.

"Who?" He couldn't keep the gruffness out of his voice.

"A new girl, Mandy," Jasmine informed him quietly. "She'd started working downtown last week. I told her to get in with AV, but she was wary."

"Anything on her?"

Jasmine hesitated, before opening the bag she carried with her and taking out a black envelope. "I found this on my car outside her crime scene. The cops had arrived and there was a crowd so I don't know who left it."

Alpha took the envelope and placed it on the desk, giving her his undivided attention.

"What's the word on the street?"

"Girls are scared," she admitted. "They all agree it's a man, with the way they've been butchered. Most of the victims have been girls who wanted an out. Some of them had already put measures in place, some were about to quit. It's keeping them in the profession out of fear, whether they want to be or not."

He hated that. There was nothing that pissed him off more than someone putting a woman where she didn't want to be.

"We're getting flooded with registration requests."

That was good for business and bad for the city, but he didn't voice that.

"That's all I got for now. I'll check in next week. Hopefully, he doesn't hit before then. I'll also get an update from the department, see if the cops have anything new that can help us."

Alpha gave her a nod. "Tell me if you need one of the guys with you."

"It's better if I work alone. Girls won't talk to me with a guy lingering in the background."

He understood that. Didn't mean he had to like it.

She started to get up, but hesitated. "The girl who was in here just before me, Zephyr?"

She knew her? He waited for her to continue, his curiosity even more piqued. Jasmine wasn't one to gaff. If it wasn't about work, she was usually on her way.

She hesitated again. "She need money?"

"No," Alpha told her, still waiting for her to get to the point. "How do you know her?"

"I met her at SLF. Her sister works there, and she volunteers. She gave me this." Jasmine touched her short, styled hair that concealed half of her facial tattoo, swallowing, emotion visible in her dark eyes. "Told me I could be whatever I wanted to be. My pa never let me cut it . . . it helped with the customers, he always told me. And that day, she just . . . chopped it.

Made me feel beautiful for the first time. Clean. New. She gave me something that day, and I owe her. If she needs money or something, I'd like to help her out."

Damn. After so many years of seeing the ugliness, nothing really moved him anymore. But listening that his little rainbow had changed this woman's life without possibly even realizing, earning herself an ally who would bat for her with a man like him, he was a bit moved. Alpha sat there, processing everything Jasmine was saying about the woman who had essentially proposed to him, making him even more curious. Would she do that to him too? Change his life, make him feel new about himself, earn his loyalty to the point he would look out for her? Could she? He was intrigued, and nothing really intrigued him anymore.

He contemplated Jasmine's words, wondering if maybe talking about her asinine idea would make it make more sense, before finally speaking. "She wants to marry me."

"Oh." Jasmine's eyes widened before a little smile curled her lips. "No offense, Alpha, but you need a wife."

"Excuse me?"

Jasmine leaned back. "If this was a fairytale, you'd have been the beast in the tower all alone, with your staff and your dogs, biting anyone who came close. I've seen the worst of people, and I didn't know men like you existed until you saved me. You deserve something good, not to be alone in that house of yours."

Is that what everyone thought?

"I have my bois," he reminded her. He had three huge German shepherds that he'd nurtured and trained since the day he saved them. They were his loyal companions. They kept him company. He didn't need shit.

"They're dogs," she pointed out correctly. "And they're great dogs. But you need human companionship. And Zephyr is good people. If I were you, I'd marry her. Just food for thought."

Alpha had never wondered if Jasmine was swung that way. Not his business, though. As long as she stayed a good sentinel and never came on to him, she could do whatever she wanted in her private life. He never mixed pleasure with any of the girls under his protection, which also made it tough to find women willing to fuck him. Normal girls took one look at him and ran in the other direction. The rebellious ones wanted a walk on the wild side and risked it, which left him feeling slightly empty. Given his background, paying for sex was something he never did, and taking advantage of the workers who came to him with trust just went against his personal code. There weren't many things he was righteous about, but vulnerable women and kids were it.

Which again begged the question, why would a girl like Zephyr, from a seemingly good family and in complete contrast to his world, run to him, jump him, kiss him, and then get on her knees to pop a crazy question? Why would she be okay with everything he said he'd do to her? She wasn't a groupie, she wasn't a rebel. And he doubted she couldn't find someone else for her scheme. So why him? What was up with her?

As Jasmine left the office, Alpha walked to his windows, mulling over her words.

So, Zephyr helped out battered and abused women at his center. He wasn't sure why, but that did something to his chest. But he still didn't understand the marriage proposal. What could she possibly know about him? There was nothing.

She was slightly crazy, he decided. But at least she was a distraction.

For the first time in years, Alpha could feel the lull of ennui breaking. Everything had become the same—the underworld remained the same, his empire remained the same, his loneliness remained the same. He realized a while ago that each fight, each fuck, each finale had become the same old shit he lived through.

Some days, he didn't understand the point. And on those days, he missed his ma. To others, she might have been a sex worker off the streets of Los Fortis; but to Alpha, she'd been nothing but an amazing mother who had lost too much too early in life. Her parents dead, she had taken care of her younger sister the only way she'd known, going to the streets and selling herself to give her sister a chance at a better life, only to have a monster rip it all away.

Lorenzo Maroni had swept in like a storm in the lives of the Villanova sisters and left behind nothing but debris. He had raped his mother, abducted his aunt, and left her for the dead. And even though Alpha had been the seed of a monster, his mother had decided to not only carry him, but also raise him to be nothing like his sire.

He grew up on the streets, surrounded by hollow humans who had once had aspirations for themselves and then had none.

And he had built an empire, fist by fist, to escape that.

As he stared out with his limited vision at the expansive jungle beyond the city from his tower, to the compound that he called home, Alpha wondered what the point of it all had been.

And then the rainbow had come barreling into him, like a burst of color after endless gray, kissing him like he wasn't a mangled man, looking at him with genuine desire in her eyes like she appreciated all that he was. In his experience, he was either a walk on the wild side for a woman or a scary monster out of her nightmares. But Zephyr, the tiny button of a woman, who'd strolled through his testosterone-filled foyer like she was a queen, looked at him differently, and he couldn't put his finger on why.

That baffled him.

"So, should I get my good suit out?" Hector joined him on the side, a grin on his face.

"Eavesdropping. Nice." Alpha shook his head, knowing Hector had listened in at the door like the nosy bastard he was. Hector and Victor, brothers and sons of the streets like him, had been with Alpha for as long as he could remember. Hector had stuck with Alpha while Victor had joined the military, coming back after an injury to his leg, angrier and darker than the young boy Alpha had remembered protecting. But Hector was the closest thing to a friend Alpha had, and when he'd asked him to give Victor a job in the company, Alpha had. He wasn't as close to the younger boy, but he wondered what had made him so volatile.

"After the way she jumped you that night," Hector said, interrupting his train of thoughts, stepping into the peripheral vision of his good eye, something Alpha always appreciated him doing. "There was no way I was missing out. Is that why you didn't get your dick sucked? Because you knew I was listening?"

"You know why." Alpha gazed out and heard Hector sigh.

"Your celibacy is wasted, boss. It was an accident."

An accident where he'd fractured a woman's hip because he'd been too rough. He liked when his partners screamed, but not in that kind of pain. Although he was usually careful because of his size and knew that most women needed adjusting to his dick, his last partner had wanted the beast, and high from a fight, he'd delivered. The sound of her bone breaking still haunted him, made him feel like a fucking monster.

It had shaken him enough to make him celibate for over an entire year.

"Who's her tail?" Alpha asked, changing the topic.

"Victor."

Of course, Hector would put the best-looking of their squad on her tail, knowing it would rile him up. He didn't know why he'd declared she was with him when she'd been talking to Victor earlier, but he'd seen her on the camera for the last two weeks, lingering, watching, essentially stalking the building. She was a curious little creature.

"Any update on why she was here this week?"

"Besides stalking you, you mean?" Hector grinned, his white teeth gleaming against his darker skin. "You must have kissed her real good if she's proposing so soon."

Or she had an ulterior motive. There was no other explanation for why someone like her would want to tie herself in matrimony to a man like him. It wasn't a lust for his money. No, had it been mercenary, she never would've suggested a prenup.

Alpha looked down at the busy street below. "Any news on Reyes dealing at the fight?" Hector's voice sobered. "Yeah, you were right. He's gambling his money on fights. Word says he'll go in debt once the season begins."

The season of illegal fights where all and anyone important enough in their level of the underworld bet their money. It was an entire industry, of buying boys, training them to fight till death, only the survivors becoming men and making it to the actual circuit, going around to different locations and fighting for either masters or money. Alpha had stumbled upon it accidentally when he'd been fighting his way up the streets, trying to make ends meet after his mother's death. And once he'd realized the potential of fortune his fists could rake in, he had taken over. The fights had no rules, just two guys in a cage, both knowing only one of them could make it out, and every fight Alpha was in, he was the one who got out.

And for that reason, they began calling him *The Finisher*.

He gave them quick deaths unless they pissed him off. And now he was pissed because the media was calling the killer *Fortis Finisher*. Oh, he'd not give that butcher a quick death, that was for sure.

"How's the Syndicate been?" Alpha asked, remembering the request his half-brother, Dante Maroni, had made a few weeks ago.

"Surprisingly quiet."

A phantom pain bloomed in his right eye socket. Even after so many years, it took him by surprise sometimes, the sensation of having the eye, of losing it, feeling a hollow ache, one he couldn't really explain. Alpha shook it off, knowing that rubbing the eye only made it worse.

"There's a note on the desk Jasmine found on her car," he told the younger man. Hector moved to the note, tearing the flap open, taking the paper out. Since losing his eye, his other senses had become more acute. He'd trained them to be.

"Ugh," Hector groaned. "Jasmine is like a sister to me, dude. I don't want to read what some asshole wants to do to her. I need to bleach my eyes out."

Alpha shook his head, disappointed. He'd been hoping for some kind of intervention, anything to remove the monster terrifying his streets.

"Cops know anything more?" he asked, focusing on the sunlight falling on the lush green in the distance.

"Not that we know of."

"Fuck."

It was a fucked-up situation. Alpha had been aware of a serial killer amongst the streets killing off high-risk sex workers for over two years now. None of his girls had been hurt, but word on the street had spread like wildfire. The police hadn't been able to piece it together much mainly because they didn't have the time or resources to spend on such victim profiles. The one cop who had wanted to solve it had been transferred to another division last month, the corruption at the seed of the system. It was one of the reasons he had taken power over the city.

"Any word on Caine's sister?" Alpha asked, taking another breath as he tried to make sense of everything happening in his world. "The feelers come back?"

"Nothing yet," Hector told him. "It was such a long time ago, it's taking a while to trace it back. Most information is either gone or deliberately suppressed. It's taking time."

Yes, it had been a long time. And if his guess was correct, the girl was either dead or deep in the clutches of the Syndicate. For her sake and Caine's, he hoped she was in a grave.

Growing up the way he had, as the son of a sex worker, living in a dilapidated red light district of the city, he'd grown up seeing what happened to women who sold themselves under a pimp. The Syndicate made it all look like a walk in the park. From what he knew about them, their depravity was much, much worse. Flesh trade was only one arm of the organization. Alpha knew there were countless others. They had their hands in everything—human fights, dog fights, organ black market trade, sick slavery, anything one could and couldn't fathom. And even after knowing so much, he had no idea who they were, where they operated, and how deep their tentacles went.

"You think she's alive?" Hector questioned, coming to stand at his side again. He was an emotional bastard, and since he'd been leading the investigation into the missing girls, Alpha knew his friend was invested.

"For her sake." Alpha squashed down Hector's wish. "I hope not."

His entanglement with The Syndicate went way back. Knowing the ways his mother had risked herself for their survival had instilled a sense of responsibility in him at a young age. He'd been twelve the first time he's used his fists, pummeling the pimp who'd beaten his mother. While the pimp had disappeared, he'd realized he couldn't just sit and do nothing. So, he had begun fighting on the streets for money and earning himself a nasty reputation. Most of the scars on his body accounted for such fights when he had been young and stupid, because on the streets, there were no rules. And while his mother had died immediately after, his sense of responsibility for those people, his people, had never really left.

Soon after, he had begun offering the workers in his neighborhood the protection of his name, and they had simply begun to give him a little money without him even asking or wanting it since he began making more than enough with his wins. He was a protector, not a pimp. But over time, the word about his pack spread—a pack where only voluntarily sex workers were allowed to work for themselves without anyone breathing down their neck, where they could keep whatever they made, and they themselves began to hand him a cut for his security. Women came looking for protection from clients, and boys came wanting to work. Alpha had given them both. Now, he had over one thousand sex workers in the country who worked under his name on their own terms, completely voluntarily, and hundreds of men protecting them.

And the Syndicate didn't like that at all. He had been a thorn in their side simply by existing and doing what he could for his people. They'd tried to get him to work for them, but Alpha being who he was, had given them the middle finger. And they couldn't touch him, not with the empire he'd built, not with the power he now had in their seedy world. It was a part of the underworld that was dirty and dark, and he wondered what he was even thinking entertaining the idea of bringing someone like Zephyr into it. His loneliness was getting to his head, nothing more.

Maybe he needed a good fuck. It had been over a year since he'd been with someone, and maybe he just needed to get his dick wet again, just like he liked it.

The only time he had entertained the thought of dating someone in the recent past had been when he'd seen Amara in the city. Given her beauty and her strength, it had been impossible not to be attracted to it all. But she belonged to his brother, and they were going to get married next week. He'd received the invitation, but he still didn't know if he would go, especially with the way everything was going to shit in his city.

He felt Victor enter the office, the youngest of the three, the best-looking, and usually the angriest.

"She quizzed me about you," Victor reported, his face more relaxed than he's seen in a while. Alpha turned around to face the boy he'd seen grow up with them. "What did she ask?"

A frown marred the handsome fucker's face. "Weird shit. Your favorite color, food, shoe size."

Hector huffed a laugh at his brother. "You know what they say about a guy's shoe size.

Maybe she was curious since you didn't whip it out."

Victor rolled his eyes at his brother's snark. "She also asked me for your number."

Alpha sighed. "Did you give it to her?"

"She was . . . persistent," Victor replied in a dry tone.

Amusement, as he'd come to expect in the little time he'd spent with her, filled him. He didn't know what it was, maybe her tiny stature, maybe her ferocity, maybe her utter disregard for predictability. But she broke the ennui, and that was the main reason Alpha was at a loss about what to do with her proposition—accept and see where it led, or refuse and let life go on as it was. For her, the second option was much safer. But he didn't like the way Victor looked relaxed after spending time with her, and he definitely didn't like the idea of her considering him as an option.

He was a selfish bastard.

"So, will you say yes to her?" Hector asked the question buzzing in his head.

Fuck if he knew.

CHAPTER 5

ZEPHYR

She'd broken the news about her breakup with Alec to her parents when it had happened while visiting them for their weekend brunch. Her mother still didn't believe it after weeks, despite Zephyr telling them she was seeing someone else. Mama thought it was a lover's tiff rather than a clean break.

As Zephyr kneaded the dough for a special dessert at her parents' home, she wondered how to break the news about the wedding thing. It had been a week since she'd gone down on her knees with her proposal, and she was yet to hear back from him.

Her father sat reading the finance section in the newspaper, his gold-rimmed glasses on the end of his nose. Her mother chatted with some friends as she typed on her phone, her coffee untouched on the table in front of her. Zen sat on the kitchen counter beside Zephyr, swinging her legs as she whisked the batter in a bowl. It was like any other weekend brunch.

And her birthday was in two days.

She took a deep breath, punching the dough with her hands. "I'm getting married on my birthday," she announced, her back to the table.

"Alec proposed?" her mother asked, her voice excited with glee.

"We're not together, Mama," she reminded her mother. "I'm in love with someone else."

Even though he didn't know it.

She'd sent him two texts over the week, and he hadn't replied or called her back. While her proposal had been unconventional, she'd been almost certain he would accept. She was pretty enough, she made him smile, and she'd rock his world in bed. What more did a man want? Ugh. She'd also loved him for a long time, but he didn't know that so she didn't hold that against him.

"What do you mean?" Esmeralda de la Vega put her hand down on the table. "He was about to propose to you!"

Zephyr sighed. She loved her mother, she truly did, but her mama had her flaws. One of them was caring about what people said, which she couldn't entirely blame her for, because people could be nasty with the backtalk. And she knew her mama only wanted a good life with all the comforts for her daughters, which was why she could get swayed by material stuff sometimes.

"He cheated on me, Mama," Zephyr reminded her for the hundredth time. "And even if he hadn't, I would have left him. I love someone else."

Her mother's voice flared. "He doted on you!"

"When he wasn't trying to tell her not to eat," Zen murmured from the side, having her back as always.

Her mother waved that off. "That's a part of relationships. I tell your father not to eat something because it's bad for his health. Alec was just looking out for you."

Zephyr looked to her father, who was watching her quietly, his eyes behind the spectacles. If someone had told her thirty years ago that Esmeralda, one of the most beautiful girls in town, who had a line of eligible bachelors lining her door, would fall in love with a slight, sweet accountant who genuinely loved numbers and was always calculating something or the other, Zephyr wouldn't have believed it. But she'd witnessed the love her parents had for each other—two polar opposite personalities, her mother loud and her father quiet—and she'd wanted that for herself. She'd wanted the romantic tale that she could tell her kids and make them believe in love, the story of two lovers who loved so deep they couldn't be without another, flaws and all. Perhaps that was why as a little girl, she'd subconsciously seen that capacity of love in the pained, violent outburst of a boy, and claimed him for herself from that day forward.

"It's happening, Mama. I'm not asking," Zephyr stated firmly and the table went quiet.

Her mother dropped her head in her hands, mumbling something too quietly for Zephyr to hear.

"Who is he?" her papa asked, folding his newspaper and speaking for the first time.

"Alpha Villanova," she told him and saw recognition flare in his eyes.

"The owner of Trident?" he asked, just to confirm.

She nodded. "I knew him a few years ago, but we lost touch and just reconnected recently. It felt like no time had passed. It was magical, Papa."

Her mother looked up. "Alpha? He owns *Trident*? The towers? What's his family like? How did you meet him?"

"Mama—"

"No, no!" Her mother stood up. "This is too much. This Alpha has corrupted your mind against Alec. Alec is a good man. His family has accepted us as their own!"

It was like hitting a wall sometimes.

Zen piped up from the side, "Mama, did you miss the part where she told you, twice, that he *cheated* on her?"

"Mind your tone, Zenith de la Vega." Her mama pointed at Zen with her death stare, before turning on her heel and walking out of the room.

Her father sighed. "Give her some time. She just wants the best for you."

"I know, Papa."

He considered her with the quiet seriousness that she associated with him. "Are you sure about this young man? He has a certain … reputation."

Zephyr gave her father a smile. "Papa, trust me. He's the one. You remember how you told me when it's right, you just know? I *know*. And I want to marry him on my birthday. We can have a big wedding later, but I just have to. Please support me."

Her father sighed again, but nodded. Giving both daughters a kiss on the head, he left to go talk to her mother and calm her down.

"That went well," Zen whistled. "What are we baking, by the way?"

Zephyr smiled as she continued pounding the dough. "Bribes."

A week. She'd given him an entire week before deciding enough was enough. Her birthday was tomorrow, her plan wasn't working, and she needed reinforcements. Thanks to their history and the interrogation with Victor, she knew just the weapons to bring.

Zephyr walked into Trident Towers with a lot more confidence this time, signing herself in as 'Miss Rainbow' at the reception, a box clutched in her hands. She grinned at the guards, at the receptionists, at everyone in the elevator, trying to hide the nerves in her stomach as the doors opened on the 28th floor. It was exactly as it had been the last time she'd been there, hot men lingering in the open area, eyes coming to her and recognizing her, them trying to seem uninterested but paying attention as she stood there.

The door to Alpha's office was open. She could see him and Hector walking out toward the elevator, both concentrating on the conversation, and she braced herself for the impact of his gaze. Alpha looked up and saw her, coming to a stop in surprise. Guess he hadn't watched the cameras this time. Disappointing.

She gave him a bright smile as Hector gave her a man-nod. "Yo."

"Yo." She tried to imitate the chin lift thing, but she was pretty sure she failed. But her beast's unscarred lip twitched, and that alone made being stupid worth it. She turned fully to him.

"So, do you want me to get on my knees here or should we go to your office?"

She heard someone choke on something, but kept her eyes on the man before her.

A vein on the side of his neck pulsed slightly, and god she wanted to lick that.

"Inside," he growled, heading back to his office.

"Whatever you say, sexy." She followed cheekily, seeing his step falter before he continued, someone coughing their laughter behind her.

Alpha shut them in and turned on her. "Don't do that."

She blinked innocently. "Do what?"

"Make suggestive comments in front of my men."

She leaned against the door, craning her neck up. "Would you prefer I make them just to you, then?"

"No."

The vein pulsed harder. Something else was hard too even though he clearly didn't want it to be. Taking pity on his circulation, she took a step closer, holding the box out for him. "This is for you."

She saw him exhale before eyeing the cardboard box curiously, raising his unscarred eyebrow at her in a silent question.

"It's a bribe." She rolled her eyes. "So you'll put me out of my misery and marry me and make me a stinking rich woman."

He scoffed, and she was glad to see that he knew she wasn't a gold-digger. He hadn't been rich when she'd loved him, and if he lost everything tomorrow, she'd still be there. He just didn't know that yet.

"Most people propose with rings, but I thought you'd prefer this."

Genuinely intrigued, he opened the box.

And completely *stilled*.

Zephyr watched him watch the contents in the box for a long minute, a slight tremor in his hand, before looking up at her, searing her with that powerful gaze.

"How?" he demanded, his voice gruff.

She let her eyes flit down to the dessert she had spent hours finding the right recipe, cooking to perfection yesterday, and refrigerating to the perfect temperature.

Alfajores.

Specifically, alfajores rolled in coconut shavings and filled with homemade jam.

When a ten-year-old Zephyr had asked a then thirty-five-year-old dying Adriana why her son, who had such a pretty name like Alessandro, was called Alpha, Adriana had laughed. She'd told her it was because Alphas led the pack and she wanted him to be a good leader, that she wanted him to be a good man.

Then, she'd conspiratorially called little Zephyr closer and told her that the real reason was a secret, one she could never tell. Zephyr had promised with her whole heart, and Adriana had spilled. Her son had a sweet tooth, and Adriana used to make alfajores for him when he was a child, with coconut shavings and jam, but as a kid, he'd never been able to pronounce the word. So every time he had craved something sweet, he'd said 'alfa', and it had become a secret joke between mother and son as he grew older and started going by Alpha.

No one knew about the significance of the sweet delicacy. And from her interrogation of Victor the other day, she knew he still had a sweet tooth, but she hadn't known if he'd had these particular desserts since his mother had passed.

She simply smiled at his question.

"Try one," she urged him, and he just looked down at the box, unmoving, his jawline tight, the scar on his face lighter than usual.

She wanted to give him a hug, but she doubted he'd appreciate it right then. Zephyr turned on her heels and headed out the door, letting him have his moment in private. A part of her was so soft to be able to give him this, something from his childhood that he'd once loved. He'd understand now that she was serious about knowing him, and he'd possibly be tempted to agree to her proposal.

A few curious eyes followed her, but she ignored them. Hector waited up ahead near the elevators, his bald head gleaming in the sunlight from the windows, a slight grin on his mouth.

"He say yes?" he asked her as she pressed the button.

Zephyr laughed. "Not yet."

"I have my suit ready whenever." Hector winked at her, before sobering. "Don't give up. I haven't seen him this interested by something in a while."

God, her beautiful beast. There was no way she was giving up, and hearing those words from someone who was clearly a friend of Alpha's buoyed her heart. "I won't."

The elevator doors opened, but before she could enter, a large hand gripped her arm and spun her around, the scent of wilderness and musk infiltrating her nose.

She looked up to see Alpha piercing her with his singular eye, his other hand coming up to hold her chin in place in a move she now recognized, his entire personality intense and aggressive in ways that made her heart begin to thunder in her chest.

He leaned closer, speaking quietly, "I'm going to Tenebrae to attend my half-brother's wedding on Wednesday."

Zephyr frowned, puzzled. "Okayyy." He had a half-brother?

"You're coming as my wife," he stated.

Her heart crashed against her ribs, her eyes widening. "Okay."

"And when we get back, you're moving in with me."

She silently nodded.

"There will be a contract."

Of course, there would be.

"Do you have a passport?"

"Yes."

"Good. Tell your family. We'll meet them before we leave."

Oh, shit.

"Mama won't like not being able to arrange a wedding," she warned him clearly.

"She can arrange a wedding for another date." He shrugged as the elevator doors opened and closed again and she stood frozen in place, his hand a warm band around her bicep, eye patch even more vivid on his scarred face in the daylight.

"We're going to the courthouse tomorrow."

"Tomorrow?" Her palms began to sweat. It was real, it was happening.

Holy shit, it was happening.

He took a step into her personal space and leaned down while tilting her chin up, his lips an inch from hers, his warm, minty breath sending little shivers up and down her body. "I don't know how, rainbow," he murmured softly, "and I don't know what secrets of mine you have, but I want them all. You've sealed your fate now. Welcome to my hell."

Dramatic, but okay. Although was it dramatic if he meant it literally? His world was the netherworld, the underworld even the media didn't cover, and she was stepping into it. But this was what she'd wanted.

He pulled back, pressing the button to call the elevator again.

Hector, who she'd forgotten had been witnessing the whole thing from the side, asked curiously, "What was in the box?"

To which Alpha replied, deadpanned, "Drugs."

Zephyr choked, her heart thudding against her ribs.

Holy shit, it was happening.

CHAPTER 6

ZEPHYR

On her twenty-ninth birthday, Zephyr stood in front of the mirror, watching herself in the cute white sundress with embroidered flowers, her sister's reflection in a pale green dress behind her.

"I can't believe you're marrying Alpha," Zen whispered, her voice reflecting the disbelief of her words. *"Your* Alpha."

Her Alpha.

She couldn't believe it either.

There was a slight twinge in her heart because her mother had refused to attend what she'd called 'this farce of a wedding'. She was still processing the news of her breakup, much less her nuptials, and Zephyr didn't entirely blame her. It was fast. But not to her; she'd been waiting for this for over a decade. Although she'd never imagined marrying him in a courthouse while being a stranger to him. In a way, she was glad it would just be Zen with her. Knowing everything her sister knew, Zephyr wouldn't have to pretend anything with her.

A knock on the door had her heartbeat tripling.

"Calm down," she told herself out loud as Zen went to open the door. She straightened her dress for the last time, tucked her wavy burgundy hair back in her low bun, fixed her fringe, fidgeting.

The door opened and he filled the frame, his large body in a black leather jacket and jeans—of course, he'd wear leather and jeans to their wedding—and that eye patch, and dear lord, he looked *fine*. Zen, seeing him for the first time, froze. Yeah, she could imagine he had that effect on people.

Zephyr quickly covered the distance between them, going on her toes to kiss the scar at the corner of his mouth. "Hey, sexy."

The other side of his lip twitched, his golden eye taking her in her dress. She took a step back and twirled for him, showing him the deep back, and stopped in a pose. "How do I look?"

"Fine," he grunted. "We're getting late." With that, he turned on his heel and went down the stairs. Zephyr rolled her eyes.

"Zee," Zen asked from the side, her face slightly apprehensive. "He's . . . a lot. Are you sure?"

He was a lot. Moreover, Zephyr knew she was stepping into a world she knew nothing about, a world she'd only seen from the fringes from her time spent volunteering. The more she'd dug, the more she'd realized he was lethal. But he was also the boy who'd walked her five miles to her home in the middle of winter just so she'd get there safely.

Zephyr gave her sister a quick hug. "He's still my Alpha, Zen." She believed that. No matter how much time had passed, deep in her soul, she believed that.

Zen inhaled, knowing what that meant to her, and nodded, putting a smile on her lips. "Okay. Flowers. Let's go."

They both got their bags and flowers and went down the stairs to the waiting black Rover, Hector in the driver's seat, checking Zen out. Alpha waited outside. He opened the passenger side's door for Zen, shut it, then turned to her, seeing the way her dress hugged her. Sighing, he picked her up casually by her hips, and put her in the backseat, closing the door behind her.

God, she loved it when he did that, picked her up like she weighed nothing, when the entire world had shoved an entirely contrary belief down her throat. It made her feel delicate, small, and so precious, and Zephyr rarely felt that around people.

He got in and Hector started the drive. "The lawyer will meet us at the courthouse," he informed them. "All the documents are ready."

Zephyr nodded, watching the man on the other end of the wide seat, his eye patch and scarred the side toward her.

Zen gave her a look in the rearview mirror, before turning to him. "Hi, Mr. Villanova," she introduced herself in her most professional voice. "We haven't met. I'm Zephyr's sister, Zenith. You can call me Zen."

"Alpha, please," he corrected her in a soft tone. "We'll be family soon."

Oh, she liked the sound of that a lot. Yes, they would be family. It made Zephyr smile.

The rest of the drive passed in companionable silence. Zephyr looked out at the city she loved, seeing people going about their lives in the early morning, and it filled her with joy. Everything filled her with joy right then. All seemed right in the world. She remembered the first time she'd talked to him. It hadn't been planned. She'd been stuck one night in the bad part of town after her friend had ditched her. She'd gone there because she liked to check up on him, and he'd been there when she'd been walking the street alone, the young man with golden eyes and the deep voice, speaking to her for the first time—

The car came to a stop outside the white courthouse building.

Shaking herself out of the memories, Zephyr opened the door, and he was there before she could get down, picking her up and placing her on her feet, his hands huge on her hips, her nose level with the middle of his ribs. God, he made her feel *tiny*, and she *loved* that.

His hands clenched on the sides of her hips, and she looked up at him, locking her eyes with his golden gaze, mourning the loss of the place his other eye had been. He held her chin in that sure way she'd always associate with him, his face fierce. "Last chance, rainbow."

There was no way she was backing out.

"Cold feet, handsome?" she teased him with a grin, and his gaze strayed to her mouth.

Inhaling, he let her go and took a step back, indicating the wide, low steps of the courthouse. Heart pounding, she took her bouquet of deep red roses and climbed up with her sister, Alpha and Hector following at their heels.

Zephyr had seen the courthouse many times in passing, but had never been inside. A man her father's age waited for them at the top, dressed in a sharp, expensive suit. He escorted them to a sparsely furnished but folder-filled chamber and indicated the seat. For the next few minutes, he explained the contract to them. Basically, they were both to marry for six months, after which she would be given access to her grandmother's treasury and he would be given whatever information she had on him. If they chose to divorce afterward, Zephyr wouldn't get anything from him, and he from her. If the marriage wasn't consummated, which she'd try her damndest to get done, they could annul it at any time.

If it was up to her, they'd never grace the courthouse again.

Giving the contract a cursory glance, she signed at the bottom.

Alpha picked up the pen, his eye squinting, and signed his name.

With that done, the lawyer sealed the contract and locked it in a cabinet. A clerk escorted them to another room, one with the officiant, and they stood as he got the papers ready. Watching the black leather jacket stretching across her husband-to-be's back as he bent and signed the documents, Zephyr felt something like nerves fluttering in her belly. The leather jacket, the eye patch, the longish, disheveled hair, the short scruff—lord, he was sexier now. She was taking a huge risk, and she didn't know if it would pay off. She didn't know what their future looked like, or how she'd fit into his world and he in hers. But god, she'd try, and she'd die knowing that she tried, that she gave it her all. If it never worked out, she didn't want to regret never taking the risk in the first place. She just hoped heartache didn't wait for her.

"Sign here, please." The clerk's voice interrupted her thoughts. She bent over and quickly signed on the dotted line, sealing their deal in the most binding way for half a year.

"Do you have any rings to exchange?" the clerk asked.

Alpha looked at her hands, the vein on the side of his neck popping. It hadn't even occurred to him that she'd need a ring. Guess she'd have to get one herself.

Zephyr waved it off. "Don't worry about it."

Zen handed her the simple gold band she'd bought yesterday for him, taking a guess at his size, hoping it fit. She took a hold of his large hand in hers, saw the contrast between them—his larger, rougher, deadlier, with blunt tips; hers smaller, softer, rounder, with slightly longer painted nails—and slid the ring home.

He was hers.

Finally.

The joy bubbled in her heart, a wide smile splitting her face as she looked up at him.

Impulsively, she went to her toes, and pressed a soft kiss on his scar, right at the corner of his mouth. One day, he would turn his face and catch her lips with his. One day, he would kiss her on his own and she would bask in the beauty of it. Until then, she'd pepper him with kisses.

A throat cleared, and she pulled back.

"Witnesses, please sign here."

Hector and Zen stepped up and completed the protocols, and then it was done.

She was Zephyr Villanova.

Damn.

She looked at Zen and saw the same happiness she was feeling reflected in her sister's eyes. She knew. She understood what this moment meant. Her sister grabbed her hand, giving it a squeeze, and Zephyr squeezed back. Alpha watched with interest, and she knew he was trying to figure out her reasons. She watched with interest as Hector stared at her sister, clearly liking what he saw.

Once the clerk was done with the paperwork, they all exited the building.

"I'll get to work." Zen gave her a hug.

Zephyr saw Alpha watching them embrace, his look blank of any expression. But the way he watched, it almost looked like . . . longing. Zen turned to Alpha and gave him a nod.

"Welcome to the family."

She saw his face soften slightly at her sister's words.

Hector took over. "I'll get you a cab." He went down to the road with her, giving them some privacy.

"Have you told your parents?" Alpha asked as they stood on the steps in broad daylight. She noticed how the people passing by stopped to gawk at her husband, because of his size or scars or missing eye, she didn't know, but she didn't like the way they looked, like he was something lesser than they were.

"Hmm," she mumbled distractedly, giving a woman to her

right who'd been staring at him a glare. "Hey, can I help you with something?"

The woman stuttered something and left quickly.

Zephyr turned back to the man before her, surprised to find him somewhat amused while she fumed. "What?"

"Nothing." He shook his head, pushing his hands in the pockets of his jacket. "When should I meet them?"

Zephyr blinked for a second, her brain catching up to their conversation. "Oh. *Oh.* Tomorrow. Zen and I are going there tonight after I pack for the trip. I'll take my bag. She'll stay with them while I'm out of town. We can head to the airport straight after, because my parents are romantics and think we're marrying out of love, and my mom is skeptical about the suddenness of it, so she'll interrogate you and we'll have an excuse to get out—"

"Breathe," he told her again, and she stopped.

Okay.

God, he was hers.

It hit her out of nowhere. Impulsively, she slid her arms around his waist and hugged him tight, exhaling a shaky breath against his chest. He stilled, his arms at his sides, holding her biceps with his large hands, not embracing her but not rebuffing, confused.

She'd seen the way he'd looked at her hugging Zen, and she wondered if anyone hugged him anymore. She wondered when was the last time he'd been embraced with love, and held him tighter. Hugs were her thing. People loved her hugs. If hugging was a contest, she'd surely be a runner-up. So she'd hug him. Every day, she'd hug him until he returned it, until he accepted that it was normal, until he began to crave it from her.

She'd break down his defenses, one hug at a time.

All in good time.

Happy birthday, Zephyr Villanova.

CHAPTER 7

ALPHA

He had forgotten what intense emotions felt like until she handed them to him in a colorful cardboard box. There was no way she could know the actual meaning of the alfajores for him, but her cryptic smile made him wonder if somehow, someway, she did.

He had stood in his office with the box in his hands, a grown man who had seen the worst of humankind and survived through times that should've killed him, and he had felt his eyes burn. His hands had trembled as he'd picked one piece up, the coconut flakes reminding him of a childhood where his ma hadn't been able to afford a more luxurious filling, but had made him the best desserts she could have. He had taken a bite and felt something inside his chest come alive, something that had been dormant, something he'd thought dead.

A man who had forgotten what it felt like to *feel* had been undone by a tiny blip of a woman. And though he'd had every intention of protecting her from his world, it was too late. She had sealed her fate, and fuck if he would let her get away without knowing everything she knew now. He didn't know what her motive was for wanting to marry him, but he would find out.

Alpha sat in the back of the black Rover as Hector drove to her parents' house to pick her up, knowing the location after receiving her message last night. As it was, Alpha couldn't have driven to the place even if he had wanted to. It was such an irony, the fact that he's always wanted to drive a Jeep but hadn't been able to afford it, and now, he had a fleet of them but couldn't drive them, not with his limited vision. Even though he used the Jeep mostly around his compound, Rover was more suited for the city.

Alpha didn't remember the incident that had partially blinded him, what or who had changed the course of his life and left him for the dead. He just remembered waking up in the hospital, his entire body broken beyond repair, his face on fire due to the pain, and his eyes taped shut into blackness. Hector had found him behind one of the underground fight clubs and brought him to the emergency. How long he'd been there, no one knew. The attending doctor had told him his memory around the incident might never return, that it was possibly his brain's way of protecting him from further trauma. Some days, he was grateful for it. Some days, the need to know the truth was a hunger gnawing inside his scarred flesh.

It had taken his body weeks to heal, and taken him months to train. His body hadn't worked the same as before, his partial vision hadn't aided his movements, and his head was fucked up even without remembering anything. That was when he'd thrown himself into the fights and made himself a fortune, a beast in a cage with nothing to lose, taking over the city block by block, making his beautiful compound brick by brick, training his body muscle by muscle. He'd worked with trainers to adapt to his vision, honed his other senses to make up for the damage in one, and over time, his sense of smell and sense of sound had seamlessly taken the place of the one eye. Still, there were certain things he'd never be able to do, like drive. Shaking his thoughts away, he looked out at the neighborhood from the backseat, a far cry from what he'd grown up in. Although it wasn't an expensive area, the houses were well-cared for. The streets were clean and lined up systematically, the houses were old but homey, the lawns all well-maintained. It was a solid good middle-class neighborhood, the kind where neighbors went to each other for little things, the kind that had never come in contact with his old residence. This was where she'd grown up, and he was glad for that.

"Wonder what growing up here must be like," Hector voiced the thought in Alpha's head. "She's good people."

Alpha didn't reply, just kept looking out, wondering if he'd been there before, a sense of familiarity to the block making him frown.

"Sure you wanna drag her into our hell completely?" Hector asked.

"She wants it."

And for the first time in his life, he wanted something just for himself. And he would be selfish, especially when she wanted him to be. He'd enjoy her company for the months, assuage his curiosity, but rebuff any romantic overtures. He'd make it clear to her not to have any expectations beyond their time together, and he'd sure as hell not fuck her, no matter how much she tempted him. He was destined to be alone, and it was the best for both of them.

Before he could respond to Hector's question, the vehicle stopped in front of a single-story house painted yellow. Zephyr stood out on the porch to greet them, her hair the same deep burgundy it had been, her curvy body in some kind of flowy dress full of flowers, and a smile so wide it split her face almost in half, a dimple popping on the left side.

Alpha felt his chest tighten just looking at her. It was an odd, unfamiliar reaction, especially to a woman he had known only for a few weeks. And why the fuck was she so happy to see him? He'd done absolutely nothing for her except agree to her asinine scheme purely for selfish reasons. Would she be like this the entire time they were to be married? And then after the time was up, she'd leave him in his own company? He didn't understand why the thought of that irritated him.

Keeping the irritation off his face, he exited the car, taking in the way an older woman, possibly her mother, took him in from the window beside the door, her eyes judging him. He couldn't entirely blame her. If it was his daughter and a big, scarred, one-eyed man showed up on his doorstep after marrying her, he'd be dead before he could get out. He understood the urge to protect. But that it was directed at him simply based on how he looked irritated him a little more. Especially because, for some reason, he had actually put in an effort to look nicer. Her proposal might have been unconventional, but they were married now in the eyes of the law, and she was his wife, and he didn't want her family to dislike him. But he guessed it was probably like dressing up a lion and expecting it to look less threatening. It wouldn't work.

The memory of her glaring at the woman who'd been staring at him popped in, sending another sliver of amusement inside him. She'd looked ready to battle for him, and while amusing, it was unfamiliar too. Unlike her mother, Zephyr watched him with nothing akin to judgment in her eyes. It was pure feminine appreciation and genuine joy, and he was entirely unfamiliar at receiving both. *That* was what hooked him and baffled him at the same time. How did a woman who didn't know him trust him like that? How did she desire him like that? And how did she leave it completely open for anyone and everyone to see without any shame or vulnerability? What did a woman like her want from a marriage like this? Was it truly about her grandmother's antiques, possibly because of some sentimental attachment to them? Alpha didn't know, and he wanted to.

"Hey, hubby." Zephyr tilted her head back to keep her gaze locked with his, and he hated to admit it, but she was adorable.

Knowing her mother was watching, and given what she'd told her family, Alpha leaned down and pressed a kiss to her cheek, her skin silky under his lips, the mild fragrance of something citrusy tickling his nose. He liked the smell. His bois would lick her up when they'd meet her. Not that he'd blame them.

But the thing that got him? The way her breath hitched when his lips made contact with her skin, like he'd taken her by surprise. It was an authentic response, and how she could see him and feel that was beyond him. Maybe she was the blind one.

Clearing his throat and ignoring the slight phantom itch in his right eye, he took out the ring he'd just bought for her from his pocket.

Her entire face lit up and that made something very odd happen in his chest. Maybe it was acidity.

"That's beautiful!" she exclaimed, taking in the ring. Fuck if he knew why he'd picked it, but he'd walked into a store, seen it, and known it had been made for her finger.

She looked up at him, her hazel eyes shimmery, the greens in them non-existent as her pupils enlarged, and the tightness in his chest got worse. It was a ring, and he was a stranger, and yet she looked at him like he'd conquered oceans for her.

She extended her hand and he slid the ring on, watching her admire it and cradle her hand against her chest like it was precious. It was in a way—a platinum band studded with tiny colorful crystals he didn't know the names of, but looked good together. The ring honestly looked like a unicorn had thrown up on it, but it screamed her, so he'd had to get it.

But he didn't like this tightness. She hadn't been married to him one day and she was causing him heart problems already. He needed to take a step back. Focus on finding her motive, find out how she knew, and what she knew about his childhood. That was it.

He straightened as her young, dark-haired sister stepped out, a sweet smile on her beautiful face. She'd been too busy trying not to gawk at him at the courthouse yesterday. Between that and trying to not get distracted by Hector, she'd been too shy or too preoccupied to properly talk to him. But she was young, so he cut her some slack.

This time at least, she extended her hand out to him. "Hi, Alpha. So good to see you here."

He shook her hand gently. "You too. I heard you work at SLF."

"Yes." The younger girl pulled her hand back. "I love working there. And I cannot thank you enough for everything you do for the organization. The women appreciate it."

He'd founded the organization soon after losing his eye. It was in honor of his mother and the countless women he had encountered in his line of work, women who wanted a way out from under oppressive systems and didn't have anywhere to go. It was for people like that—women, children, and men—that he had established Survivors of Los Fortis, so that in a city of millions, they would have a safe haven when they needed it. And even after so many years, it angered him that the number of people seeking refuge hadn't dwindled.

Zephyr's younger sister was a good one.

"I appreciate you helping out there," he told her honestly.

"Oh, Zee volunteers on the weekends too." Zenith gave her sister a coy look. "She gives the ladies a makeover, whatever they want."

Alpha knew that already. "Does that help them?"

"Immensely."

Interesting.

"Welcome. Please have a seat," the older woman who'd been watching him, his mother-in-law obviously, said as she walked out with a tray of iced drinks, indicating the iron sitting area on the side of the large porch, followed by a lean man with a mustache, obviously the girls' father.

So he wasn't being invited in. He got it.

Giving them a respectful nod, he took a seat on a chair too small and watched her mother place the tray on the table. Zenith took a seat on one side, her mother took another, and her father sat opposite him. Zephyr planted her very delectable ass on the arm of his chair, sliding her arm around his shoulder, clearly presenting them a united front. He appreciated that. Introductions were made and after an awkward silence for a few seconds, her father finally spoke, "You understand why this is a bit disconcerting for us."

"Of course." Yeah, he understood. Had he been in his father-in-law's place though, the boy would've been six feet under before he could utter a word.

"Zephyr was seeing someone else one day and then she's telling us she's in love with you, and she's married you at a courthouse." The older man picked up a glass, and Alpha followed to be polite. "Is it because of her grandmother's will?"

Alpha appreciated the man's straight question. But Zephyr had told him her parents couldn't know she was marrying him for that. He shook his head once. "No. Your daughter ... she's like a ray of sunshine in my very dark life." *What the fuck just came out of his mouth?*

He heard Zephyr inhale sharply, her fingers gripping his shoulder tightly. He'd have to tell her later not to take it to heart. He didn't mean anything by it.

Her mother finally leaned forward, a beautiful woman with grays in her hair, and Alpha wondered for a moment if his mother would've had gray hair too had she been alive.

"How did you meet my daughter?"

The question broke his thoughts.

Zephyr answered from his side, "I told you we met at SLF, Mama. I was there with Zen, he was there, and we just . . . clicked."

That was a surprisingly realistic scenario. He looked to the younger sister to see her nodding, having her sister's back, and that earned her another point in his book.

"And how did you meet the first time?" her mother persisted.

The first time? What exactly had she told her parents?

"I'd gone to a party with friends. They ditched me, and Alpha walked me home."

His little rainbow was quite the storyteller. He was half-interested by her account of the fictional events, half-weary wondering what she was lying to him about.

"And your family, Alpha?" her mother questioned.

"Mama," Zephyr chided.

"I have a half-brother." He took a sip of the iced drink. Too fruity. "He's getting married tomorrow, so we're attending his wedding. Other than that, no one."

He could see where Zephyr got it from, the compassion, as her mother finally softened slightly. "Yes, Zephyr told us. I'm sorry to hear that."

Shaking off the quiet mood, Zephyr clapped her hand once. "And we need to get going." She hopped off from the arm of the chair, rushing inside to probably get her bag, and everyone stood up.

"I don't know if she told you," Alpha began, wanting to make something clear to them, "but she'll be moving in with me once we're back. You're welcome to visit anytime. We can plan for a proper ceremony later."

Her mother's lips pursed. "Yes, she told us. She's packed everything at her apartment already. It's just all . . . very sudden, and very suspicious. I asked her if she was pregnant, if that was the hurry, but she said no. Just said she'd married her love and that was that. She was with Alec Reyes for two years and not once talked about marriage, so it's very hard for us to wrap our heads around this."

Fucking gambling Reyes. He might've spent two years with her, but he'd be damned if he tried anything again. Alpha didn't share, and for the duration of the time together, she was his even if he didn't plan on fucking her. How hard could it be to resist the little vixen?

Seeing her mother's reaction, the news of their marriage probably hadn't gone over well.

And that again made him wonder, why risk a fight with her family for *him?*

What the hell was she up to?

CHAPTER 8

ZEPHYR

Zephyr had once gone on a school trip from Los Fortis a hundred miles south, and that had been the most adventurous she'd ever been. Aside from that, the only trips she'd been on had been to visit her aunts who lived an hour away. She'd never left the country, much less the continent, and never been on a flight, much less one like this.

Victor and Diaz, the other guy she'd been introduced to, less hot but more charming, sat in the back of the private plane as their security detail on the trip. Hector was staying back, clearly being Alpha's second-in-command, to keep everything under control for the two days they'd be gone.

She looked around the inside of the private jet she'd been ushered and strapped onto, at the lush beige seats and gleaming wooden table and the neat walls, and it truly sank in for the first time—he'd made it. From the boy she had first seen with the torn clothes to the man who now wore an expensive leather jacket and owned a private jet, he'd made it out, and though she couldn't tell him, she felt something like pride bubble inside her. And lord, she wished Adriana—the kind, dying woman who had befriended a scared little girl in a strange place to give her comfort—could have seen her son now. She'd have been proud.

Zephyr turned to the window and blinked rapidly, trying to clear away the burn in her eyes and the sting in her nose. He was suspicious about her motives anyway, and she didn't need to give him more reason to think she was crazier and cried at nothing.

A slender blonde with really nice hair handed them some water. "Would you like anything else?"

Zephyr thanked her. "Just a quick question, is that your natural hair color?"

The blonde blinked in surprise. "Yes."

Damn. "It's a lovely shade. You're rocking it."

The attendant gave her a surprised smile and left, and she turned to see the man across from her, watching her as though he was trying to figure her out.

"What?" she demanded, slightly conscious of the way he was analyzing her.

He didn't say anything for a while, just studying her, and Zephyr tried to relax, wondering what went on in his head.

"Let's get some things straight between us," he said as preamble, and Zephyr braced herself. "Your grandmother's fund might be the excuse you're giving to me, and a whirlwind romance an excuse you're giving your family, but I know you have another motive for marrying me. The only reason you're my wife right now is that I'm intrigued. I don't know what your endgame is, but I will figure it out, so don't think I'm fooled for one second."

God, she hoped he figured it out, but if he didn't remember her after spending all the time with her, she doubted he would. But she wouldn't tell him that. Knowing how cynical he was, it would backfire in her own face. His lack of memory probably had something to do with his eye injury. Maybe, his brain had blocked some stuff out to protect him. She'd seen that happen in movies, but it was realistically plausible, and until she spoke to someone who knew trauma about it, she wasn't going to say a thing and risk retraumatizing him.

No, she had to make him love her all over again, this new him with this new her. It could happen.

"And I don't know where you got your information about me," he continued, his voice rough and deep, reminding her of the wilderness "but I will find that out too. I hope it ends up being only for your grandmother's heirlooms because you won't like the alternative."

He was kinda hot when he was threatening her, though she doubted he'd appreciate it if she said that to his face at the moment.

"Now I just need to figure out if you're one hell of a liar or not."

Zephyr took a sip of her water. "I'm an open book."

Alpha mimicked her movement and drank his water, the motion of the muscles in his neck very sexy. God, he'd gotten sexier over the years, and she had no shame in admitting she wanted him in bed, out of bed, against the wall, whatever way she could have him.

"Just in case you're not a liar"—he placed his glass on the table between them, his hand enhancing the fragility of the glass—"consider this a simple warning not to expect anything romantic from this relationship. My curiosity about you does not equal romantic interest. If you expect anything on those lines, you will be disappointed. I don't love."

Liar. He did love; he just didn't want to. But she knew he had his shields in place, and this Alpha clearly had a shit ton of trust issues, so she didn't take his warning lightly. She'd have to wade through these waters with the baggage of his past and hope they could make it to the shore.

"Too bad." She shrugged lightly. "I tend to get attached to my lovers."

"I'm not your lover," he reminded her.

She smiled.

"I won't be your lover either." The side of his jaw ticced. "Lust leaves me empty now. It's better in the long run, anyway."

"So I'll be what . . . your roommate?" She huffed a laugh.

He tapped his fingers on the table between them. He liked tapping things. God, her brain was a smutwreck.

"You can have your own room." *Tap, tap, tap.* "For the duration of the marriage, let's just share each other's company. I find you interesting enough. We can be cordial, but it's best not to complicate things more by adding anything sexual in the mix."

"We have chemistry," she pointed out.

"A pity kiss doesn't count."

Pity kiss, her ass. He'd been as into it as her.

"It's hot chemistry." She leaned forward.

He shrugged. "I had chemistry with my sister-in-law-to-be. Doesn't mean I acted on it."

Oh, wow. Zephyr blinked and processed the fact that she would get to meet someone he'd considered being with.

"Chemistry lies, Zephyr," he went on after dropping that bomb.

"Then what tells the truth?" She tilted her head to the side, curious about his thought process.

"Heart," he stated, no affliction in his voice.

"And what does yours say?"

The unscarred side of his lips lifted. "Nothing. Fucker hasn't spoken in years. It's a dead, scarred piece of useless muscle."

God, it hurt her. It hurt her that he'd built himself a tower with walls so high it had become impenetrable.

'You are hope, sunshine. Hope for a better life.'

The boy who'd told her that clearly lived in the tower, unreachable. But she would scale the walls if she had to, get to the top, and rescue her lover. She would give him hope again if it was the last thing that she did.

His plan to stay away from her wouldn't work, but she kept that to herself. She would tempt him and seduce him until he gave in. There was nothing more powerful than a woman on a mission. Telling him her plans involved some solid skin slapping probably wasn't for the best for now.

She raised her glass of water to him. "To chemistries that lie."

He raised his. "And hearts that die."

Oh boy, he had no idea the CPR she had planned for him.

They went quiet, but comfortably. Zephyr took out her ebook reader and pretended to be engrossed in a novel while covertly watching him; he simply looked out the window, lost in thought. The attendant came again with some overloaded sandwiches and Zephyr put her reader down, happy to have an excuse to engage him in conversation again.

"I thought you'd be working on your laptop or something, master of the universe as you are," she teased, unwrapping her sandwich.

"I can't read," he told her simply.

Zephyr paused, completely taken aback. She hadn't been expecting that reply.

Her surprise must have been evident on her face because he explained. "I didn't grow up with much money. My ma sent me to school, but I dropped out after she passed away."

"I'm sorry." She extended her hand and gave him a soft squeeze, surprising him. "You must've learned to read by then."

"Yeah, but when this happened"—he pointed to his eye patch—"reading smaller things got hard. I just stopped after a while." He seemed to shake himself, watching her curiously with his single eye. "I don't usually talk about it."

A little piece of her heart melted. "Your secret is safe with me." She gave him a small smile and watched him look away, clearly uncomfortable at having shared so much. She let him be, noticing now how he slowly peeled the wrapper on his sandwich mostly with his left hand and wondered what little everyday things that most people took for granted he had to work hard to accomplish. Was everything in his house sound-controlled? Did the injury affect more than his vision and memory? His hearing? His sense of balance? She'd seen him fighting and moving well enough, but was that natural or something he'd trained himself to do?

Something occurred to her, then. "Is that why you didn't reply to my texts?"

He looked up, putting the sandwich down. "I don't like phones. And I don't text anyone. People who have my number are business contacts. They just call."

And there she'd thought he'd ghosted her. She needed to be more considerate of his new body, and the ways it affected him. "So I can just call you now?"

He grunted, focusing on his sandwich.

"Will you save my contact as wifey?"

The look she got would have flayed the flesh from a lesser mortal.

Chuckling, she took a bite of the chicken sandwich, the cheese melting in her mouth, and groaned before stopping herself, finding him looking at her. The insecurity reared its ugly head, especially when eating with people. Used to people nagging her about what she ate, she half expected him to do the same, half expected him to go *'that's a lot of cheese'* or *'you should eat only two'*.

He looked at her mouth, simply picked up his own sandwich, took a bite, and nodded. "Hmm."

And that was that.

Zephyr sat for a second, looking down at the bread, processing what just happened.

Nothing had really happened, but *something* had happened.

Born in a family of tall women with perfect figures who didn't gain an inch no matter what they put in their bodies, Zephyr had always been well-intentionally teased about being short and full-figured by her mom, her aunts, her cousins, everyone. Zen, though adopted, fit in more with their family's genetics than she did.

When she'd been nineteen, a hormonal imbalance had made her rapidly gain weight. She'd spent the next few years on medication, bringing the hormones and the weight down, and ended up being curvy as hell, only amplified by her short height. She did pilates diligently, her body was flexible and strong, and now even though she was the healthiest that she'd ever been, people around her somehow always ended up telling her, in the most well-meaning way possible, to lose a few more pounds. She'd look *so much prettier*. She was already fucking pretty. She had her own sense of style, she took her medication, and took care of her body. But it was the first time someone, aside from Zen, had eaten with her and not pointed it out. Maybe it was because his own body was imperfect by other people's standards. Maybe it was because he was a man who didn't even notice or think about it.

Whatever it was, he just did it.

And then, he expected her not to have any romantic notions. She was already a goner.

She took another bite of the delicious sandwich, enjoying the companionable silence as they both ate, silently falling a little more in love with the new him, enough for the both of them until he could catch up.

CHAPTER 9

ZEPHYR

Alpha's half-brother was seriously *hot*.

She didn't know what she'd expected, but a suave, stunning, perfectly sculpted man greeting them at the airport hadn't been it. And he was a charmer to the boot. He'd taken one look at her, asked Alpha, "Who's this gorgeous creature on your arm?" and promptly kissed her cheek platonically in greeting. Had she not already been in love with the grumpy giant by her side, she would've *swooned*.

"Where's your bride?" Alpha asked after introducing her, keeping his distance from her. He'd pulled back after opening up on the flight, taken a step far enough back that she could feel the cold seep in the gap between them, because of his idiotic sense of keeping it platonic or because of his vulnerability on the plane; she didn't know. And being in a new environment as she was, she didn't know how to close the gap yet.

Dante grinned. "Letting Tempest have quality time with her grandmother and sneaking a beauty nap. Not that she needs it, but motherhood is tiring for her."

Zephyr looked at the man. She was surprised by the openness of his affection for his wife-to-be. The men she'd encountered rarely wore their love with the kind of pride he did *and* still managed to pull off the self-assured, cocky vibe that was kinda hot. Damn, the girl was lucky. He had an interesting personality.

He escorted them to a large, black Range Rover, slightly different from Alpha's back home, and opened the door in the back for Zephyr. *Oh, a gentleman too.*

Smiling, she thanked him and climbed in, glad she'd worn leggings instead of a skirt. She was surprised though that her husband didn't just pick her up and plop her down as he'd taken to doing in their city. He was definitely taking the platonic, keeping his distance thing seriously.

She settled in, as did both men, and Dante smoothly pulled out of the airport, another dark car tailing behind them with the security. She wasn't surprised. From her internet search alone, she'd learned Dante Maroni was a pretty big deal in the mafia world, recently having taken over after his father's death. The only thing she was curious about, however, was how he and Alpha had met, and precisely what Alpha was involved in. It couldn't have been mafia, because Los Fortis had never really been the center for one. She knew he was into something with security, just not what exactly it was. She'd find out eventually, and she just hoped it wasn't something she couldn't live with because there were some lines that just shouldn't be crossed. Knowing who he had once been though, Alpha had always been a protector. She could not imagine a world where he could be crossing those inhumane boundaries.

All in good time.

Tenebrae City was vastly different from Los Fortis. For one, the climate was more temperate than tropical, the hills in the distance a darker shade of green than the jungles around her city, the cover of the dark clouds something she only saw during the heavy rains.

She rolled the window down, enjoying the cool, dry wind on her face, her eyes taking in everything.

"Thanks for coming." Dante broke the silence after a while. "It means a lot."

Alpha grunted. *Grunted*.

Zephyr observed him quietly from the back, trying to understand why he was more reserved with his own blood. He was more aloof, more rigid than he had been on the flight, and she didn't know if it was because of her or Dante. Alpha attending something like a wedding had made her assume that he was on good terms with his half-brother. Was that not the case?

"So when did you get married?" Dante went on, seemingly unbothered by the silence, with such ease she liked him immediately.

"Monday," her husband replied. "Courthouse wedding."

Dante looked at her in the rearview mirror. "Are you pregnant?"

Zephyr loved how everyone automatically assumed she was knocked up because of the whirlwind wedding. She shook her head. "No, we haven't even—"

"It's just for six months," Alpha interrupted her, quite rudely. "Not a real marriage."

Ouch.

She knew that's what they'd talked about, but saying it out loud like that just made it all so … clinical. Reductive. *Lesser*. Like the little moments they'd had never happened.

Dante was considerate enough not to comment, simply shifting the conversation to include Zephyr, asking her questions about her family, her work, normal generic talk that she appreciated more than she could say.

She looked down at the ring on her finger, the beautiful piece unlike any she'd seen, a band of platinum adorned with tiny rubies, amethysts, sapphires, and emeralds, colorful and unique.

'One day, when I have money, I'm going to buy you the prettiest ring, sunshine.'

Zephyr felt her nose burn and looked out, remembering the whispered promise on the last night she'd seen him before he'd disappeared from her life. The ring was more precious to her than he'd ever realize. She hadn't expected him to get her one, had been fully prepared to buy one for herself, but he had and it was perfect, and Zephyr tucked that moment he slid it on her finger in a corner of her heart, cupping it like a flame in the fluttering wind, keeping it alive, warm and loved, to revisit if she failed in making him love again.

It scared her sometimes, the enormity of the task she had undertaken. She didn't know what he'd been through in the years between then and now. She didn't know what kind of traumas he had, didn't know what his triggers were, didn't know if the walls he'd built around his heart could be scaled at all. She'd bruise and bleed if they could be, drag herself to the corner where he rested and lay her head down with him if he let her. But she had to take her time. He would get spooked and run the other way if he figured out what she wanted—him.

The men talked about something related to work using code words because she didn't understand a thing. Within thirty minutes, they were out of the city and driving up a rolling green hill toward a large mansion she could see. The tall gates, manned by security guards who nodded at Dante respectfully, opened, and it looked like a different world inside. The huge mansion, a few buildings off to the other side, all over the green hill and fenced within a wall, was like a movie set. Her entire neighborhood could've fit in the area easily. People were bustling about, decorating the venue, some carrying chairs, some carrying boxes, and some carrying guns.

Zephyr had never seen so many guns in real life. She'd seen one in Victor's jacket when she'd interrogated him, but that had been it.

The driveway stopped and Dante pulled the car right next to the mansion's double doors. Zephyr jumped out without waiting for anyone to open her door, taking all of it in.

Wow.

A member of the staff ran to them, and Dante directed him to get their luggage to the guest wing. They had a *wing* for guests. *Bougie shit.*

An older woman with graying hair came out with a tiny bundle wrapped in a green blanket in her arms, and Zephyr watched in awe as Dante took the baby from the woman, cradled her against his broad chest, uncaring for the drool he got on his suit, cooing to her. "You missed Daddy, didn't you, princess?"

Then the fluffiest cat she'd seen walked out and rubbed against Dante's legs, getting fur over his pants.

Zephyr's ovaries *melted*. What was it about a big man with babies and kittens? It was like catnip, pun intended.

Dante finally turned to his guests, his smile huge.

"Alpha, Zephyr, I'd like you to meet my princess, Tempest. Tempest, this is your uncle and aunt."

Aunt.

She was that little baby's *aunt*. Holy shit, she'd never been an aunt before.

She looked at Alpha and saw that it had affected him too. *Dead heart, my ass.*

Knowing what she did about his family, she couldn't imagine what being an uncle must be doing to him. Quietly, she took his large hand in hers and gave it a squeeze, and though he didn't squeeze it back, he didn't let go either.

"Oh my god, she's absolutely scrumptious!" Zephyr stepped

forward since Alpha seemed frozen in place, and touched Tempest's soft cheek.

The baby yawned, her eyes like emeralds opening wide, her mouth opening in a wet, gummy smile at seeing her father. She made those happy baby noises and flapped her arms before her eyes went to the larger, scarier-looking man.

Zephyr took Alpha's hand she was holding and brought it up, making his fingers touch Tempest's soft skin, praying that the baby didn't cry.

She didn't. Little Tempest Maroni gurgled and drooled and gave Alpha the same gummy smile, and she saw her husband get wrapped around her minuscule pinkie.

Oh yeah, it affected him all right. He didn't even try to hide it on his face.

"You came." A husky tone of surprise made Zephyr look up at the entrance, and her jaw dropped. A stunning, and she meant *stunning*, goddess of a woman walked toward them with the grace of a swan gliding through the water, a gentle smile on her perfect face, tall and classy and oozing poise, her glinting green eyes popping against her tan skin, her dark hair voluminous with natural waves and curls. That was some *good* hair. She didn't think women like this could exist outside of mythologies.

The woman, clearly Tempest's mother and Dante's bride, took in the man beside her.

Zephyr looked up at Alpha and saw him watching her with a look she knew.

Chemistry.

He'd *liked her* liked her.

Zephyr had never really been jealous, especially never of other women. Her family had beautiful women, she saw absolute knockouts at work every day, and she loved making women feel good about themselves on a daily basis. Jealousy was an entirely antithetical emotion to that. But standing there, at the side of the man she had loved once and wanted to love again, a man who had just moments ago reduced her attempt at making their future into something lesser, a man who clearly didn't remember her but remembered the goddess in front of her, something ugly took root in the pit of her stomach. Not anything against the goddess, who was clearly in love with Dante and happy with her family, or even against Alpha for admiring something even she admitted was admirable.

No. The ugly was old insecurity, one she'd fought off for years and thought had laid to rest, an insecurity that maybe she wasn't enough. Maybe she'd never be enough. Maybe anything she did wouldn't make a difference. She loved too much, trusted too easily, got hurt too often, and maybe she needed to harden herself. But she would lose the essence of who she was if she did, and so she never did. Feeling hurt was more acceptable than feeling dead. The ugly in her head got awful.

'Almost thirty and no boyfriend? There must be something wrong with you.'

'Such a nice girl, how has no man fallen in love with you?'

'Flings and flings, and your one long-term relationship? He cheated.'

'The one man you truly loved left you. He doesn't even remember you. You were that inconsequential.'

'Your husband doesn't want you.'

Zephyr blinked the burn away and withdrew her hand, pasting a smile on her face as introductions were made. Dante put a hand around Amara's waist, and Zephyr hoped her husband would touch her, maybe hold her shoulder, do anything to indicate she was with him. He didn't. Dante asked Alpha for a quiet word.

Zephyr, already a bit lost and a bit sad, simply told them she'd take a look around the grounds, and excused herself. Diaz followed her at a safe distance.

She hated when she got like this sometimes when something completely random would trigger her down a spiral of questioning her self-worth even though she knew it wasn't *real*. It *felt* real.

Walking around the mansion toward the gazebo where people were putting up the frame for the wedding, she took her phone out from her pocket and called the one person with who she could be honest about everything.

"Zee! How was the flight?" Zen's happy greeting immediately had her heart feeling lighter. Even though she was five years younger, Zenith was her best friend. Since they were kids, they'd had a ritual of snuggling together every night and talking about everything that had happened in their day, from a lame catcalling to a serious crush to bad clients. Now, they did their night routines while chatting. Though it had only been Zephyr doing the sharing in the beginning, over the years, Zen had joined in. Now, Zephyr knew she was her sister's person and vice versa.

"Really good," Zephyr told her, walking around the hill, her eyes taking in every facet of the mansion.

"Oh, no," she heard her sister mumble. "What happened?"

"Nothing really." Zephyr felt her lips tremble. "It just . . . I wish he remembered me sometimes."

"Oh, honey." Zen knew exactly how she felt. Zen had been the one who'd looked out for her every time she'd snuck out, the one she'd spilled everything to when she'd returned. Zen knew it all, from the first time she saw him to the last. "Are you sure you want to do this? You can still back out, you know."

"I have to try," Zephyr whispered, her chest tight. "He's different now, but I have to try, Zen. I can't live knowing I found him again and didn't do anything."

Zen sighed. "And how's that going for you?"

Zephyr huffed a laugh. "He wants us to be roommates only."

Zen was quiet for a moment on the other end. "Then be his roommate. Be the best roommate he'd ever have. You know him, Zee. You know his buttons. Push them, test them. If anyone can make a scary man like that fall in love, it's you."

Zephyr sniffled. "This is why you're my favorite sister," she declared into the phone and heard Zen chuckle. "I'm your only sister."

They talked for a few minutes, mostly about her mother believing Alpha was the devil's kin who had brainwashed her, and how she couldn't *'wait for him to get out of her life.'* If she did end up separating, she knew one person who would be happy. At least Zen had convinced her father to keep a more open mind. That counted.

Zephyr bid her sister goodbye, her mood still low, and asked a staff member for directions to her room, heading to the guest wing. The sun was setting down, the sky more dark than light, portions of the hill completely submerged in the shadows as she made her way to the building, her eyes taking in the mansion.

Her perusal came to a stop at a large window of some kind of study. Dante and Amara sat with another couple, her husband sitting with his back to her, all having a drink, Amara laughing at something, the fluffy cat napping on the windowsill.

Zephyr stood outside at a slight distance, alone for the first time in a new city of strangers, watching it all. And she didn't know why, but it hurt her. She may have married him, but she wasn't a part of whatever this group was. She wanted to be.

Stop wallowing, she chided herself. She'd chosen this path, and she knew it wouldn't be easy. Dante, the only one facing her, looked up and locked eyes with her. She saw him glance at where Alpha sat before looking at her again, something akin to compassion in his dark eyes. Zephyr gave him a little smile that hopefully looked reassuring, pretending she was completely unbothered, and went on her way to her room, married, miserable, and alone.

CHAPTER 10

ZEPHYR

He hadn't come to their room the entire night, and she'd known it was their room because both their weekend bags were there.

Zephyr had lain awake in bed, staring at the ceiling of the unfamiliar room, tossing and turning, and shedding a few tears because she cried at everything. Sometimes, she watched videos of puppies and cried. One time, she'd been on her period at work and a client had complimented her hair and she'd gotten teary-eyed. Her tear ducts were just extra hydrated, always had been.

Every time she felt dejected, she looked at her ring and reminded herself that it meant something. Him finding that particular ring meant *something* even if he didn't realize it. It would take time, but she had to keep fighting for them.

But it was early morning and Zephyr just couldn't stay in anymore.

She changed from her sexy pajamas—that she'd put on, expecting to at least have their first night of sleepover together—and into leggings and a thin sweater, venturing out of their room on the first floor. Down the stairs she went, and out into the gazebo she'd seen the previous evening, enjoying the foggy morning, which was a rarity in her city.

A few members of the staff were up and about, already prepping for the big wedding, the lawn behind the mansion turned into something out of a beautiful fairytale. Zephyr simply sat her ass on a cold stone bench in the gazebo, watching them all, wondering if she'd ever get her own big wedding. Zephyr had always wanted one with all her extended family in attendance, with a gorgeous dress and veil, letting everyone see her commit to her love for life. It hadn't been until she'd met Alpha that she'd ever thought she could spend her life with this guy, definitely not something she ever felt for Alec, even though she gave him two years of her life. She was going to try and delay her mother from planning something for six months until the contract ended, and see at the end if she needed a wedding or a divorce. "Congratulations on your nuptials."

A dark voice from the side made her glance up. A man stood against one of the pillars of the gazebo, facing away from her, wearing a black hooded sweatshirt, his hands in his pockets, his face not visible to her from the angle.

"Um, thanks," she replied lightly, looking back at the staff again. "Who are you?"

"A friend," he answered, something off in his voice. Zephyr glanced at his form again. He appeared tall, muscular, but not overly. She could see the muscle definition in his back, but his body didn't look like a hardcore gym body.

"Have you heard about the murders in Los Fortis?" he asked, a slight accent in his tone, and Zephyr straightened, wondering if he was making small talk or not.

"The hooker murders, right?" That's what the media had been calling them. The murders had been in the papers recently, but nothing had been solved yet.

"Yes." The man straightened. "Tell your husband to be alert."

Zephyr felt herself stiffen, a cold shiver passing over her, suddenly realizing she was in the compound of a mafia boss and sitting alone far away from anyone to call for help.

The man chuckled. "If I'd wanted to kill you, you'd have been dead coming out of the salon last week when your heel snapped, Mrs. Villanova. You need better security."

What the hell?

She froze on the cold stone bench, watching the man as he brought out a gloved hand from his pocket, dropping a black envelope on the empty stone railing that went around the gazebo. "Give this to your husband. And make sure he reads it."

Zephyr glanced down at the envelope and looked up, only to see an empty space where he'd been. He'd disappeared, like she'd imagined the entire thing.

Taking a fortifying breath, her body covered in chills, she went to the railing and picked up the paper. The stationery was thick, good quality. The urge to pry it open was strong, but she knew she shouldn't. It could be something confidential meant only for Alpha, and until he gave her the okay, she couldn't dig in.

Gripping it in her hand, she went in search of her errant husband.

It took a while.

Not one staff member knew where he was, which was ridiculous, because how could someone miss a giant man with an eye patch? It was the wedding day, the sun was already rising and bright, and

Zephyr was getting seriously pissed, walking around the strange mansion, trying to find one place where her husband could be. For a split second, she wondered if he was in another woman's room, but she discarded the thought immediately. Until he gave her a reason to think that, she'd keep her overactive imagination contained. He hadn't been with anyone in a while, and if he needed to be with someone, she was right there. Trust was the cornerstone for any relationship, and she needed to give him trust in order to earn it back.

Finally, she caught a break and bumped into one of the guards who told her Alpha was in the training wing. Of course, he'd be in there punching at something. Getting directions, her hand holding the envelope, she brisk-walked down the hill to the training building. No wonder people on the property looked extra fit with all the walking they must do daily.

Finally, she reached the gray building and stopped at the entrance, gaping.

Five shirtless men stood around the mats in the middle, cheering and cursing as her very shirtless husband and a very shirtless Dante went at each other with knives. Honest-to-god *knives*.

Her jaw open, she watched with fascination as Alpha, despite having a physical disadvantage, danced around the mats, escaping each and every hit coming at him from different angles, counter-attacking with his own set of knives, his hands wrapped in tape, his body a study of scars and ink and sweat. Her face started getting hot watching him move, over and over, the playfulness with which he chuckled when Dante missed, goading him. They were bonding with weapons, and it was bizarre to her, since her idea of sibling bonding involved heart-to-hearts and ice cream, but hey, whatever floated their boat.

They finished their mock-fight, and Dante slapped him on the back, turning to see her standing at the entrance. His eyebrows hit the hairline, but he came forward with a smile. "Sister-in-law. To what do we owe this pleasure?"

God, the man was a treasure. The way he'd made her comfortable yesterday, and the way he did so now, she could've hugged him.

Before she could say anything, she saw her husband coming up behind Dante, a glower on his face. "You shouldn't be here."

She suddenly remembered she was pissed at him.

Shoving the envelope against his sweaty chest, she hissed, "And you should've been in our room last night, but life is full of disappointments."

With that, she turned to Dante and gave him a soft smile. "Thank you for having me here."

"Of course." He inclined his head, giving her husband a side-eye. "I can have one of the guys escort you back." He indicated one of the shirtless men in the building.

"She's fine," Alpha grit out before she could respond. What the hell was his problem?

Whatever.

Without a word, she turned on her heel and left, heading to her room to get ready for the wedding. She was halfway there when her steps faltered and she realized he wouldn't be able to read the note, and he was prideful enough to not admit it to the others. Sighing, some of her fury seeping out, she went back to see them coming out, Alpha walking to the side, slightly apart from everyone else. She slowed to a walk, meeting him halfway.

"I'll read that for you if you'd like," she offered softly, tilting her head back to keep their gazes locked.

He didn't say anything, just handed her the envelope quietly, and she softened a bit more.

Taking it from his hand, she opened the flap, and pulled the white paper out, looking down at the words, sobering.

"What does it say?" he asked, his voice gruff.

She swallowed, and read the note verbatim.

"I know who he is. As a gesture of goodwill, I will share that he will frame you in his next kill. I'll be in touch."

What the hell?

"It's unsigned."

She looked up at her husband to find his jaw clenched tight. "How did you get this?"

"A man gave it to me." She swallowed. "What does he mean?"

His hand fisted, and he took a step closer. "Did you see him?

She shook her head. "He was tall, wearing a sweatshirt. He had the hood up."

He took the paper from her hand, staring at it for a long minute with his single gaze, before letting out a breath. "I'll deal with it later."

This was serious. Who was the guy and why the hell was he talking about a killer framing her husband?

Zephyr frowned as he purposely headed up the hill to the guest wing, leaving her standing there alone.

Her earlier annoyance returned. "Is there a reason you're being deliberately rude to me or are you just this delightful every morning?" she asked, injecting joviality into her tone as she caught up with his longer strides.

He gave her a side glance, but kept on quietly.

"It's quite a feast for the eyes right now." She poked at the bear, deliberately eyeing all the shirtless men coming out of the training building.

He didn't respond, just began walking faster like he could outrun her.

"I mean, not that my eyes don't appreciate it, but what was even the point of bringing me here?" she kept on. "A girl has her pride, you know? You don't have to go around telling people it's not a 'real marriage'." She emphasized the words with finger quotes. "Dante probably thinks I'm a hussy who's tied you down, which, granted I am, but he doesn't need to know about that."

He was listening, with the way his head was slightly tilted as he walked, his eye patch and scar visible to her in profile. Time to test the waters.

"I mean, just yesterday someone asked me if it wasn't a 'real marriage' and if I wanted to hook up for the wedding, which was very flattering, but—"

He pivoted so suddenly she barely had a second to stop before tripping.

"Who?"

Bingo.

Zephyr shook her head. "Doesn't matter. My point is you saying that will give people the impression that we're in some kind of open relationship here—"

His free, scarred right hand came to her chin, interrupting her as his golden gaze seared her. "This is not an open marriage. I don't share."

Oh, she liked that.

"Great. I don't want to be shared." She nodded profusely and threw her hands out. "But they don't know that. Not with the way you've been acting. I've already had someone flirt with me"—his grip tightened on her chin—"and if you don't make it clear that I'm taken, I think it'll just escalate, me being so irresistible and all. Someone might even risk your wrath and steal me away like we're in some B-grade crime movie—"

Before she knew what was happening, she was up and over his shoulder, her world tilted upside down, blood rushing to her head, her leggings stretched over her ass as his palm covered it.

"You talk to my wife, you die," he announced coldly.

Dante whistled in the distance, and Zephyr flushed. That was the most *'Me Tarzan, You Jane'* thing she'd ever seen in her life. She was as taken as she could get.

He declared to the men lingering on the ground and simply carried her to their room to get ready for the wedding. Zephyr shut up after that, satisfied that his possessive streak still existed somewhere deep down, and while he was being cold, he wasn't unaffected by her. If the last twenty-four hours had been any indication, it was a long, long road ahead of her. But today began with a win, and she'd take that.

Happy as a clam, she hung over his shoulder as he carried her away.

Dante and Amara's wedding was beautiful. Not just the setting and the day itself, but the couple. She didn't even know them, but she cried when Amara came out with little Tempest on her hip. Zephyr looked at the way Dante gazed at her, the love so visceral in his look it reminded her of a time long ago when the man at her side had looked at her like that. And it wasn't just Dante, but the dangerous-looking man at his side looking at the spectacled woman beside Amara. What the hell did these guys eat up here? She needed to bottle that love. Maybe she could sell it on the black market and become a mafia lordess. Lordess? Was that even a word? It should be. She wondered if her husband would ever look at her like that again, and that made her sniffle.

He handed her a tissue silently, sitting in a white formal shirt that she was sure he'd had tailored because there was absolutely no way they made it in his size. The shirt was left open at the collar, the fabric taut over his chest, a smart navy jacket covering the rest of him. His short beard was trimmed, his hair pushed back, and damn he cleaned up so well. And why he had tissues in his pocket, she didn't know, but Zephyr took it, blowing her nose as delicately as she could.

"You cry a lot." A young voice from her side made her look down at a boy with blue eyes who just sat down at her side. He was around ten years old, but the way he was studying her made him seem older.

Zephyr wiped her nose with the tissue. "I'm an emotional girl."

The boy kept staring at her unnervingly for his age. "How do you do that? Cry?"

Zephyr focused on her little companion, intrigued by his line of questioning. "I just feel it, and tears come out. You don't cry?"

The boy shook his head.

Damn. "Do you want to?"

He gave a nod.

Poor baby.

"Tell you what." She leaned closer to him to whisper. "I'll cry for you, so that way you don't have to waste your tears. What do you say?"

He blinked, his leg restlessly moving up and down. "Someone else can cry for me?"

That was a weird question. Before she could reply, Tempest's grandmother came to take the boy. "Come, Xander. We have to sit up in the front."

The boy left to go to the front from the seating area, and Zephyr turned to the wedding too, momentarily distracted by musing about what kind of a world she'd stepped into where little kids didn't know how to cry. It reminded her of seeing Alpha that first time, roaring with the pain of losing his mother. She looked at him now, sitting still with a permanent scowl on his face, and it made her wonder if this world had killed that boy completely or if he still existed somewhere inside the one-eyed beast he'd become.

CHAPTER 11

ALPHA

His new wife was infuriating.

Since that morning at the wedding, where she'd goaded him into a reaction, she'd been wearing a self-satisfied look on her face, and it was partially amusing, partially fascinating, and mostly annoying.

He'd stayed away from her that night, staying in another one of the rooms in Dante's mansion after bringing Tristan, Dante, and their partners up-to-date on everything from his end. Tristan's partner, Moarana, in particular was a curious case. She had pretty much dug up his life and recited it without compunction, and he got the sense that she was wary of him. Not that he'd blame her. Tristan wasn't particularly fond of him either. But Dante and Amara seemed to be the mutual point of interest, and he was okay with that. He was there for his brother anyway, who seemed to be a pretty cool man, and he was wicked good with knives, which Alpha respected.

A part of him wondered if he'd ever get to meet his other half-brother, Damien. But if he'd not made an appearance at Dante's wedding, Alpha doubted it. Good for him though, making a life for himself away from everything. Although Alpha hadn't known Dante for long, seeing Amara and Tempest at the ceremony, he was happy for the fucker. It was a rarity to find any semblance of love and keep it in their world, and the fact that he'd done that for almost a decade was truly admirable.

He and his new wife had left soon after the ceremony, mostly because he'd been eager to be back on his own turf and share the note with Hector. He had a suspicion about who'd left the note with Zephyr, which was chilling in itself, but he wanted to discuss it with his friend. While Alpha couldn't read and do shit, Hector was a whiz with paperwork. He read, managed all the documents in place, and kept them out of trouble. The younger man had a fantastic eye for details, and a loyalty to Alpha and his empire like nobody would've expected. If it truly was a pack, Hector was his Beta.

Victor was excellent too, but he had hair-trigger and anger issues he needed to work on, possibly learn the ropes for a few more years before he could and help his brother in running the company. But he was good with security, and since he already had a rapport with his little wife, he was on bodyguard duty for her.

"I didn't know you lived in the jungle," the infuriating little firecracker said from his side in the Jeep as they drove out of the city limits. Victor drove quietly, and Alpha just stayed silent. He'd just picked her up from her apartment with all her endless boxes and suitcases. What such a tiny woman needed all that stuff for, god only knew.

The only person who seemed as happy about their union as his wife seemed to be her sister. The two had stood on the doorstep, hugging and crying for a solid time before they had left. And it made him wonder, given how close the two sisters were, if Zenith knew the real reason for this entire venture.

"Do you wear a leafy skirt and swing from the vines too?" Zephyr quipped from the side, and he finally turned to give her a look that scared most people. She just smiled up at him, and he swore he wanted to turn her upside and smack her delectable ass.

Fucking infuriating.

Victor choked on his laugh at the front, and Alpha grit his teeth. He liked Victor, but he didn't like that the good-looking boy had already established such an easy camaraderie with his wife when he usually hated people. He didn't like that she had that light effect on Victor too. But he pretended to ignore it all. That was the best way. Just like he'd been ignoring her teasing little touches, the breathy little sounds she made when she called him for the most random reasons, the way her eyes checked him out and lingered deliberately on the hard parts of his body. He didn't think about how full her lips looked when she spoke, or how her citrusy scent teased his nose sometimes when she stepped into his personal space, or how he could see down her cleavage from his height, and it made him think of what his dick would look like nestled between her tits.

A month since she knocked him on his ass at the fight with that kiss, and he still remembered her taste, was tempted to taste her again at least twice a day. Minimum.

But it was best for her that he didn't, both physically and emotionally. She was small, and he could hurt her seriously if he lost control. After his last sexual encounter, it was best he didn't tempt fate. And the fact that she'd told him she got attached to her lovers just made him keep his distance more. When this time was up and the marriage ended—and it would end because he would find out her reasons and his curiosity would be satisfied—they'd simply move on without any attachments. He'd give her another room, enjoy her company because she did make him feel lighter, and probably have her bake him some more alfajores because he couldn't remember the last time he'd had them. Yes, that was the perfect plan.

The view outside changed as the city was left behind, the solid road becoming rougher, the foliage thickening as it closed in slowly.

A small hand gripped his thigh as the Jeep jerked over a boulder, and he looked down at it, her ring glinting in the daylight. He wondered how it'd look with her hand wrapped around him. He doubted her fingers would even touch.

She gave a nervous laugh, breaking his thoughts. "You guys aren't taking me to the jungle to drop me in the middle of nowhere with all my stuff, right? I wouldn't survive a day in the wild. The extent of my survival skills involve burning something with a curling iron, and even for that, I'd need electricity. And I don't like anything that slithers. I mean, I know I've been a pain in your very nice ass, but you wouldn't do—"

A laugh bubbled up in his chest, trapping itself in his throat as he looked out the window and heard her prattle on. The urge to smile, to try and lift the scarred side of his mouth, was a new sensation. And that was the other reason he'd wanted to assuage his curiosity, right there. He couldn't remember the last time he'd wanted to smile before she jumped into his world, a burst of colorful explosions in the stark gray of his sky, a sprout of life blooming in the land of death, a festival in a field that had only witnessed funerals. And now that he'd experienced that, like an addict, he wanted more.

"Breathe," he instructed as he'd naturally begun to when she started hyperventilating with her own imagination, her words coming too fast one after the other. She shut up, inhaled, mumbled an apology, and fell silent.

He thought it was fucking cute, and he didn't even like the word. She was, though. He was actually looking forward to seeing her reaction to his compound and his bois. And he was juggling whether he wanted to put her in the guest house or tempt fate by putting her in the adjoining bedroom. Maybe he needed a middle ground, to give her the bedroom near the kitchen. But that would be the most susceptible to any external attack. No, just for the sake of her safety, he'd give her the room adjoining his. Only for safety. It had nothing to do with how attractive he found her. Nothing to do with how he wanted to both cuddle her and smear her with his cum, the dual urges in him equally strong, the pure and the filthy desires colliding in perfect balance. He could imagine coming on her tits after fucking her mouth, fingering her while she screamed for release, one he wouldn't give until she begged. Fuck, she'd look good with him on her.

And he could just imagine how happy she'd be, sitting there all fucked up, looking like his little personal slut he'd threatened to call her, with her bright eyes and flushed skin and happy smile, right before she called him by some ridiculous term of endearment like 'lobster' (which she'd done that morning when he'd picked her up). It was ridiculous.

He subtly adjusted himself even as a part of him wanted to smile. Fucking infuriating.

CHAPTER 12

ZEPHYR

She'd gotten out of the jeep after a short bumpy ride and made her way down the stone path, covered with trellises in an arch, the scent of flowers and foliage strong as she walked through the space, enjoying the swish of her dress against her thighs, the sound of water rushing somewhere close by. As she'd reached the end of the path, the view became clearer, and she'd frozen.

When they'd told her he lived on the edge of the jungle, she'd expected a cottage in a clearing, maybe a large house. What she'd not expected was the architectural monstrosity that stood before her. Zephyr leaned her head back, her jaw dropping at the marvel of something like this actually existing just twenty minutes away from the city, much less being lived in. "Welcome home." Hector smiled as he received them, carrying one of her boxes inside the ... compound. That's what they'd referred to it as.

It was a *beast*, like the man who stood beside her. He'd made this?

"Holy shit," she breathed as she took everything in, and there was a *lot* to take in.

Three tiers of construction were done in levels on the hill. The first and lowest level had over twelve little cottages with slanting roofs that had eroded with time to a light sandstone shade. She could see a few women, men, and even two kids around the level. On the other end was a gray single-story building, outside which she saw two guards lingering. The second level had larger but fewer cottages of the same build, more spaced out and evenly spread. But it was the last and highest level that had a gasp leaving her lips.

A large mansion sat atop the highest point of the hill, wood and stone and glass that she was dying to see up close. Stone stairs from the bottom led to the top, a black metal railing running parallel to it on the sides, connecting all the levels with each other.

Having just visited the Maroni property, she'd not thought anything could have been more extra than that. She'd been wrong.

Standing there, seeing the empire he had created for himself, a wave of emotion burned her eyes.

'I'll get out of this shithole one day. You'll see.'

He had. He fucking had. He'd done it. It hit her then that he truly had lifted himself out of his circumstances, left behind the boy on the streets, and become the ruler of the city, with his own compound.

Her heart full, she wiped away an errant tear, aware of his gaze on her.

She looked to the side, locking their eyes together, something so acute sitting heavily on her chest as she watched him watch her, suffocating the words in her throat.

His large hand came to her chin, tilting her face up as he trailed the line of her tears with a golden eye, his thumb touching the wetness.

"This is not a reaction my home has ever had," he spoke softly, the puzzlement on his face clear.

Zephyr sniffled once. "I live to surprise."

He wiped her tear with the pad of his thumb, letting it linger on her cheek where her dimple appeared. "I don't like these."

Poor man, he'd have to learn. She was a crier.

She wiped her face with her palms and took a deep breath to steady herself. He left her chin and led the way to the stairs. Hector took the lead with one of her boxes in his muscular arms, Victor taking the Jeep away to park somewhere, she assumed.

The sun shone brightly on the entire hill, coating her skin with a sheen of sweat even though it was almost spring. The heat would be brutal in the summer.

"We have over two hundred guys in security in total." Hector began giving her a tour as they climbed the stairs. "A few fighters too, and most of them stay in the city. Our main training happens in the industrial district. All the cottages on Level One are for the in-house staff. There's a housekeeper and her family, her husband who's the chief of security, and her kids. You'll meet them all later."

Zephyr took it all in, completely in awe. "And the other staff?"

"There are the guards, of course," Hector informed her. "Five guys who maintain the grounds and keep the jungle from taking over. A cook, other helpers around the place, and so on. They all live on Level One. That"—he pointed to the gray building on the side—"is for them to relax, enjoy time together. More like a communal building. Boss doesn't really intrude on their time, so it's chill there."

The wind got stronger as they got higher, whipping up her dress, and she covered it with her hands on the back of her thighs, not wanting to flash anyone who climbed behind her. Zephyr watched Alpha ahead of her, his ass solid and very biteable in those jeans. The urge to grab it suddenly gave her an idea.

"Hubby," she called him sweetly and watched his back still as he turned to give her a questioning, slightly exasperated look. "Do you mind walking behind me?"

The unscarred side of his face frowned, matching the scarred side, but he sighed, moving to the side so she could precede him. Zephyr gave him her sweetest smile, making sure the dimple popped, and moved her hands from her ass, letting the wind do the rest of the work. She heard his little inhale as he got an eyeful of her backside, one of her best assets, and smiled to herself, glad she'd worn the sexy red thong, as uncomfortable as it was. She added an extra sway to her hips, knowing from his vantage, he'd be looking up her dress, seeing her ass cheeks being split by a line of red lace that was wedged in her crack, but he didn't have to know that.

Oh, she was enjoying this.

"What about these middle cottages?" she asked, continuing the conversation with Hector while making sure to sway her ass as she climbed to torment her stubborn husband further.

"They're for the sentinels."

"Sentinels?" Her eyebrows hit her hairline at the word.

"That's what we call ourselves. There are six of us in total. Five guys, one girl. We're the boss's main team. But only Victor and I are here right now. The rest are on . . . assignments." That was a very interesting power structure not only in the compound but the organization. Zephyr bit her lip as they crossed the larger cottages, curious about how he had made his fortune, wanting to know the specifics of what he did.

They finally got to the top, and Zephyr just halted at the visual overload. A large wooden deck with bamboo furniture sat on her left, overlooking a vista of endless green that made her realize how close on the precipice of wilderness they were. On her right, a large, curved swimming pool with clear blue water went to the edge of the structure, so anyone standing there could see straight out. The pool wrapped around the side of the mansion and disappeared behind it.

Zephyr looked at the house itself, a stunning design of cement, stone, wood, and glass. Behind the deck, a glass wall spanned the space, currently hidden behind tall beige curtains that hid everything. But lord, the view from the inside on a rainy day must be mesmerizing. Right in front of her and the hill stairs, was a tall, wide wooden door with a hinge slightly toward the center.

The sound of loud, multiple barks broke through her admiration.

Alpha stepped up beside her just as an older lady with weathered skin swung the large door open. Three huge dogs shot forward toward her husband, their tails wagging aggressively as they barked and danced around his legs, yapping away at seeing him home again.

Zephyr had never been around dogs. She liked them, and she loved puppy videos, but actually seeing them, three of them who came up to her waist and had jaws of wicked-looking teeth, had her freezing. Alpha, on the other hand, bent down and gave them each solid rubs behind their ears, on their heads, their bellies, a softness on his face that made her heart melt, his affection for the canines visible and palpable. Okay, men with babies and kittens and dogs, she was a simp for them.

The dogs, satisfied with their master being there, finally turned to her. One of them trotted forward immediately, giving her legs a sniff, his nose velvety and warm. His tongue lolled out and he licked her knee, tickling her slightly, the sensation making her giggle.

"That's Bear," Alpha spoke, watching the dog's behavior toward her.

"Can I pet him?" she asked, not knowing the protocol for this furry introduction.

He gave her a nod, and she extended her hand. Bear gave it a sniff before giving it a lick and moving his head for a scratch. Zephyr pet the soft fur on his head, and he immediately flopped his ears down and raised his head higher for more.

Smiling, she scratched him harder. "Oh, you and I will get along just fine, Mr. Bear, won't we? You're a big ball of love, aren't you?"

His tongue lolled out in answer.

Another dog joined his brother. This one was more tentative in his approach, his coat a deeper brown than Bear's on the snout. He sniffed her open-toed flats, giving her toes a lick, before trotting to the side of the deck, sniffing at different plants that lined the wooden boundary wall.

"That was Bandit," Alpha introduced the second one. "Be careful with your socks around him. You'll never find them again."

That made her chuckle. She looked at the third dog, the one watching her with somber eyes from Alpha's side, his ears perked up.

"And who is this distinguished gentleman?" she asked, noticing the scars on his snout. Alpha gave his head a pat. "This is Baron. He's not very social. As long as you don't do something sudden around him, he'll mostly leave you alone. And this"—he turned to the older woman eyeing her curiously—"is Leah. She's been my housekeeper for many years. Leah, this is Zephyr."

Zephyr gave the lady a smile. "I'm his wife. Call me Zee, please."

Leah wasn't surprised at the *wife* word, which made her realize she'd probably been already updated about her arrival. "Welcome, Zee. Where are her bags?"

Hector nodded at the house. "Vic and the boys are bringing it up from the back." He turned to Zephyr, explaining, "There's an elevator at the back you can use. I'll get your things settled in."

"Put them in the adjoining bedroom," Alpha commanded, still giving Baron a scratch absently as Bear settled his head on her feet.

Zephyr kept her smile on her face, not letting him see that she didn't want the adjoining room. She wanted to cuddle in his bed.

All in good time, Zee. You're here now. This is the win of the day.

"Leah," her husband addressed their housekeeper. "Would you please give Zephyr a tour and help her settle in? I'll be back for dinner. Please tell Nala to prepare accordingly."

If Leah found it odd that he was dumping her there and going on his way, she hid it well with a smile that creased her face and put laugh lines at the corner of her eyes. "Of course, Alpha. Come with me." She took Zephyr's hand and pulled her toward the door.

Zephyr saw Alpha whistle and the dogs—one lazing, one roaming, one scratching his ear with his paw—snapped to attention.

"Inside," he commanded, which did something to her insides, and the dogs followed her in. Damn, he was sexy when he was assertive like that. She wondered if he'd do that in bed, command her to do something, make her do it if she resisted, and manhandle her into position if she took too long to follow through.

She fanned her face thinking about it and watched his single eye darken.

She smiled.

He looked even more annoyed.

She would win him over, one tease at a time. For now, she had his home to make her own.

CHAPTER 13

ZEPHYR

Bear loved her. There was no other explanation for the way he followed her on her tour, right behind her, sniffing her legs, giving her little licks, and wagging his tail, giving her looks with his hopeful brown eyes that made her stop and give him head rubs. She was in love with him already.

Baron, on the other hand, couldn't care less. He plopped down on what she understood was his perch on a windowsill and simply watched the view outside, completely unbothered by her or anyone else. Bandit was nowhere to be seen.

Leah started her tour right from the main door. "There are four bedrooms in the house, besides the master. They're all en-suites. This is just a living area, but the dogs spend more time here than Alpha, mostly because they enjoy the view and the sun. The entire house is designed around this interior garden."

Zephyr took in the garden in question, genuinely awed at the design. An amazing indoor garden surrounded a sunken living area. Comfortable-looking beige couches took up half the living space in a three-sided rectangle, a center table in the shape of a chopped wooden log seated upon an oriental rug. A large flat screen was mounted on the wall in front of the couch, the area semi-private due to the garden that surrounded it. Glass took up the wall on the left of the main door, and a set of wide, wooden, unconnected stairs went up to another level on the far right. Immediately in front of the door, two low steps led to the raised open kitchen and a wooden, rustic-looking dining table with six seats. Behind that, sliding doors opened on to another decked area, the pool from the front of the house wrapping around to the back. It was *extraordinary*.

"Wow," she breathed, taking everything in, and heard Leah laugh.

"Yes, it takes some getting used to. But it is beautiful, no?"

"Oh, yes," she mumbled, rotating in her spot to not miss a single detail. "Were you here when this was built?"

"No," Leah replied, leading her through the kitchen to the back deck. Surprisingly, there was another smaller structure at the back. A wooden bridge went from the upper half of the mansion to the upper half of the outhouse. On the ground, stone steps connected the back deck to the door.

"That is a guest house," Leah informed her. "Usually, Alpha makes the guests stay at the hotel in the city, but sometimes, important people want to visit here, and Alpha does not like strangers in his house. He blames it on the dogs." The older woman gave her a grin. "Says they bite strangers. They go into that house happily, then."

Zephyr laughed. She could see him doing that to keep his space his own, threatening to sic his dogs on them.

The sound of running water was louder on the back deck. "Is there flowing water here?"

The other woman pointed to the side of the compound. "A little bit away, there's a waterfall. You can see it from the master bedroom."

Zephyr's eyes widened. "Really?"

"Yes, come, I'll show you."

The woman took her on a tour of the kitchen first, showing her where everything was kept, explaining the routines as she went. The cook came early in the mornings, cooked for the day, and stored everything for whenever Alpha wanted to eat. He didn't have any fixed meal time since he mostly worked and came home late, and everyone left the house in the evening since they knew he liked his quiet.

Leah took care of the house and fed the dogs on time. Alpha took them for a run in the morning, and if he was out of town, Leah's husband took them.

There was a bedroom off the living room that Leah showed her. Alpha had turned it into a study. Another bedroom, smaller than the first, was next to it, clean, but completely empty. Zephyr wondered what it was like for him, having all this space and being alone with his dogs, coming home after a day to a solitary house. Maybe he liked that, but Zephyr couldn't imagine what it must be like. She'd always come home to someone, her parents or Zen, and she hoped now to come home to him and the dogs.

Leah kept telling her everything as they went up the stairs. "This level has only two rooms. This is the master." She opened a heavy, rustic wooden door to reveal a room big enough to fit her parents' house.

The largest bed she'd ever seen dominated the left of the room, with a large carved headboard. It was a four-poster bed, pushed up against a plain white wall, netting folded back on top of its wooden frame. That bed could've fit four Alphas and still have space. She would drown in that bed. There was nothing much in the room though, which she found odd. The walls were barren, the space aside from the bed empty. It looked *too* clean.

Removing her eyes from it, she went to the sliding glass doors that opened into a covered balcony, a hammock hanging from the iron frame of the covering. From this side of the house, she could see a small waterfall in the distance between the thick green. It was absolutely *magical*.

"Your suite is through here," Leah brought her back to the present, indicating a single connecting door opposite the bed. Zephyr went through and saw a much smaller room without a balcony, but a large window facing the waterfall view. Four of her boxes were already in place, and Bandit was sniffing around one of them.

"Thank you." She gave the older housekeeper a smile as she left.

Dropping down on the small but comfortable bed, Zephyr let the entire house sink inside, realizing that though beautiful, there was absolutely nothing personal in his home. No pictures, no objects of his interest, nothing that screamed it was *his*. It almost looked like he'd had the compound made and forgotten what to do with his own house. And though beautiful, it was kind of tragic. Did he simply not know that there was more involved in making it a home, or did he not know how to make it one? Did he feel at home in this beautiful paradise he'd made or did he sleep restlessly? There were questions in her mind, and sadness in her heart as she unpacked.

She spent the next few hours setting things, emptying her boxes and bags as they kept arriving, carried by two young men and Victor. Hector had probably gone with Alpha wherever they had gone.

Bear ran from door to box each time someone came in, excited about all the new stuff, while Bandit sniffed everything she took out, his particular interest not in her socks but her underwear. She'd caught him trying to sneak off with her yellow lacy bra and tugged it back just in time, even though he kept his eyes fixated on that one.

The cook came around dusk and introduced herself as Nala, telling Zephyr she'd cook them a special dinner since it was her first night in their house, and left for the kitchen. By the time Zephyr was done unpacking and putting everything away, it was eight in the evening and she was both hungry and exhausted. She hadn't been able to sleep properly since the courthouse wedding, and she could feel it catching up to her.

Bear sat in a corner of her room, napping, her one solid companion throughout the day.

Zephyr looked around her settled room, happy with the way she'd brought it to life temporarily, and decided to take a shower before going down to eat. She went to her lingerie drawer, took out her sexiest peach-colored semi-transparent baby doll, and laid it on the bed, along with her small vibrator. Stripping, she entered her smaller en suite with a shower cabin and washed off the tiredness of the day.

Sudden multiple barks from downstairs alerted her to her husband's arrival.

Wrapping herself in a towel, her burgundy hair wet and shining, she entered her room, only to find Alpha standing in the doorway of their connected rooms, his eye on the lingerie and toy on the bed.

She couldn't have timed it more perfectly if she'd tried. He looked up, perusing her towel-clad body with heat in his golden gaze, such heat that she could feel it on her cool skin. Her nipples hardened. His eye stopped on them, lingering on the knot of her towel, and boy did she want it to drop.

She casually raised her hands to her hair, the towel hitching up her thighs, exposing them, lifting her breasts higher, and he noticed every bit of it, and from the very sizable tent in his jeans, she'd say he liked it.

"Have you eaten?" she asked innocently, aware that he was stripping her naked in his mind.

"No," he growled, his voice deeper with arousal. His hands fisted by his side, and he suddenly pivoted on his heels, stalking out of the doorway and into his shower, slamming the door behind him.

Satisfied with the reaction she'd incited, Zephyr changed into her baby doll, loving the way it hugged and fell on her curves. She loved the way lingerie made her feel—confident and sexy and desirable—and this one, in particular, made her full boobs look incredible. Covering it up with a long silk robe, and tying it loosely so it could give a peek with movement, she went down the stairs to the kitchen.

Bear joined her, trotting on her heels. Baron raised his neck from the rug where he was now lying with Bandit dozing, gave her a hard look before going back to ignoring her.

The house was otherwise empty, doors locked, drapes drawn.

They were alone.

The sun had set a while ago, the house lighting up automatically around dusk. The view that had been incredible during the day was a bit scary at night because it was pitch black, and Zephyr had never been this close to the jungle and this far out of the city before. Her eyes saw absolutely nothing in the distance, even though she could hear the sounds of animals, the water, and the lack of civilization. In the distance on the far left, the lights of the city twinkled. It was freaky how he'd comfortably lived here alone for so long. She wouldn't be able to last one night.

Knowing where everything in the kitchen was, thanks to Leah's tour, Zephyr went about setting the table for two, taking the delicious-smelling carbonara and garlic bread Nala had cooked for them. She took out some red wine, poured them in two glasses to accompany the dinner, along with two glasses of water, and lit up a candle in the middle.

Perfect.

Footsteps coming down made her turn to find her husband, wearing loose gym shorts and a loose t-shirt, his hair wet and curling from the shower. He looked at the setup, but didn't comment on it, simply taking a seat where she indicated.

"It smells great, doesn't it?" She broke the silence, serving them the food. "How long have you had Nala?"

"A few years," he replied, taking the dish with the bread and putting two slices on her plate before taking his. "She was the mother of one of the girls who'd worked with AV Security."

That was her opening. "What does AV Security actually do? I know you give some kind of protection to people off the streets, but how does that actually work?"

Alpha considered her, before tearing the bread. "AV gives security to sex workers mainly, but we also do extraction from places people don't want to go."

Zephyr leaned forward, interested. "Security to sex workers?"

He explained, "Sex workers are constantly in danger, from their pimps, their clients, anyone walking on the street." He paused, as though contemplating whether to tell her more, and then continued, "My mother was a sex worker, and I was the result of her rape. She also got beat up once, and I decided I wasn't okay with any of that. I had a reputation on the streets. Gave my name to anyone who wanted the protection."

She was surprised he'd spoken about his mother. She was also surprised at how kind the woman who'd been through what his mother had been through had been to a young girl like her. That alone made her remarkable. But she held off on commenting on it, sticking to the other side of the conversation.

"And they pay you for it?"

"I don't ask for a payment, but most of them want to. I make enough with the fights."

Zephyr took a bite of her pasta, groaning in delight at the sheer deliciousness, before asking, "How does the fight money work?"

"People bet, I fight. I win, I get the money."

He used words like they were going out of fashion. Zephyr shook her head. "And fighting made you enough to buy half the city?"

He chewed on his bite of pasta slowly, watching her. "I only fight big fights now. People bet in hundreds of thousands."

She choked on her mouthful, her eyes widening. "Are you serious? They just throw that kind of money around?"

"It's a well-plotted bet usually." He shrugged.

Fascinating. Zephyr had never really given any thought to sex workers or fights, much less the entire industry, and now questions whirled in her head.

"What happened to the girl, Nala's daughter?" Zephyr asked.

"She died."

"I'm sorry."

The dogs trotted to the table, quietly sitting on the side while their eyes stayed up on the food.

"And these three?" Zephyr smiled at the dogs, taking a bite of the bread. Damn, it was amazing. She made a sound out loud, and Alpha cleared his throat.

"I found them about four years ago," he hesitated, contemplating something. "There had been an underground dogfight. I'd gone to meet an informant. These three"—he indicated the canines with his fork—"had been dumped in an alley. It was a cold night and they'd been crying, so I took them to my car just to warm them up. Couldn't let them go after."

She went soft. He was a protector; he always had been. That was one of the things she'd loved the most about him.

She extended her hand and touched his, her skin loving the sensation of his, and gave his fingers a squeeze. "You're a good man."

Alpha pulled his hand away. "Don't look at me with those stars in your eyes, Zephyr. You're fooling yourself if you think I'm anything but a beast under this skin."

Zephyr raised her wine glass to him. "Then the world needs more beasts like you."

His golden eye widened, the unscarred side of his mouth turning down at her defiance of his belief. His dark scruff caught her eye, and she wondered for the hundredth time how it would feel on her skin. Her breath caught, and she saw his fingers tighten over his fork.

"This feels like a date," she breathed.

"It's not a date."

Stubborn man. She would break him, though.

"Whatever you say, sexy."

He didn't respond to that, just quietened down and quickly finished his food. He was up and clearing his dishes before she was done, rushing out of the room with a gruff 'goodnight' thrown her way, the dogs seeing him leave and settling down in the living room.

Zephyr sighed and finished eating, texting Zen about the day to keep herself from feeling alone. After she was done, she cleared up and walked up the stairs, the motion-sensor lights automatically dimming as she left.

His bedroom door was shut tight as she went to her room, the connecting door closed too. Zephyr undid her robe and put it on the dresser, lowered the netting around the bed, and got in, staring at the ceiling fan slowly circulating the air in the room.

She picked up her vibrator from the side, her nipples tight in the cool air with arousal, and finally turned it on. The quiet buzz filled the room as she closed her eyes, sliding her hands under her panties, her wetness meeting her fingers.

She exhaled, palming her breast with one hand, remembering the way he'd pulled her hair back during their kiss. She let her mind drift to old times when he'd stared at her hotly with both his golden eyes on fire, when he'd kissed her softly, his mouth exploratory, his hands tender on her young breasts. She doubted he'd be tender now with the way he watched her. No, he'd pull her hair and smack her ass and impale her on his cock, whispering filthy things to her as she tried to fit him in.

Her heartbeat picked up at the fantasy, her fingers penetrating her as she placed her vibrator on her clit, a quiet moan escaping her mouth as the device shot the pleasure through her. She kept her eyes closed, stuck in the fantasy, remembering the words he'd threatened her with at his office, her mind making it more profane. He'd hold her hair in a ponytail, pulling her head back until he could kiss her, thrusting into her so deep the motion would push her up the bed, her sensitive nipples scraping over the sheets, but his hold on her hair would keep her in place.

Oh god.

She tried to push deeper with her fingers, her hands making a wet, filthy noise as she fucked herself, imagining it was him as she drenched the sheets with arousal, pressing the vibrator harder on her clit as pleasure zinged through her body, on the precipice of an orgasm but not quite there yet.

A noise from her side suddenly had her eyes flying open, her heart pounding as she watched the shirtless mass of a man lean over her with one hand by her head, his golden eye focused on her like a hawk about to swoop down on his feast.

She hovered on the edge of the orgasm, knowing she needed more, needed him, and she had no shame in asking him for it. "Please," she begged, her body writhing on the bed.

"Give me a taste," he commanded, and she brought her hand to his mouth, touching his scar, coating his lips in her essence before his mouth sucked her fingers in, in a deep pull that she could feel in her nipples, in her stomach, in her core, as her walls clenched emptily around nothing. He swirled his tongue around her fingers, his eyes hot, and she felt the motion on her clit where the vibrator was pressed.

"Oh god," she moaned, biting her lips.

His hand, his large, scarred, rough hand went straight between her legs, his fingers not exploring, not teasing, but penetrating her, going so deep she felt herself squeeze him as he stretched her with two thick digits.

She started to remove the vibrator, but he growled, "Keep the toy there."

Her breath caught at the command, her breasts heaving as he fucked her with his fingers, hard and fast and deep, imitating what his cock would do, and she bent her legs, spreading her thighs wider, her heels digging into the bed as an unknown pleasure began to build up. Between her vibrator rubbing over her clit and his fingers penetrating deep, she was rushing toward an explosion that would splinter and shatter her to pieces. There was understated confidence with the way he handled her body, confidence her lizard brain appreciated because that's all he rendered her to—a basic, primitive instinct to mate. His motion was vigorous as he loomed over her, his fingers scissoring through her pussy walls roughly, with such disregard it was insanely arousing.

And then he shifted the angle of his wrist, curving his fingers upward, finding the spot inside her that had her screaming. Her neck tightened as molten fire seared through her veins, burning through her in pleasure so intense her thighs started to jerk, her head digging into the pillow, her back arching as she came, dots behind the blacks of her eyes, her walls clenching around his merciless fingers that stayed inside her, feeling each contraction.

"You remove your toy, I'll remove my fingers."

The threat had her gripping her vibrator harder, her other hand finding his chest and digging into his skin, the vibrations on her clit combined with his relentless fingers making her body have one orgasm after the other, the endless cycle making her scream and cry and whimper as her body wrung out every last drop of pleasure it could, her heart beating so rapidly she thought it would explode out of her chest.

The sensory overload went on for minutes, for hours, for days; she didn't know. She lost track of every thought, everything, and became nothing but sensation, too much sensation, so much more than she could take, but he didn't stop, no. He kept fucking her with his fingers and kept the vibrator pressed to her clit with his thumb as her hand started to fall, keeping her floating in a space where the pleasure became too much, too intense, too unbearable.

She possibly passed out.

She didn't know.

When consciousness slowly drifted back, her body was lax, unmoving, heavy, and the hand holding the vibrator had fallen to the side, small pulses of pleasure still weaving through her muscles as her heart slowly came back to its regular pace, still tripping every alternate beat at his proximity.

She opened her eyes to see him watching her, the line of his jaw tense, the heat in his eyes so palpable her pussy gave an exhausted flutter, making her realize his fingers were still inside her.

She didn't know what had just happened.

Holy shit.

He pulled his digits out of her sore pussy and straightened. Zephyr saw the bulge in his shorts, but was too exhausted to move, much less do anything about it. She watched as he turned and went to his room, closing the door behind her, leaving her alone on sheets he'd made her drench.

CHAPTER 14

ZEPHYR

He'd made her squirt.

Zephyr had never squirted in her life, and it wasn't like she didn't have any sexual experience. She'd had a few partners; two of them had made her orgasm. She had always enjoyed sex and had never felt shame in wanting her pleasure, but she'd genuinely believed she was just one of those women who weren't built to ejaculate.

She'd been wrong. With a few thrusts of his strong fingers, he'd unraveled that belief. The next morning, as Zephyr changed the sheets and got ready to go to work, she thought back to the previous night. With her head cleared from arousal and post-orgasmic bliss, she realized he'd sought her out, despite saying he didn't want to complicate anything with sexual attraction. It didn't get more sexual than what they'd done; a first for them.

A decade ago, their relationship hadn't been as sexual, though not for the lack of trying on her part. She'd been eighteen and he almost twenty-two, and he'd been adamant about not sleeping with her until he could do better for himself, like she'd even cared about that. But she'd seen him before that, seen him fuck a girl once against a wall, and god, her teenage self had burned up with jealousy. She remembered she'd cried to Zen that night, and it had been her younger sister who had very sensibly told her to just talk to him because he didn't even know of her existence. She had taken the advice and gathered her courage, and approached him one evening.

And he'd fallen for her. Only to not remember a thing about it.

Zephyr took a deep breath. He was hers now, and that was all that mattered. He had initiated something between them, and that was her win of the day.

One step forward.

Zephyr loved the way her ring glinted in the salon lights. Throughout the day, as she'd worked on two of her regular clients, her eyes kept drifting to the way the gems sparkled in the bright lights in her workspace, and god, she loved it. She loved the weight of it on her finger, the reminder that he had given her the perfect ring for her, the way anyone who saw it 'oohed' and 'aahed' over it. She loved the feeling of soreness between her legs, the memory of his fingers inside her every time she moved, the glow on her face as she caught her reflection. Her eyes were shining and she *loved* it. Marriage suited her. Marriage to *him* suited her.

As she snipped one of her newest client's hair, her eagerness to return to their new home built up. She didn't know how the night would go, but she knew she wanted to just be in his presence again. Odd as it sounded, she missed him.

Shaking off her thoughts, she focused on what her newest client was saying.

"That's a nice ring on your finger."

Zephyr had been receiving compliments about it all day and she'd been smiling like an idiot about it, but something in the woman's tone had her gaze sharpening. It wasn't something obvious that she could put her finger on, just something . . . *off*.

"Thank you," she smiled politely and simply cut the lock of mahogany hair between her fingers.

"Mrs. Villanova, right?" the client pressed.

Zephyr kept the polite smile as she checked the lady out. Mid-forties, crow's feet on the corner of her hardened brown eyes.

She stayed silent.

"Your husband manages girls, did you know that?" She didn't wait for a response. "Girls on the streets, he takes them under his security, gives them better choices. It's bad for business. But at least you won't have to wonder where he's spending his nights when he's not at home. A man like that wouldn't be content to settle, you know."

Zephyr didn't react outwardly as ants crawled up her skin. Something about this woman was unsettling, and not just what she knew about her husband. It felt icky, like she'd dragged the scent of something rotten inside with her.

Turning on the blow-dryer so she wouldn't have to listen to any more of her words, Zephyr quickly finished with her hair as soon as she could, barely spending any time to actually make it look as good as she was known for. She nodded to one of the assistants and indicated for him to take over the final setting, leaving the repugnant woman behind as she went to the main counter for a breather.

The receptionist raised her eyebrows. "Bad lunch?" Which was code for an awful client. She gave a weak smile, her mind swirling with questions, not about Alpha, because she knew what he did already, but about the woman and who the hell she was. How did she know all that about her husband, and more importantly, what was she doing at Zephyr's workplace telling her all of it? What was the point of that?

The demoness in question came to the counter and paid, all the while watching Zephyr with sharp eyes. Just as she stepped out from her side, she bent from her height.

"The Syndicate is watching you now."

And she left.

Zephyr didn't know what The Syndicate was but it sure as hell didn't sound like a club she wanted the membership to. Frowning at the bizarre encounter, Zephyr shook her head and wrapped up her day, totally weirded out by the random woman. She clocked out and exited the salon to find Victor, her bonafide bodyguard and driver, reading a newspaper as he leaned against the large Rover, a few women checking him out as they walked past him.

"Serial killer on the streets?" jumped out from the front page. Was that the killer the note had been about at the wedding in Tenebrae?

"Is he at Trident?" she asked about her husband without preamble.

Victor folded the newspaper and nodded.

"Good. Take me to him, please."

Since her salon was just a few blocks away, it didn't take them more than a few minutes to get to the towers, even less for them to get to the 28th floor.

This late in the evening, with the sun setting over the city, there were surprisingly more guys in the open area than there had been during the daytime. All of them turned to look at her when she exited the elevator, most of them gave her the respectful version of the man-nod. Being wifed by their boss had put her on a higher scale.

"Yo," Hector came to greet her, his bald head gleaming as always in the light.

"Yo, he in?" she greeted back with a smile. It should have unsettled her, being the only woman in a room full of men who were taller, stronger, and definitely meaner than she was.

But knowing they were all Alpha's men, that he was the tallest, strongest, meanest of the bunch, and that she was *his* made a warm ball of butterflies erupt in her stomach. It made her feel safe, protected, knowing that even though he didn't love her yet, not one of these guys could put a finger on her without feeling her husband's wrath.

"He's on a call." Hector grinned. "But go ahead."

Nodding to them, she hiked her purse on her shoulder, fixed her top to show more cleavage, and knocked on his door, entering.

His golden eye came to her as he leaned back in his chair, watching her lock the door behind her.

"She's setting herself up to get out of the business," a woman's voice said from the speaker on the desk. Zephyr hesitated, expecting him to make the call private, but he didn't, simply keeping his gaze steady on her.

Intrigued to get a glimpse of this side of him, she dropped her bag to the floor and walked around the desk, perching herself on his lap, and put her arms around him, tucking her head under his chin. She felt his body stiffen at the contact, and she gave him a squeeze, closing her eyes and breathing his scent in. God, she loved his smell, all warm and musky and masculine, like the wild forest and wet earth, like home.

"And she's not keeping it quiet," the woman's voice continued. "I have a feeling she might be the next one he hits."

His hands stayed on the arms of his chair, his body rigid under her.

If he thought she was going to be rebuffed by his lack of reciprocation, he was wrong. She was made of stubbornness and willfulness. She would break him down hug by hug until he had to put his arms around her out of sheer exasperation. She nuzzled into his chest, watching the V exposed by the top three buttons of his black shirt, the edge of one scar peeking out on his pec.

"Keep an eye on her," he commanded the woman on the line, his voice gruffer than usual. Zephyr liked to think it was thanks to her proximity. "I want to know the moment something is off."

"You got it, boss," the woman signed off, disconnecting the call. Silence reigned in the office, the lights turning on one by one as the sun went down over the forest, burnishing the entire city.

"What are you doing?" he asked, still keeping his hands to himself.

Zephyr smiled. "Cuddling."

She felt him inhale, his chest expanding against her cheek, before deflating as he let out a breath. Damn, she should've sat the other way around. She missed out on his heartbeats. *Next time.*

"This isn't a part of the contract," he reminded her, his hands gripping the armrests.

God, he was cute sometimes.

"You giving me mind-blowing orgasms isn't either, but hey, you don't hear me complaining."

"Mind-blowing?"

Of course, he'd focus on that.

"Mind-blowing, bone-melting, toe-curling, earth-shattering orgasms."

He didn't respond, but she sensed he was pleased. *Men.*

"So, these girls under AV?" she started, picking at his shirt button. "Do you know them?" His left-hand fingers began tapping the armrest, the ring she'd given him looking delicate on his rough, large hand. "Not all of them, no."

"But they're all there voluntarily, right?" She needed to be certain. "They're not . . . coerced or anything?"

She felt him pull back and look down at her. "Where's this coming from?"

She told him about the encounter with the woman, feeling him stiffen again. He pressed the speaker.

"Victor. Get the cameras from Zephyr's work today. I want to see every client who walked in and out of there."

Zephyr kept fiddling with the button. "It's the Syndicate, isn't it? It's bad news."

He didn't confirm or deny it.

"The girls under AV"—he distracted her while they waited—"they might not have come into this world voluntarily, but it's not easy to get out. Many get too used to it, scared of the normal. Many enjoy the money it can rake. And many want to escape, but don't know how."

"You can't help them get out?" Zephyr asked, genuinely wanting to know. His world had begun to seep into hers, but she still didn't understand how it worked.

He gave a humorless chuckle. "I'm not a savior, Zephyr. And it's best if you don't think of me as one. The most I can give these women is a choice—to join me and be safe, or remain unsafe. And once they join me, they're free to leave any time. But I'm not a good, moral man. I can kill you as easily as I can make you orgasm. Blood or cum, my hands wear them both well."

That was probably the most he'd ever said to her in one go, and it was a lot to take in. Zephyr liked to think she was righteous, but how much of that was her upbringing? Would she have felt the same had she led a life alone on the streets and not one with a warm, loving family? Would she have cared about right or wrong when the goal had been survival?

She didn't know. And she had to accept who he had become now, and not the boy he'd once been, even though his morality had always been skewed.

She gave him a squeeze, and though he didn't return it, she felt him relax slightly.

One day at a time.

PART 2

THE MANTLE

"And in the end, we were all humans, drunk on the idea that love, only love, could heal our brokenness."

-Christopher Poindexter

CHAPTER 15

ZEPHYR

Over the next month, they fell into a routine.

On Mondays through Thursdays, Alpha got up early to run the dogs and then train with his men while she got ready for work. She only saw Nala, who came to cook, and Leah, who came to take care of the house, and the dogs post-run. Bear—who she had become most attached to, because he was just a ball of love who needed pets and cuddles—was usually the one following on her heels since she woke up. Bandit—who had succeeded in finding one of her favorite bras and making it his toy—was moody and came to her when he wanted.

Baron—who still didn't give a shit about anything but his grumpy master—barely even glanced at her, no matter how much she tried to get his attention.

Through those weekdays, she went to the salon, finished with her day, and went to find Alpha at Trident, where she sat on his lap, while he usually finished calls. Sometimes, Hector came in and they talked, and he let her sit there, never taking his hands off the armrests. But the fact that he allowed her in on his private meetings gave her hope.

She'd learned a lot about this new Alpha through that. She'd learned that he met with his sentinels once a week to get updates, that he was worried about the killer murdering girls who wanted to get out of the business, that The Syndicate was an organization that didn't like him. She also learned, through listening in on his calls and watching his men defer to him, that he was both respected and feared, that his girls were grateful to him, that he had built something for himself that the rest of the world didn't see. To the outsiders, he was just a real estate mogul. To the underworld, he was a man to be taken very seriously. And she, from her completely normal background, was surprised at every little morsel about him that she learned.

After Trident, they went back home together, ate dinner together, and if she could rope him into watching a show or a movie, which she usually did, they did that together. The time they spent fed life into her blood, pumping it through her heart, making her more alive than she'd ever felt. Even though she was the talker between them, he listened, and that made her soft. She'd chatter about her family, her day, her dreams, and he listened to every word. He didn't respond to most of it, but he was receptive, and that alone made her hold on to hope, even as he constantly reminded her that it was only for a few months and the deadline was approaching.

On Fridays, he went out of the city to check up on his empire, and Zephyr had dinner with her parents, spending the night with Zen before returning the next morning. Though her father had warmed up to Alpha, mostly because she was stinking happy, her mother still hadn't, even though their marriage had definitely benefited her. Her daughter marrying the elusive but filthy rich Villanova had definitely boosted up her social points.

On weekends, she spent her time with her sister at SLF before coming home and spending time with her husband. And it was all great domestic bliss.

Except he held back.

Emotionally, physically, there was a chasm between them she didn't know how to bridge. No matter how much she tried to seduce him, it didn't work. He never came into her room, never touched her when she cuddled him, never looked at her if she was half naked. She bought the raunchiest bikinis and swam around the ridiculously large pool when he sat on the deck with earplugs in, listening to rock music she didn't have taste for, but his eye never went to her. She deliberately wore lingerie for dinner, and he kept his gaze above her neck. She put on her vibrator with the loudest setting, and his door stayed locked.

Weeks passed and her frustration climbed. While it felt like she was making progress in some ways, she felt stuck in others. He still called them temporary, still stuck to the contract, and while she'd become his housemate, it still felt reluctant. It felt fleeting, like she could walk away and nothing would change.

And it really pulled her low sometimes.

But she didn't let him see it. She didn't let him see the ways his deliberate distance chipped at her day by day, little by little, piece by piece. She didn't let him see how a dry remark sometimes brought back memories that she wished he'd remember, so he could take her into his arms and she'd stop battling for them. She didn't let him see any of it; just gave him her love and smiles and hoped he fell for her as he once had.

And every day, her hope withered a bit.

Zephyr stood at the entrance to the tower after her day of work, her shoulders slumped. It was slowly catching up to her, giving and giving and giving, hoping and hoping and hoping. They had been married for a month, and he'd not kissed her, not embraced her, not returned her affection in any form. That one time he'd come to her room seemed nothing but a slip.

"You okay?" Victor asked her as she stood at the tower entrance, not entering.

She gave a smile, even though she didn't want to.

"Yeah, just . . . lost in thought, I guess."

Victor hesitated, before giving her shoulder a squeeze.

She appreciated it. Victor had been a good friend to her. Part of her wanted to not go into the building, only to hold him when he didn't hold her.

"You know what?" She made up her mind. "I'm going to go grab something to eat there." She pointed to the café across the street in the other tower. "You go on ahead."

Before Victor could respond, she crossed the street and entered the café, finding a seat in a corner and ordering herself a cappuccino. Zephyr played with her ring as she waited, quiet and contemplating some questions, doubt seeping in. She'd talked to Zen about finding a medical professional for their opinion on his amnesia, and her sister had told her not to approach anyone in the city. With the connections he had, and the fact that she was his wife, she didn't want to raise any red flags for anyone about the situation.

She sipped the coffee and looked down at her phone, hesitating before hitting call on the number.

It rang a few times before a husky feminine voice answered, "Dr. Amara Maroni."

Zephyr had a girl-crush on Amara and she wasn't even ashamed about it. A few days ago, she'd found Amara's contact in her husband's study next to Dante's, and saved it, knowing she was a practicing therapist. More importantly, she was family, and she wouldn't pose a danger to Alpha.

"Hi Amara," Zephyr greeted. "This is Zephyr Villanova. Alpha's wife. We met briefly at your wedding."

"Of course." She could hear the surprise in the other woman's voice.

"Is this a good time to talk?" Zephyr asked, tracing the rim of her mug with her finger. "I need your professional opinion about ... someone."

There was some background noise, and Amara returned, sounding serious. "Okay. First, I want you to know whatever you tell me will stay confidential between us. You can be open about whatever you want to discuss. I'm here."

Total goddess.

Zephyr took a deep breath, making sure she was alone in the corner. "Someone I knew a few years ago met with an accident. I recently met ... him again, but he has no memory of me or the accident. My question is, is it possible that reminding him of our time would affect him adversely? Because his brain had to be keeping certain things away from him for protecting him, right? Or is ..." She trailed off, controlling her mouth before it ran away in her nervousness.

Amara listened, taking her time to reply, her voice soft. "The brain is very tricky, Zephyr. It can lock away traumas for entire lifetimes to protect people. Have you spent any time with this person now?"

"Yes."

"And he doesn't remember you? Not one thing? Even a hint of familiarity?" she asked to confirm.

"No." Zephyr shook her head.

Amara's tone turned sympathetic. "Then I'm sorry. My suggestion in cases like this is to not remind the patient of the traumatic incident or anything that surrounds it. It can trigger some extremely adverse responses, even psychotic breakdowns in certain cases. If his brain is suppressing you or your memories, the kind thing would be simply starting fresh."

Zephyr stared at the table. "I tried that, and it's not working."

Amara hesitated. "Is it Alpha?"

"Yeah."

"I'm sorry." The compassion in the other woman's voice almost undid her.

Zephyr felt her nose tingle. "Thank you for your help. I'm just at a loss at what to do now." And she spilled the entire story, the scheme about the marriage, the distance he kept between them, everything to the woman who listened on without judgment.

When she was done, Amara spoke again, "I have some advice, but more as a friend than a professional."

"Shoot."

Amara chuckled. "Don't say that around these people. They'll take you literally."

Zephyr smiled, but waited for the other woman to talk.

"I don't know Alpha very well," Amara began. "But he and Dante are very similar in some ways, and it makes sense. In my case, the one thing that always pushed Dante over the edge to act was distance. Specifically, me putting distance between us in any way. I'm not saying it'll work with Alpha, but given that you're at an impasse, it might tip you over either way."

"But at least I'll know if there's any hope or if we're doomed." Zephyr mulled over the idea. She liked it, mainly because she was already feeling drained with always closing the gap between them. Maybe she needed to stop for a bit, just recharge, not go anywhere but not walk to him either. It had merit. Plus, the woman giving the advice had sustained a relationship with a guy like Dante for over a decade, so it had *good merit*.

"Thank you, Amara," Zephyr spoke sincerely. "You've been really helpful."

"Of course. I'm really glad you felt you could reach out to me."

Tempest's wail came in the background, and Amara sighed. "Remind me to never have another kid."

Zephyr felt her lips curl. "Dante doesn't help? I thought he was a hands-on dad."

"Oh, he is," Amara confirmed. "When she's playing and happy. Is he hands-on when she's cranky and driving me up a wall? Nope. He's nowhere in the house. It's like the man has an internal radar or something. I'm thinking of giving him some distance treatment myself." Chuckling at that, Zephyr let Amara go and attend to her niece, and she sipped the coffee, her mood dipping again. She took as much time and space as she wanted, ordered a caramel latte, and read a gothic romance set in a castle on her phone app. Customers came and went, it got dark outside, and finally, after two hours of sitting there, she paid the bill and got out, still feeling low.

And she just wanted to go home.

Thankfully, Victor was in the car outside the café, waiting, despite her telling him to go, and she got in, asking him to take her back. It was a weekday and she was supposed to be at Trident, but she felt off. Victor gave her a questioning glance in the rearview mirror, but she ignored it. In half an hour, despite the traffic, she saw the familiar trellis come into sight. She left the car and walked around the hill to the back where the elevator was, greeting members of the staff on the way. The simple elevator took her up, the bark of Bear and Bandit greeting her before she even cleared the level, putting an automatic smile on her face. They greeted her with licks and wagging tails, happy to see her back, and even Baron gave her an *'oh, you're back'* bark before lying down on the deck. This late, the house was already empty. Zephyr quickly took a shower and had dinner alone for the first time in weeks, breaking their routine of eating together. Then, even though it was dark, she went for a walk on the track around the perimeter, taking Bear with her to clear her head. Though she didn't walk the path a lot, the trail was familiar enough for her to be comfortable with the green. It also helped that there were patrolling security guards every twenty feet or so.

Getting back to the house after a while, she opened the door, letting Bear off the leash, only to be met with her husband's thunderous gaze.

And for the first time since their meeting, she ignored him, turning toward the stairs.

His hand gripped her arm as she passed, turning her to face him.

"Where were you?" he grit out, and Zephyr stared at his chest.

His fingers gripped her chin, and after such a long time, she'd almost forgotten what his touch had felt like. How fucking sad was that?

He tilted her face up, his golden eye taking her in. She let him. She stayed silent, which was unlike her, and let him see whatever he wanted to see.

"Where were you?" he asked, quieter now.

She shrugged. "Just went for a walk."

His thumb traced her chin. "You didn't come to the tower today."

Hope. Stupid, idiotic hope.

"Were you waiting?" she asked, hating the way her voice didn't hide the hope in it.

He didn't reply, and she sighed. What had she expected? That he would hold her and tell her he'd been waiting for her, that he'd been worried, that he'd come home early to see what was wrong? He might have done all those things, but he'd never admit to them, not when he was intent on denying anything serious between them.

Swallowing, she pulled out of his hold. "Goodnight, Alpha."

She heard his sharp intake behind her.

Yeah, she never called him Alpha, either.

Guess there was a first time for everything.

CHAPTER 16

ZEPHYR

For two days, she'd been in a funk and avoided going to his office. But her stupid heart didn't let her skip their dining ritual, knowing he'd started to enjoy their time eating together, especially when he'd never had a companion before. Eating alone sucked and she knew that, so even though she was grumpy, she didn't bow out of their dinners. But she did stop dressing in lingerie for the meals. Instead, she'd begun wearing her usual pajamas, not intent on seducing him in her current mood. If he chalked her mood swing up to PMS or something else, she didn't know, and he didn't say.

But Amara had been right.

While her husband hadn't outright done anything, he'd begin to watch her more. He called Victor more to check up on her. He sat at the table even after finishing his food if she was eating. He'd even left the adjoining door between their rooms slightly ajar last night. But none of it felt like a victory. Instead, she got the sense that he was testing her. She just needed to see where it led. Now that she wasn't easing the tension with her humor and chatter, now that she stayed silent and forced him to face what thickened the air when they were in the same room, something was building, activating, like a volcano, dormant from the outside, bubbling with lava, waiting for the right moment to erupt and cause destruction. She stood at the mouth of the volcano, watching the lava come forth from the mantle of the earth, knowing it could wreck her, but waiting for it. She wanted to be the rain that fell upon the magma and sizzled, drenched it until it became rich. She wanted to seep down to his dried roots, nourish the soil of his heart, and fill him with life again.

Standing in his office for the first time in two days, married but without much progress for over a month, Zephyr watched the sun setting over the forest in the distance, mulling over her thoughts, her shoulders slumped. She'd come into Trident because staying away from him wasn't doing a thing except making her more miserable. While something had shifted, it still wasn't enough.

The sound of the office door locking shut echoed in the space, breaking her thoughts.

A presence at her back made her aware of him, his heat warming her freezing heart. She'd always loved that about him, how he could dwarf her but make her feel safe, how he could ignite and warm her at the same time. Before she'd met him, the idea of him had fascinated the little girl, but afterward, the reality of him had paled the thought. Whatever had or hadn't happened over the weeks, Zephyr had begun to fall deeper for the reality of him now. She loved the man he had become, the way he was with his staff, the way he was with his dogs, the way he just was. She loved that he carried his scars without shame, that he had survived whatever he had and come through the other side stronger. The perseverance he wore on his skin, the respect he commanded from his people, the kindness he showed the vulnerable—he was a man worth falling down the hell for. And sometimes, when he let his guard down a bit and looked at her with softness, it kindled the hope in her heart.

She still loved him. And he didn't.

And she was both okay with that and agonized by that knowledge.

She walked away from the window to get her bag from the desk, and his hand on her arm stopped her again. He'd been doing that a lot, just stopping her in her tracks and staring at her, trying to figure her out.

"What game are you playing?" he finally asked, breaking the tension that had been building for the last few days, his eye narrowing on her.

Nice.

She tried to pull her arm out. He held her steady, firm but not tight.

She wished she could shout about the game she had been playing, but she couldn't. She couldn't do that to him, and now she was trapped in a situation of her own making with a husband she loved, one who didn't remember her, love her, or even trust her. And it made her mad. Her dying hope made her *livid*.

Zephyr shoved at his chest, glaring up at him. "Let me go."

"Not until you tell me what your agenda has been, Zephyr."

He'd not called her rainbow in a while, just like she'd not called him anything but Alpha.

"My agenda," she hissed, "was to make you love me."

His grip tightened on her arm. "It didn't work, because I don't believe you."

Ouch. A little crack.

"Tell me the truth," he demanded, cool and collected, completely unaffected, unlike her insides. "I'm losing my patience now."

"Your impatience isn't my problem."

"But my anger is," he said dangerously. "You don't want me angry, Zephyr."

She looked at him, unable to understand what to do. Telling him anything meant risking his mental state, and he had healed enough to be okay. There was only one way to divert his attention. "What are you going to do, you beast?" she deliberately goaded him, pulling her arm out of his grip.

Something flared in his eye. He looked at her, his nostrils flaring, tension building as they stayed locked.

Before she could take another breath, he had her up against the window, her front pressed to the glass, his large form behind her, startling her with the suddenness, as his familiar scent drifted through her nose.

What game was *he* playing?

"I'm going to give you what you've been begging me for. Yes or no?" he growled against her ear, fisting her hair and tugging her head back with one hand, touching her after so long she drowned in the sensations.

There was something dark about it, the way he questioned her, the way he pulled her head, the way he pressed her into the glass. Zephyr didn't know what had happened to trigger him suddenly, and even though she'd wanted nothing more than their bodies to connect, she tried to turn her head to look at him to understand what was going on.

His hand in her hair limited her movement.

"What—"

"Yes"—he didn't let her finish, pulling her neck back—"or no?"

This was one of the things she'd discovered about the man he'd become—his obsession with her hair. He enjoyed pulling it, playing with the strands, for control or something else, she didn't know. She enjoyed it too, the tug on her scalp, the way it made her submit to his will, the way it made her feel desired, like she'd pushed the boundaries of his control and he just couldn't help himself anymore. His fist in her hair had become her anchor. And she didn't know what was riding him, but whatever it was, he was there. That had to mean something, right?

"Yes," she whispered.

The words weren't out of her lips before she felt his large, rough hand going under her dress, lifting it. She felt him fist her panties on one side, pulling the silk sharply until it dug into her hip enough to bite, right before it snapped and ripped from the seam, the sound loud in the room.

Her breathing escalated, her immobility and his roughness making her hands press into the glass, the coldness against her palms and the heat behind her body making her flesh quiver in anticipation as her body readied itself for him.

Finally.

She'd wanted this, wanted him, for so long, she didn't remember a time before it. Their first kiss had been something like that too, her against a metal fence and him at her back, him kneeling behind her, spreading her before diving in. He had eaten her out, right where anyone could have walked in, and then he had stood up, whirled her around, kissing her with her juices on his mouth, pushing her so hard against the fence she'd felt it on her back for days.

As first kisses went, it had been dirty, but it had been them, and perfect, and something she remembered as he pushed her against the glass.

In some ways, he hadn't changed at all.

She felt his fingers checking her wetness and widened her legs wider to give him access, enjoying the certainty with which his digits prodded her nether lips, teasing her clit, dipping into her lightly before pulling out, enough to give her just the taste of what was to come.

"Fucking soaked," he ground out against her neck, hooking his hand under her right knee and pulling her leg up over it, spreading her obscenely wide as she went on her toes on the other foot. "Does my anger turn you on?"

It did. She didn't even have to answer him; he knew. The fact that she was pressed into the glass, that the lights were on behind her and anyone who looked up could see her, that she was rendered immobile in the position he had her in, it made her pulse pound.

She heard his zipper behind her, felt him take himself out, and felt the head of his cock against her weeping pussy. And god, she wanted it. She wanted him so bad, inside her, rutting her like the beast she'd called him, claiming her for the world to know she was just his, loving her good enough she'd remember it for the years to come.

She held her breath, her heart in her throat, the thrill, the finality, the inevitability of it making her fluid against him. He didn't say another word, just tightened his grip on her hair and knee, and with one thrust, the thundercloud that had been hanging over her for weeks burst.

A loud yelp escaped her, her hands pushing on the glass for support as she breathed out harshly, adjusting to his size, her walls fluttering around him in keen pleasure that felt on the knife end of pain. He slowly started to push in, sinking into her inch by inch, and dear lord, he was massive, his warm flesh inside her a weight making her feel so full her head tipped back, not knowing where he ended and she began. He felt huge, bigger than anyone she'd ever had, and she wasn't surprised, given his bulk that he was proportional, but she was surprised by how good the stretch felt as her walls grappled to welcome him, accommodate him, pleasure him.

Her breasts pressed against the cool glass, the contrast of his warm body behind her making her nipples tight. The tug on her scalp pushed her blood south, her hips gyrating against him to move restlessly, needing the friction, needing to coast that pain-pleasure line again. He pulled out a few inches and rammed in again, the force of the thrust pushing her against the glass, her eyes looking down below and realizing how deep down she'd fall if the glass broke. That added layer of danger woke something dark inside her, something that responded to it by pushing her arousal higher, making her juices run between her thighs in ways she'd remember tomorrow and blush. Right then, she didn't care. She felt consumed, in the best way possible, his desire something so tangible it pulsed inside her, matching her heartbeats. God, she was turned on, so turned on it didn't even matter to her why he was giving in to temptation, just that he was.

"Harder," she urged him, her voice a breathless demand as she held on to the glass, bracing herself, feeling his jeans against her ass. The fact that he'd hiked up her dress, ripped off her panties, and just unzipped to push inside her made her walls clench around him, his urgency catching up to her.

She caught their reflection in the glass, his dark, hulking form huge against her, his eye patch shadowed and his golden eye on her ass, his scar disappearing into his short beard. Zephyr put one hand on the side of his neck, touching his warm flesh, and watched his eye close at her touch.

Shit.

Weeks, months, years of longing bled into that moment, her heart clenching as her eyes burned. She let them, knowing he couldn't see it, and focused on his hardness inside her, pressing up so deep it almost felt a bit uncomfortable.

He didn't go harder as she asked, instead, he pulled out slowly and pushed back in so slow; she felt the ridge, the veins, the heat, all of it entering her what felt like endlessly. A wrangled moan escaped her, her head falling back, her fingers digging into the side of his neck as he held her in place, completely at his mercy, impaling her at his pace.

No matter how much she moved her hips, how deeply she clenched him, he didn't go any faster. But he went deep, so deep she felt uncomfortably full when he bottomed out, felt him press somewhere inside her at the angle that made her walls milk him faster, felt his breaths ragged against her ear.

"Harder, please," she begged, needing more, needing the relentless friction that would push her over the edge instead of teasing her right on it, giving her a taste of ecstasy before taking it away, over and over. And with the way she was pressed, she couldn't move her hand down to help herself.

He stayed in control against her plea, rotating his hips once in a deliberate move, and her eyes closed, stars bursting behind her lids as he hit that sweet, elusive spot inside her. He did it again, and again, and again—*ram, pull, rotate*—over and over, slow and controlled and deliberate, and her heartbeats quickened, pulsing in her throat, in her neck, in her pussy. Lust coiled in her belly like a serpent of sin, slithering through her veins, unfurling and biting until she felt the poisonous heat consuming every inch of her skin, making her feverish, fervent, fanatic in her desire.

He hammered into that spot, unceasingly, steadily, his other hand sneaking to her clit, rubbing her mercilessly until she felt her legs begin to shake, her knees jerking, her hard breaths turning into moans. Everything focused on the place they were joined, from where the burn spread and spread and spread until she was a quivering mess, her thighs jerking in his hold, her body falling but held up only by his cock in her pussy and his fist in her hair. She felt truly impaled by him, controlled by his body, and she came, so hard her nails dug into the side of his neck for purchase, making him bleed with the force of her orgasm, her eyes closed, her body on fire, her mouth open on a scream gone silent. She still felt a tremble in her throat as she gulped air.

He slipped out and she gushed, her jaw trembling, her body falling into the glass as his hands left her. Before she was finished, his hands went to his cock, and in a few seconds, she felt the warm spurts of his seed on her exposed ass, the filthiness of it turning her on even though she'd just come, making her want more.

It was over within minutes or hours; she didn't know.

She stayed lax against the glass as he let her leg down, taking a step back.

She heard his zipper again and opened her eyes to see him in the reflection, straightening his clothes. She waited, for him to say something, give her a touch, a soft kiss, anything. His gaze stayed on her back for a few seconds, his fists clenching and unclenching, and she watched, her post-orgasmic bliss turning hollow as he turned and left the office, leaving her cold against the glass, with his cum dripping down her ass and a tight weight in her stomach.

CHAPTER 17

ALPHA

"You're a dick, you know?" Dante's wry tone caught him off-guard over the phone. Alpha watched Jasmine talking to one of the girls in the AV headquarters, his mind preoccupied.

"Good to hear from you too," Alpha ground out, distracted. Distracted by too much happening around him. The killer had finally left his DNA at his last scene. His wife had been screwing with his head for days. His feelers had come back about the missing girls. The Syndicate was clearly trying to get him out of the picture. Too fucking much was happening, and his head felt out of the game.

And his missing eye itched like a bitch.

Fuck, he sounded whiny. Alpha wasn't whiny. He didn't know what was up with him these days.

He heard Dante sigh. "Amara was upset at how soon you left after the wedding. Tempest too."

Alpha grunted, "She's barely one."

"So?" Dante argued. Alpha knew better than to say anything about Dante's little princess. Fucker was whipped by both girls in his life, and shamelessly so.

"How's your marriage?" the younger man asked, with no sense of boundary or self-preservation. His marriage. It had started as a farce, a game, and now he didn't know. He hated to admit how much he'd begun to enjoy her company, how she amused him with her cuteness and seduced him with her antics. He'd begun to doubt that there was a secret at all, her motives for the marriage unknown to him, and with the way she was, he knew it best to ride out the months with some distance. Everything had been going great. Until she didn't show up at the tower.

Alpha remembered sitting in his office, watching the door, something twisting in his gut when she didn't come. He'd called Victor, who'd told him she'd gone home. Thinking maybe she was unwell, he'd wrapped everything up and gotten home, only to find it empty, her dinner plate washed and drying. She'd eaten without him. And that ... they did that together. She'd come back, and she'd been off. Not herself.

And then she'd called him Alpha. Not hubby, not handsome, not some absolutely ridiculous name like 'pumpkin pie'. *Alpha*.

That had pissed him off, and he'd been even more pissed at getting pissed. For the first time in his life, Alpha had hated hearing his name. Standing there, watching her quiet form duck away from him, something nasty, ugly had taken root in his gut. And it didn't go away, not when she'd started to have dinner with him in her pajamas, not when she simply went to sleep and didn't even try to engage with him, not when she didn't cuddle him anymore. She had slipped in behind his defenses, and he did not like that.

Alpha wasn't defenseless, much less against a little woman. And yet, last night, when she'd been about to duck away again, his defenses had shattered against the office windows. She'd pushed him over the edge, and he'd fucked her, and fuck if it hadn't felt good. But being inside her, he'd not lost control like he'd thought he would. And that had given him a plan to get the upper hand back in their dynamic. He'd fuck her slow, satisfy them both, break the sexual tension, keep her happy, and keep his distance. He was best alone, and she was nothing but a distraction, one who was getting too close, too sneaky under his skin. He didn't even care anymore what her motives were; he just wanted to let his promised time pass in pleasure. Their time together would end and they would go their own ways, mutually satisfied.

It was a good plan.

"Is that why you called?" he asked in response to Dante's question.

Dante chuckled. "That bad, huh?"

Fucker.

"Anyway." His half-brother's voice turned sober. "Morana found something. The Syndicate did put that building here in your name, but they got tipped off by someone. The username on the account was 'f_finisher'. The IP address originated from central Los Fortis. I'll text you the address."

Fortis Finisher.

What the fuck?

Was the killer a part of The Syndicate? One of their operatives told to target Alpha and his empire? Or was it a freelancer, someone Alpha had wronged in the past? He didn't have a dearth of enemies who would happily see him fall, and clearly, the killer was framing him for some reason.

"I'll check it out," he told the other man, keeping most of his thoughts to himself. While he appreciated Dante and the fact that he was nothing like his father, a part of him couldn't help but feel bitter about their shared past. He wasn't a good man by any means, and the fact that Dante had grown up with resources Alpha had to bleed to earn and beg Lorenzo Maroni to save his mother, was still a thorn in his side. He tried to not let his previous experience color his relationship with Dante, especially since the other man had been persistent in wanting to have a good relationship with him, but sometimes it bled through. Alpha didn't trust people easily, and while he'd been trying to keep an open mind, eventually, he hoped to be completely okay with the man, simply because the desire of having some family, any family, was acute in his heart.

He'd never thought he'd have any of his own, especially because he never really gave thought to bringing a life into his world without a mother. From his own experience, he knew how formative a mother's love was for a child, and he'd never seen a woman and felt he wanted her to birth his kids. Zephyr would make a great mother, he was sure, but he didn't trust her. She hid something from him, and though he didn't get the feeling it was nefarious, it unsettled him. And what a girl like her, from as different a background from his as one could imagine, would hide he didn't know.

He saw Jasmine give him a slight nod, and wrapped up his call with Dante, telling him he'd touch base soon.

"She said she saw a guy in a black hoodie," Jasmine started as she came up to him. "And another guy running off. The hoodie is the one who left the envelope on the car for me."

Another envelope. This time, with a smear of his semen found at the crime scene—a crime scene his people had been able to cover up, thanks to that warning.

Alpha was completely baffled. The only place he'd left his semen recently had been on his wife's ass, and he doubted anyone could have swiped it from her without his knowledge, especially with all the surveillance in the building. Still, he'd check to be double sure once he was alone.

"Anything else?" Alpha asked, keeping their conversation on track.

Jasmine shook her head and left. Hector entered, followed by Alpha's wife. She looked tired. He didn't like that, and he didn't like that he didn't like that. She hesitated on the threshold, uncertainty in her eyes as she wondered how things might have changed after last night, and Alpha wondered how a woman who wore everything on her face could be hiding something from him.

Hector raised his eyebrows at her, looking between them, clearly sending some kind of tension. That spurred her into pasting a fake smile on her face, one he absolutely didn't like, and coming to his side. She perched on the arm of his chair, and not on his lap like she'd been doing every evening for the last few weeks, and fuck, he *did not* like that.

He scowled, but he doubted she would see with the scarred side of his face toward her.

"We need to put this asshole down, boss," Hector grit out, folding his arms across his chest.

"Girls haven't been this terrified in a long time."

It was terrifying. With the speed with which bodies were dropping, the entire city had gone on alert. The police had finally started working on the cases seriously, his guys in the department keeping him up-to-date on everything they discovered, which wasn't anything he hadn't found out on his own. The press was blowing it up, calling the perpetrator everything from Street Slasher to Fortis Finisher to the Red Ripper. Fear entrenched his streets, and now, he had been pulled down from the observer to smack in the middle of it. The killer needed to be found, fast.

"You think he's a ... house cleaner?" Zephyr surmised from his side, referring to the common theory the police had cooked up about the guy being someone cleaning up the streets and ridding them of the high-risk individuals. The media had run with that theory, splashing it all over newspapers and channels. And they were all wrong.

"No. There's a pattern to his kills," he mused out loud. "He's not killing people on the streets randomly. His victims, at least those we know of so far, have all been girls who wanted out of the streets."

"So he's keeping them in the business?" Zephyr's voice was incredulous. "But why?"

"I think it's bigger than that." Hector looked at him pointedly. "They are his victims, but you are his target. He's coming after what he knows is important to you and setting you up for it. The question is why. Why you? And why now? If he's been actively killing for over two years, why just begin to frame you and plant false evidence at the crime scenes now? Something must have set him off. And we need to catch him before he does more harm." Alpha agreed with every word. "Take Jasmine and Victor with you to the last scene. Go check it out yourself. Ask around. I want to know anything anyone could've seen. And I want to know how to contact the man leaving me messages."

Hector gave a nod and left, closing the door behind him.

Alpha woke his computer screen, clicking on the voice icon in the corner that had been specifically designed for his voice. "Bring up the security feed from 8PM yesterday."

The icon whirred as his command registered, and in a few seconds, he had the split screens showing different angles of the building last night. Everything looked as it should have been. He clicked on the screen with his office, and it zoomed in.

He heard Zephyr's breath catch as she watched them on the black-and-white feed, her body entirely hidden from the view as he covered her, his jeans low as he pumped into her, only her shapely leg visible as he held it up.

Blood rushed to his cock, the audio from the speakers recalling his heavy breathing and her whimpers. He was big, and his cock was big, and he didn't know how she'd taken him, but fuck if the feel of her wet pussy tightening around him hadn't been the best thing he'd felt in a long time.

He unzipped his jeans, taking his cock out, and felt her eyes swivel to him as he ran his hand over it. It was like the dam inside him had a crack. It hadn't broken free completely, but more and more seeped out, and he wanted more.

"Yes or no?" he asked her the same question he'd asked before, keeping to his decision to simply keep it physical now. The tension between them was too much. He'd tried to resist it as much as he could, but the moment she'd called him a beast, something inside him had snapped. Thankfully, he'd still retained enough control to not let his actual beast out. As long as he kept it under control, it could work and it would be a lot less dangerous for her. The hesitation in her response made him look up to the side at her, where she was perched on the arm of his chair.

Her beautiful, chameleon eyes were watching him, the green in the hazel disappearing as her pupils blew up, her gaze on his face, not his cock. She leaned closer, pressing her lips to the corner of his mouth, right over the scar, in a kiss that went to his chest, making something rumble inside.

He wanted to turn his head and catch her lips entirely, taste her again and revel in the way she responded to him with such abundance. But kissing her was dangerous.

Thankfully, she pulled back before he could.

"Yes," she breathed softly, arousal clear in her voice.

Before she could take it back or rethink, he tugged her down on his lap, keeping her back to himself and making her face the monitor. Thanking whoever was up there that she wore dresses, he pushed her panties aside. He had the ones he'd ripped yesterday, tucked in his drawer after he'd jerked off to it before bed.

She was wet, but not as much as she usually got.

"Watch yourself be a little slut for me. Just for me," he said in a low voice against her ear, and felt her slicken, with his words or with the visual or the memory; he didn't know and didn't care. She was lubricated enough, and he angled himself, sliding in, keeping his hands on her hips.

Her curvy ass fell plush against his pelvis, her back bowing with the pleasure as he went deep, her hands falling to the desk in front of her. Landing her feet on the ground, he sat as she worked herself up and down on his cock, her pussy walls milking him, and fuck, the pleasure shot up his spine. He wanted to impale her hard, push deep into her, and fill her in her womb. He imagined what she'd be like, round with his seed, gushing with his touch, and it fucking did something to his brain.

He grabbed her hips as she slowed, and helped her move, leaning his head back against his chair as she flexed.

A knock on the door had her stilling over him.

He paused the video and pushed his chair closer to the desk, her walls fluttering around him with the motion, and kept her seated on his lap, the table covering their lower bodies.

"Come in."

He felt her surprise at his command, her knuckles turning white as she stayed utterly still, keeping her head straight and looking at the monitor like something very important was on the screen and she was focused on it.

Two of his guys who'd been on a recon mission stepped into the office, not surprised at finding her on his lap. Over the weeks, everyone in the headquarters had seen her there at one point or the other, and it didn't raise any eyebrows anymore.

"Boss." One of the guys gave him a nod. "There was a shipment of girls to the Syndicate twenty years ago. Came from Tenebrae to Xalin to Los Fortis. Fifteen girls. There hadn't been any underworld activity in the city back then, so the girls were disbursed from here. We tracked down twelve of them. Nine are dead. Three are under the Syndicate. Three are missing."

The fact that Alpha stayed hard inside her while listening to the gruesome report would have disturbed most people. He didn't give a shit, keeping her still and feeling every single way her walls quivered around his length as she watched him have a conversation, a slight tremor in her body the only indication she was barely holding on to composure.

"And Luna Caine?" he asked, only interested in the information he'd promised to his half-brother.

"One of the missing," the other guy answered. "We're tracking her, but it's taking some time."

Alpha gave them a nod. He could have let them leave, but he was enjoying the torment of his little wife, enjoying the way she tried to appear completely innocent and focused on the monitor while clenching around his cock, like his private little slut in the presence of the company.

Fuck, he was *aroused*.

So, he kept the guys talking. Asked them for every detail of the report. If they thought it odd, they didn't comment on it. Nor did they glance at his wife, which he was glad for, because they were skilled and he'd have hated to lose them. The possessiveness was both surprising and unsettling, but he'd chalked it up to her having his name. He had a reputation, and while she was attached to his name, she was a part of it. It only made sense that he'd want everyone to remember that and treat her the same.

He kept them talking, and slowly put his hand under her skirt, pressing on her clit.

Her body froze, her fingers gripping the edge of the table so hard he was afraid she'd break her pink-painted nails.

He rubbed her clit.

The men reported.

Her pussy squeezed him so hard he felt it shoot fire up the line of his spine, straight to his head.

He kept rubbing.

The men kept talking.

She kept trembling, her thighs quaking as she tried to keep her upper body still.

He pinched it between his fingers hard.

And with a wet flutter, she came all over his lap, her shoulders sagging like she just sighed, a loud breath leaving her.

He dismissed the guys, uncomfortably close to exploding but not wanting to inside her, for the sake of his plan.

Giving her ass a smack, he pushed her up, took some tissues from the desk, and came into his hand.

After the pleasure ebbed, he cleaned himself up and tucked his dick back in.

The moment he was done, she collapsed, her entire body shaking. He let her catch her breath, playing the video again, focusing on the aftermath of the session onscreen.

He watched the entire video, saw himself leave, saw her straighten on the black-and-white screen, and clean herself up with the tissues on his desk. She threw the used tissues in the bin in the corner, and the office stayed empty until the cleaning staff came in the morning to take out the trash. The killer could've taken the tissues from anywhere once they left his office. But the question was, how did the killer know to find the sample? Was it by luck or something more nefarious?

Alpha didn't know. Ignoring the way her soft, pliant body cuddled close to him, he watched the video again.

CHAPTER 18

ZEPHYR

To say Zephyr was confused would be an understatement. She had no idea what the hell had happened.

For the last two weeks, her husband had gone back on his 'no sexual contact' policy, their relationship going from roommates to fuck buddies in the blink of an eye, with terms and conditions applied that she had no idea about.

After the very thrilling and mildly scandalizing way he'd taken her in his office while casually chatting with his men like she'd not been a hair-trigger away from a massive orgasm, he'd taken her home. He'd greeted the dogs, they'd had dinner, and then while she'd been putting the dishes away, he'd bent her over the kitchen counter, fisted her hair, and growled, "Yes or no?"

She'd said yes, and she'd gotten fucked. Slowly, deliberately, in a manner so controlled it made her want to break whatever leash he was putting on his pace, try to get the beast out to play. She'd tried to talk, and he'd just pulled her hair back, craning her neck and hitting somewhere so deep inside her she'd lost all rational thought. After she'd been lax, he'd picked her up and put her in her bed, leaving her alone in the aftermath.

And since then he'd fucked her all over the house—in her bed, on the couch, over his balcony, bent over his hammock, pushed against her shower stall. Everywhere. And not that she was sorry, but it left her confused and mildly unsatisfied. Because while he took her everywhere he could, whenever he wanted, he kept himself distant. It was always controlled, always slow-paced, and left her cold afterward. He also never came inside her. In the beginning, she'd thought it had been for protection and he'd simply forgotten condoms in the heat of passion, so she'd told him it was okay and she was on the pill. It hadn't changed anything. He didn't come inside her, he didn't cuddle her, he didn't kiss her, and though they were more physically intimate than they'd ever been, she'd never felt as far away from him as she did then.

They'd stopped talking the way they used to. Every time she began a conversation, deciding she was going to succumb and tell him the truth, he would bend her over. Always from the back. Always slow and steady. Always distant.

It made her want to cry.

She hated when he did that—slowly fuck her brains out and then leave her unfulfilled, wanting more. And over the two weeks, he did it a lot. She was unable to say no every time he asked, both because she enjoyed the feeling of his body pressed into her and because she carried the hope that *this* time would be better, that *this* time he would hold her.

And he never did.

She'd become moodier in the last week, more withdrawn, and she hated that. The more she reached out to hold him, the further he slipped away. The more she wanted to talk to him and communicate, the higher his walls went. She didn't even know what she could do anymore.

Zephyr leaned on the side of the pool, looking out at the vista that had lost its beauty for her. It was a weekend, her day off, and she was spending the morning in the pool under the sun before she had to go to SLF. The dogs lazed around on the deck, and while Zephyr had never been much of a swimmer, she liked the pool and liked being in the water. Floating on her back, looking up at the blue sky and listening to the sounds of nature, she could almost forget herself for a few minutes and escape into a world inside her head.

A loud splash on the other side of the pool had her opening her eyes, shattering her fantasy. Her husband cut through the water smoothly, going under before coming up, slicking water back with his large hand, his gold eye light in the sun.

She hated how her heart still fluttered every time he was close.

Little sucker.

Zephyr put her elbows on the sides, leaning against the wall of the pool, and watched him cut through to her in powerful strokes. He stopped before her, their faces leveled, and Zephyr kept watching him, trying to understand where his head was at. He was probably doing the same.

Quietly, she raised her hand and touched her fingers to the scar on the side of his face, running it to the corner of his mouth, trying one more time.

"How did you get this?" she asked softly, feeling the deep groove of the marred flesh.

"I don't know." His voice was gruff, his arms coming to her sides to cage her in.

Just as she'd thought. The possibility of his memory being permanently gone or warped was becoming more and more real. And if he didn't remember the reason for his scarring in the last decade, and didn't remember her after the last months of being together, she doubted he ever would, and she had to make peace with that.

And that was one of the reasons that held her back from telling him the truth about their past, no matter how much she'd wanted to let it slip—there was a reason his brain had forgotten her. What if she triggered something in his memory that his brain was clearly trying to protect him from? What if she unleashed some heavy trauma that his mind had suppressed? She couldn't risk that, not after seeing how far he'd come, how much he'd trained to overcome his disadvantage, how at ease he'd become with his missing eye.

She slowly let her fingers drift, up to his eye patch, feeling the texture in the leather. He stayed still, letting her explore.

Hesitating, she looked at him for permission. "May I?"

His arms tightened as he gripped the side of the pool. Zephyr was aware of his breathing escalating as her finger stayed on his eye patch. Something was happening right there, in that pool of water, in the broad daylight. As his single eye stayed on her, as he gave a perceptible nod, something was happening, shifting, realigning. Heart pounding, she lifted the flap up, slowly, until it was on his head.

And her heart broke.

His eyelids were healed shut. The skin was most probably sewn together back when he'd had the injury. The scar that began from his scalp was a vertical, ugly line that went over the flesh of the lids. Once, there had been a powerful, beautiful golden orb there that had looked at her with love. She'd seen it light up in amusement, in heat, in affection.

Something had taken that from him, ripped it from his being, and left him with nothing but the scar.

Her eyes burning, she gently touched the slash over his eyelid, letting her finger feel the raised flesh. He tensed when her fingers made the contact, watching her with keen alertness with his other eye.

Zephyr studied the scar he hid under the leather patch, and leaned forward, placing a soft kiss over it.

He inhaled sharply, his breath warm on her neck.

Whatever was going on between them, whatever thoughts he had about them, he had shared something intimate, something important, something deeply private with her. And that counted more than anything ever could, right? That gave her more hope than anything else could have.

He had let her under his skin. She just needed to make herself at home there.

Pressing soft, gentle kisses to his scar, she followed the trail of the jagged line, holding the sides of his jaw in her hands, feeling his facial hair cushion her palms. She kissed him over his cheek, down the line to the corner of his mouth, all the while aware of the way he held himself, taut and rigid, while still taking her affection. And she gave it freely, loving him as her heart desired—openly, shamelessly, abundantly.

She stopped at the corner of his mouth, pulling back an inch to look at him, her chest heaving.

Since that first night at the fight when she'd jumped him, he hadn't kissed her. Through all their romps and ruckus around the house, he'd not once kissed her, even though she'd been dying for his mouth, gnawing for his taste, hungry in ways she'd never been because he'd been right there, yet so far away.

She held his gaze, the moment suspended between them, the invitation, the plea, the call clear as she closed her eyes, waiting, praying, hoping that he didn't leave her cold again, that he closed the distance and restarted her heart where it lay struggling in her chest.

He pushed her into the back of the pool subtly, his minty breath over her face, his bulky arms contracting at her sides, the wall of his chest pressing against her breasts. Her nipples, as sensitive as they were, pebbled against him. She stayed still, like a river waiting for the earth to change its course, flowing where it took her, turning as it bent.

"You shouldn't have done that, Zephyr."

His words had a soft, lethal edge to them that made her squeeze her eyes shut tighter. Zephyr. Still not 'rainbow' in so long it had become a memory like 'sunshine' had, a name she kept tucked safely in a mental drawer, to pull out when she needed the comfort.

She didn't say anything, simply held his face, the urge to tell him who she'd once been to him clashing with the urge to protect his mind from itself. She'd take the burden gladly if it kept him sane and safe.

And it was really sad, but she missed him.

He was right there against her, and she missed him with every cell in her body.

"Look at me," he commanded, and she complied, her eyes opening, her gaze locking with his. His thumb came to her chin, held her face in place, and his face dipped.

Heart thundering in her chest, Zephyr held his gaze as he pressed his mouth to hers, her lips parting on a gasp as he pulled back, watching her like a hawk, swooped in again, pressing another soft kiss to her mouth that belied the aggression simmering in his body.

She closed her eyes, surrendering to the sensation of his lips on hers, his facial hair rubbing around her mouth, his tongue flicking over the edge for a little taste, his chin holding her steady. She took it and touched his scar with her fingers again.

And the dam *burst*.

In a heartbeat, he pressed her flush against the pool wall, her mouth opening as he plundered it like a savage in a treasure cove, taking and claiming and controlling everything he could reach. Water lapped around her as she wrapped her legs around his muscular waist, tilting her head to the side, going where he took her, following his lead as he fed on her soul.

It was sloppy and hungry and aggressive, all lips and teeth and tongue. And Zephyr had never felt as cherished, as desired, as wanted as she did right then.

They made out in the pool for long minutes, kissed and kissed and kissed. At one point, he slid aside her bikini top and squeezed her breast, and tugged her nipple until she was writhing against him. At one point, she scratched her nails down his back and rode against the hardness pressing into her core. At one point, he let her breathe as he bit her chin before diving in for another taste, like he couldn't get enough of her, like he needed her kiss to make it through, like she was a salvation for his sins.

She didn't know how long they stayed in the pool, just kissing, dancing the oldest dance in the world with bodies that knew the steps even before they thought it, in synchronicity that made it seem like they'd been doing it for years.

The sound of barks broke their bubble.

Alpha pulled back, his chest heaving, his lips slightly swollen, the pupil in his golden eye blown as she panted, catching her breath, her heart full and body on fire, watching him. His hands flexed on her hips once, and he inhaled, letting her go. He fixed his eye patch and ducked under the water, swimming to the other side.

Zephyr watched as he heaved himself out, water sluicing down his powerful body, and went to the pool chair with the towel on it. As he wrapped the large towel around his hips, she turned to look at what had made the dogs bark. Hector stood on the deck, his face grim, waiting for her husband, the dogs standing around him. The look on his face wasn't good, and Zephyr wondered if everything was okay.

She would've gotten out of the water had she been wearing her usual swimsuit, but she'd started wearing minuscule bikinis at the house, comfortable in her body and skin as she'd never been before, not giving a thought to her buddha belly or butt cellulite or lack of thigh gap or untoned arms, not in front of Alpha, not with the way he looked at her, not with the way he made her feel around him. But she sure as hell wasn't going to get out and give Hector a view of it all.

Alpha knotted the towel around his hip as he strode to the deck, the man who'd been in the pool with her disappearing with each step, the dark underworld leader taking his place. The dogs gave him a sniff before dispersing, Bear coming to where Zephyr floated at the edge of the pool. He bent his head for a scratch and she obliged.

"You think he'll detach again, Mr. Bear?" she asked the canine softly, rubbing his head, her eyes on her husband and his right-hand man, both of them talking seriously. The dog gave a woof.

"I hope he doesn't, too."

CHAPTER 19

ZEPHYR

She didn't know if he'd detached, but he'd certainly disappeared. And she didn't want to automatically assume it was because of her.

He didn't come home that night, or the next, or the next, and Zephyr waited, waited, and waited some more.

After leaving with Hector post-steamy kiss, he'd not returned. She'd gone home after her volunteering, had dinner while watching a movie, and when it became clear that he wouldn't be back, she'd crashed on the couch surrounded by the dogs. That was mostly because she'd never slept alone in any house, and the thought of going up to her room in the house surrounded by wilderness had made her shiver. At least with those dogs, it hadn't been as bad. Bear especially, sweetheart that he was, had curled up on her feet, the expansion and contraction of his sleek body easing her nerves a bit.

Nala had come in the morning and woken her up. Leah had come in soon after to take care of the dogs, and Zephyr had gone to work with Victor, returned, and waited. Rinse and repeat. The next evening, she'd gone down to the first level to hang out with other members of the staff on the property, had her dinner talking to Zen, and crashed on the couch again in the company of the dogs, Bear laying his head on her stomach with canine compassion.

Alpha hadn't had any contact with her for days either. And while her instinct was to think it was because of her, she overrode that. It was possible that something urgent had come up and he got occupied enough not to give her a call. He'd just told Victor to relay the message that he would be away for a few days, and that had been it. And it could very well be the underworld shit or the killer shit or some other shit she had no idea about, because he didn't communicate with her.

So, she was trying not to take it personally, even though she knew for a fact he was getting updates on her from Victor. And that sucked because she didn't know if she was more pissed or more hurt.

"Hey, Zee!" her sister called out from the back of the long common room in the SLF building, where the women who stayed there watched television or played board games. Zephyr glanced at her in question.

"A little lady wants to see you."

Zephyr let her eyes drift down to a young girl at Zen's side, something fiery taking root in her stomach. The girl, with straight black hair and half-dead eyes, couldn't have been more than fourteen. But it was the purple bruise on the right side of her face that made Zephyr grit her teeth.

Oh, the monster.

She kept the smile tight on her face and waved the girl forward to the chair in front of her. "Come here, honey," she cajoled, keeping her voice light and soft.

The girl walked forward slowly as though sore, and Zephyr's fingers curled around her scissors.

"Is it okay if I touch your hair, sweetheart?" Zephyr asked once she sat down tentatively, knowing from experience that some survivors didn't want anyone touching their hair or certain parts of their head. As much as it broke her heart, she knew she had to ask the girl. The girl nodded.

Zephyr gave her a soft, encouraging smile. "You've got such beautiful hair. Do you know what you want me to do with it?"

The girl shook her head.

Zephyr lifted her blonde locks to the side of her face, keeping her eyes off the bruise. Someone had beat up the little angel in the worst way, and Zephyr wanted to find the bastard, drown him in a bathtub and throw her hairdryer in.

She locked eyes with the girl's gray ones in the mirror across her. "What do you think? I'll cut it like this so it's all feathery and falls right here, hmm?"

The girl's jaw trembled, but she nodded.

Zephyr got to work, adjusting her chair and moving the portable sink behind her head, giving the girl's hair a quick wash. Massaging the pressure points on her scalp to give her some relief, Zephyr chattered away, telling the nameless girl what she was doing every step of the way, talking about different nerves in the head, seeing her relax at the sound of her voice. She never asked her anything personal, having learned early on that the survivors didn't talk unless they wanted to. Once she was done and her hair was clean, she wrapped a towel around her head and straightened her chair.

Zen joined her on the side, removing the portable sink.

"You're about to be blown away, honey," Zen told the girl, taking a seat. "You know about Cinderella?"

The girl nodded as Zephyr took off the towel, getting her scissors and comb ready.

Zen took over the conversation. "Zee is like the fairy godmother. You'll feel so new after she's done. Look at all that beautiful blonde hair!"

God, she loved her sister, and how she genuinely cared so much, the way she hyped people up into believing in themselves.

She got to work, and after almost twenty minutes, she was very pleased. The girl's entire look had changed, a sleek bob falling against her jaw, feathery side bangs adding a feminine flair to the style, making her gray eyes pop.

"You like it?" Zephyr asked, happy to see her work bring something to the young girl's eyes. "Yes," the girl whispered, speaking for the first time, her eyes taking in her own face. She locked eyes with Zephyr's in the mirror, telling her so much more with one look than her words ever could have. Zephyr gave her shoulder a slight squeeze. "You look beautiful." The girl wiped a tear away and sat straighter. She gave Zen a nod, and they left.

As Zephyr cleaned up the station, she thought about the look in the young girl's eyes. That look was exactly the reason Zephyr spent hours on her weekends in this place, even though her fingers hurt in the end, even though she went home and cried afterward some days that hit hard. But every second of it was worth it.

"Mrs. Villanova."

The feminine voice came from behind her. She turned around to see Jasmine, one of the girls she'd given a makeover a long time ago. She remembered her because of the brand she'd had on her face back then, a brand she'd covered with a floral tattoo, making the line of her jaw a work of art.

"Jasmine?"

The woman's eyes widened. "You remember me?"

"Of course." Zephyr smiled, checking out how different she looked compared to the last time she'd seen her. "You look good," she complimented the other woman. "Wait, how did you know I'm Mrs. Villanova now?"

Jasmine plopped down in the vacant chair in front of her. "I'm one of Alpha's sentinels.

Victor told me you'd moved in. I thought it was time I introduced myself properly."

Wait, she was the same Jasmine he'd been talking about the other day? Small world.

The young woman eyed Zephyr. "Victor also told me you'd been left alone."

Zephyr slumped. She hadn't slept well at nights, she had a crick in her neck from sleeping on the couch, her period was about to come, and her emotional well-being was unwell. The last thing she wanted to do was talk about her husband because she was too tired to dredge up being pissed. She fussed with Jasmine's hair just for something to do.

"There was an incident last year," Jasmine spoke quietly since there were others in the vicinity, watching her in the mirror. "He broke a girl's hip by accident during ... Well, while he was with her. He hadn't been with anyone since."

Zephyr paused, listening intently. He'd severely hurt a woman. That was why he never went full-throttle with her. He didn't want to let the beast out again. God, his protective streak must have been driving him mad. *It all made sense.*

"Why are you telling me this?" Zephyr asked the other woman, curious.

"Because I owe you," Jasmine stated, her eyes fierce. "I don't know why you married him, but I felt like I should give you a heads-up. He's entered one of the big fight tournaments, and he's not done that in a few years. The fact that he's been in the arena for nights in a row instead of being home with you says something."

"That he wants to avoid me?"

"Exactly. And Alpha Villanova is many things, but a coward isn't one of them."

Jasmine hopped down from the chair. "Just some food for thought."

Zephyr looked down at the ring on her finger, at the ring he had brought her right before he'd withdrawn, and decided she needed to do the heavy legwork again. Just one last try.

Stupid heart.

She wrapped up her volunteering time at SLF, giving her sister a hug, and exited the building to find Victor on the phone, leaning against the car.

"Take me to him," she demanded, and the young man looked up at her in surprise.

"Eh," he hesitated. "He's at a fight tonight."

"I know. Take me or I'll go myself." She slid into the SUV. Victor finished his call and got in the driver's seat, pulling out of the parking lot and onto the busy street.

"Does he fight often?" she quizzed the one guy she'd made her friend on this side. Owing to the fact that she spent most of her time with Victor being her security detail, it only seemed logical to her. Plus, she knew from previous experience that he was susceptible to her interrogations.

Victor smoothly swerved right toward the industrial area. "No. Usually, it's only when he's got some pent-up energy. He used to fight every night on the streets when we were younger, but he's not been in the big arena for a few years."

"But he's been fighting for the last week?" She wanted to confirm.

"Yes, ma'am."

"Oh, for heaven's sake, stop calling me that."

"Yes, ma'am."

Ugh.

Victor pulled into the parking lot of a warehouse, moving his chin toward it. "That's the location."

Cool. She ushered him out of the car for a few seconds, and quickly undid her bra. Usually, she wouldn't leave her boobs free, since they needed the support, but she needed to push him over the edge. Undoing her hair, she fluffed it up with her fingers to give them a just-rolled-out-of-bed look, adjusted her bangs, and made sure her blue top showed a little cleavage. Climbing out of the car, she tucked it into her jean shorts, glad she'd chosen the fishnets for the day, and hitched her cute white backpack on.

"Let's go."

Victor led her to the largest warehouse on the block, and the closer they got, the louder the cheering came from the inside, much louder than that first fight she'd seen.

She was kind of excited to see him in his element. He'd never let her come to a fight a decade ago, told her it wasn't a place for a girl like her. They'd met in the dark parking lots, much like the one she was walking through, and they'd—

"Seems like a big fight tonight," Victor murmured, breaking her train of thought.

Zephyr shook herself to clear her head, and focused on the present.

They entered, and right off the bat, she knew it was a much, much bigger fight. For one, the warehouse interior was converted into some kind of fighting ring, the middle being one of those elevated squares with the ropes that she didn't know the names of. For another, there was a much, much bigger and more elite crowd this time. Mostly men, and a few women, sat around the ring in chairs on one side, roped off from the other crowd that was cheering. There were more bouncers positioned in the corners, this time with weapons, and a guy taking bets on the players.

Victor led her to an empty chair up front and sat her down. From her place, she wasn't even ten feet from the ring.

An announcer jumped in the ring, raising both arms to silence the crowd.

"Ladies and gentleman!" His voice boomed through the large space. "Welcome to the preliminary fight of the season! Our first match, between the man famous for slicing his opponents down one cut at a time, the man who trains the best fighters on his continent, all the way from Russia. Ladies and gentleman, The Ravager!"

Zephyr watched as a surprisingly good-looking, tall, shirtless man with ice-blond hair calmly jumped in the ring, his muscles well-defined, a platinum wedding band shining on his left hand. He looked at the spectators, still, almost as if he was bored, his light eyes taking in everything. "And from the Riviera, slaughtering his opponents, Hellhound!"

Jeez, who even came up with these names?

A lean, spry boy who looked in his early twenties jumped up, smiling and waving to the crowd.

The announcer rang the bell and stepped back.

The Hellhound guy put some kind of connected punching thing on his knuckles, and came at the Ravager, who ducked, got the boy's neck in a chokehold, and broke it, all within five seconds flat.

Zephyr gasped as the boy dropped to the ring dead, her hands going to her mouth. The crowd went wild, money exchanged hands. Two bouncers picked the boy up and took him away.

Just like that.

Dead.

The boy was *dead*.

She tugged at Victor's sleeve. "What just happened? What kind of a fight is this? This didn't happen last time!"

Victor shook his head. "That was a local fight. They can go whichever way. This is international. Death makes the most money."

"And Alpha's been ... fighting these death matches? Killing his opponents?"

Victor laughed. "Why do you think he's still breathing? They don't call him The *Finisher* for nothing."

Holy shit.

Holy shit.

Knowing he fought was one thing, but seeing it. God, she was going to throw up.

Zephyr put her head between her knees and breathed deeply, her hands shaking, questions that had been swirling in her mind for weeks crashing through her head. Was she truly out of her depth with him? Had pulling him into the marriage to love him again been a mistake? Would he ever even be able to love now after so many years of walking these dark streets? For the first time since she'd found him again, Zephyr felt more unsure about her own decision. She saw darkness, she knew darkness existed, she tried to help those who survived through it, but she didn't belong to it. In her heart, she was light, in so many ways still untainted by the brutalities that existed in the world, and she was grateful for that.

What the hell was she doing?

"Zee?"

Oh god, not now. Not when she was on the verge of a massive anxiety attack.

She exhaled and straightened as Alec, her cheating ex, took a seat at her side, his handsome face creasing in confusion at seeing her there, his eyes dropping to her boobs.

God, she was an idiot.

"You know this guy?" Victor asked, his hand going to the gun on his hip, ready to remove him.

Zephyr sighed. "Yes. Go away, Alec," she told her ex, keeping her eyes straight ahead on the ring.

She felt his fingers brush her burgundy hair. "Nice color. I heard you're Villanova's whore these days."

Wife, but she didn't correct him, well aware of how Alec operated. He goaded her into giving him attention and took it as an opening, so Zephyr ignored him.

"He knows how good you suck a cock?"

He was just asking for a reaction, and she grit her teeth, keeping her head straight ahead. He tugged at her strand. "I love you, Zee. I miss your tight little body. Come to the back with me."

God, she couldn't believe she'd been with this toad for two years. Had he always been this slimy?

The announcer jumped on again, clapping for silence. "Our last prelim match, ladies and gentlemen," his voice boomed again, "is between last year's champion, the Kraken of Killroy, and the notorious one-eyed beast, our very own, The Finisher!"

Zephyr watched with concentration as last year's champion, a large dark-skinned man jumped on the stage and into the ring, bouncing on his feet and shaking his muscles loose, his demeanor confident, his intent focused.

And then, her husband, no, the *Finisher* got in the ring.

She'd never seen him like that.

Zephyr held her breath, her hands fisting on her thighs as she watched him walk to the center as he did, fixing the tape around his hands. He wore a bandana around his forehead, probably to keep his longish hair away from his face, his massive body and its marks exposed to every naked eye in the room, only clad in black gym shorts.

She wondered how he fought with just one eye, how he made up for the disadvantage with his perfect-visioned opponent.

Alpha cracked his neck, flexed his fingers, and looked up, his eye coming to her.

She saw the surprise on his face at seeing her there, followed by something very, very dark as his eye went to Alec at her side, who she'd completely forgotten about. She saw his jaw clench, his fingers flex again, his eye taking in every detail of her seated body before lingering on the hand Alex had on her hair.

Alpha loved her hair.

Her heart in her throat, Zephyr watched as he turned to his opponent when the bell rang. Her entire body felt tight, on edge, as if she was about to fall down a very high, very steep cliff. The announcer went off with the ring, and the match began.

The men circled each other, both observing, but not making a move. The Kraken took out a knife, ducked to the right before suddenly going left, in Alpha's blind spot, and swiped at him, slicing his chest.

Zephyr gripped the arms of her chair, her knuckles turning white, her body shaking from the adrenaline she could feel flooding her system upon his injury.

Alpha didn't even react to the cut, just turned and did a body roll on the ground, landing on his feet in an agile movement. The Kraken turned with him, never letting him get to his back. He swiped again but missed as Alpha kicked him hard in the stomach, the force of which sent him staggering back. The Kraken recovered, shaking it off, and coming at Alpha again, angered, and the *Finisher* took a hold of his wrist, twisting his arm behind his back as he positioned himself behind the Kraken. With his free hand, he caught the other wrist of the hand holding the knife and brought it to the Kraken's neck.

Zephyr watched, both enthralled and aghast, as he turned them to face her, making sure she was watching.

She couldn't look away if she tried.

And keeping their gazes locked, he sliced the man's throat open, inch by inch.

The crowd went wild around her, chanting his name, yelling words that were all a buzz in the blood rushing through her ears.

She kept watching, unable to move.

Alpha stepped away from the body, letting it drop down, his chest and arms covered in sweat and blood, and his eye on her. Knife in his hand, he jumped off the ring, searing her with his intensity to the point breathing became difficult, and strode toward her.

She tilted her head back as he stepped between her legs, close enough that her chin touched his thigh. He raised the knife and her eyes widened, not understanding what was happening. Finally, he broke their gaze, his eye shifting to the side.

Zephyr turned to see Alec frozen in his seat, the knife under the wrist of his hand that had touched her hair, the edge of the blade pressing on it until she could see a line of blood break the skin.

"It's going to be your neck the next time I see you near my wife," Alpha growled softly. "Are we clear?"

Alec swallowed and nodded.

"Then fuck off."

The blade came to her chin then, almost like his fingers always did, directing her focus back to himself.

"Who am I?" he demanded quietly, her face level with his waist, her eyes enraptured with his.

"What?"

"Who. Am. I?"

She swallowed. "My husband."

The unscarred side of his mouth lifted, but the amusement didn't reach his eye. Before she could take another breath, he gathered her hair in his free hand, gripping it in the way that made her scalp singe with sensation. The blade traveled down from her chin, and her breath hitched, her body in flux of sensations at the confusing signals as it went down her neck, down the slope of her heaving chest, coming to rest in her cleavage.

"And who are you?"

Her mouth parted. "Your wife."

He let the knife travel down the slope of her right breast to her peaked nipple, slapping it with the width of the blade, and she gasped, heat spreading through her body, pooling between her legs.

"Mine."

With that one word, she was destroyed, decimated, done for; every cell in her body sizzling at the very public, very dominating claiming of her.

To drive the point home, even more, he threw the knife to the side, bent down, hauled her over his shoulder, tilting her world upside down once again.

CHAPTER 20

ZEPHYR

She hung on as he took her through the crowd to somewhere at the back of the warehouse, her body jostling on his wide shoulder, her thighs sticky with the blood on his chest, her free breasts hanging down and almost threatening to pop out of her neckline due to gravity. There were whoops and catcalls and filthy suggestions shouted as he just walked with purpose, his hand on her ass in a way that screamed proprietary.

A door opened and shut, and then she was upright and sitting on a table in some kind of locker room, and before she could process anything else, his hand was wrapped around her hair, tugging her head back, his body flush against her, the blood of his dead opponent smearing on her chest from his, the large bulge in his shorts pressing into her pussy. "You wanted the beast," he growled against her lips. "Here he fucking is."

His mouth slashed in an angry kiss on hers—deep, dark, decadent.

It was carnal, consuming, claiming, singeing her from the roots of her scalp where he pulled, to the tips of her curling toes. It was what she imagined a neanderthal would've given to his woman after hunting down a bear, what a pirate would've given to the maiden after taking over her ship, what a warlord would've given to his mistress after slaying his dragons.

It was a kiss of claim, of power, of hunger, one to make the blood simmer and head spin, and she fell into the spiral with his tongue in her mouth. His mouth stayed on hers, his free hand grabbing her breast and squeezing it painfully. Her mouth opened on a gasp and he pulled back, watching her with that golden eye, his face darker, harder, hotter than ever before. His hand loosened on her breast, their gazes locked, and he slapped her nipple.

A yelp escaped her.

"Louder," he commanded, slapping her other breast with his large palm, right on the nipple, and fuck if heat didn't flare out from the points to pool low in her belly, her thighs squeezing his waist in. It was the first time he was doing something like this, and god, she wanted him even more. She leaned closer, wanting his mouth again, but he evaded. His fingers pulled her over-sensitized nipple harshly, before giving it another smack. "Louder."

She moaned, her eyes closing as the heaviness in her breasts increased with the blood, her nipples turgid with the sensations.

He wrapped his fist in another loop of her hair and pulled her head back, inhaling the line of her neck, his lips stopping at her ear. "Did you like that outside?"

"Yes," she breathed as his fingers plucked at her rigid nipple, squeezing it over and over again, making her hips move rhythmically against his erection, chasing the pleasure he promised.

"You want the beast, my little slut?" His deep voice in her ear had her panting, his words tugging something dirty free out of her. God, yes, she wanted to be the most shameless for him, wanted him to do whatever he desired to her.

"Yes." She tried to move more to no avail. He'd immobilized her, and that just pushed her arousal through the roof, knowing she was completely at his mercy as he did whatever he wanted to her in there.

He pressed his bulge right into her clit over their clothes, pulling her hair and nipple at the same time, biting her earlobe, the blood and sweat on his body covering hers, and her jaw trembled, her pleasure peaking. She was going to come if he didn't stop. She didn't know if it was the baser instincts reacting to the blood and his pheromones, or just the fact that she'd gone without any pleasure for a week after he'd made her come daily, or just the very possessive nature of his claim. But as he tugged and slapped and twisted her nipples, grinding his hard length against her over and over, right over her clit, Zephyr felt the beginnings of her orgasm, pleasure coasting through her blood, her head falling back, everything from his hand in her hair, to his fingers on her breasts, to his mouth on her neck, to his cock against her clit, hypersensitizing her body to the point she couldn't take the barrage of sensations anymore. With a loud noise, something between a moan and a scream, she shattered in his arms.

"Look at you soaking me." He pointed out the very obvious wetness between her legs, her body lubricating itself in hopes that he would ravage it.

"You sat out there, fucking naked under this, and let another man breathe your air," he whispered softly, dangerously into her neck. "Next time, it'll be his blood on your skin when I'll fuck you so raw you wouldn't be able to move for weeks. Get on your knees."

She swallowed, her heart crashing against her ribs, her mind reeling as she dropped down, his hand in her hair keeping her still. He pushed down his shorts, exposing himself to her like that for the first time, and Zephyr's breath hitched. She'd always felt him from behind or over clothes, and knew he was well endowed, but seeing it made her realize just *how* well endowed. He could very well fuck her raw and make her feel it for weeks.

She leaned forward to take him in her mouth, wanting to taste him for the first time, but he held her in place with one hand, jerking off with the other, watching her. His large hand moved up and down his shaft, his cock aimed at her breasts. She pressed them together, deepening her cleavage, and tugged down her top, exposing them to him, her nipples hard and sore from his rough fingers.

He groaned at the sight, his head falling back, veins popping on his forearm, adjacent to his scar and on his neck as he came, ropes of his warm seed hitting her chest.

Zephyr breathed harder as he finished. She didn't get to finish him as she'd wanted, but she didn't mind, not at seeing him come undone like that.

He let go of her hair and went to one of the lockers in the room, throwing her a towel to clean up. Zephyr got to her feet, her legs shaky, her knees aching, and wiped the fluids off her chest the best she could, adjusting her top as she looked at him standing a few feet away, back to his cool, composed self.

"You shouldn't have come here."

He was putting distance between them. Again.

Her lips pursed, the anger, the hurt, the longing coming back.

"You didn't come back."

He hadn't. Not for days. Not for weeks. Not for years. She'd waited.

He'd left her alone, standing on the side of a road and never returned, and god, a part of her hated him so much for it.

She closed the distance between them, pushing against his chest. "You left me." She hated the way her jaw trembled as memories she'd been keeping at bay flooded her in her vulnerable state. "You forgot me," she whispered, unable to keep it in any longer. The secret had become poison in her veins, corroding her from the inside as she tried to protect him. The unscarred side of his face frowned, his gaze sharpening on her. "I didn't forget you." "You did." Her eyes flitted to his throat as hers tightened. "And you don't even know it." His hand came to her chin, drawing her eyes to see a fierce look on his face as he tried to understand what she meant. He wouldn't get it. He'd never get it.

And suddenly, she felt so completely *exhausted*. He pulled and pushed and pulled and pushed, and now, she was drained. She didn't have anything left to give anymore.

She slumped, her head coming to rest on his chest. She should probably care that they were covered in someone's blood, but she just couldn't bring herself to be bothered. She could feel her heart plummeting, her emotions going on another downward spiral of the ugly, and all she wanted was to go home and sleep and not move until she felt better. But she didn't know where she could sleep—her room in the mansion was unsettling alone, the couch hurt and he didn't want her in his bed.

Everything crashed on her.

What had she been *thinking?*

That was the thing; she hadn't been. She'd been *feeling*, and she'd made her decisions from her heart and not her head. He didn't remember her because of whatever injury had taken his eye, and it seemed he would never remember. But she'd been hoping, somewhere deep down, that maybe spending time together would trigger some emotional response in him, not taking into consideration the fact that he'd spent the last ten years not wanting to feel. And she could tell him about their history, but what was the point? He was sexually attracted to her, he felt territorial about her, but that didn't equate any emotional attachment. For him, putting distance between them was easy. He had no issues detaching because he wasn't attached in the first place. He'd taken her to a new city and left her alone; taken her to his house and abandoned her for days. And had she not come here to find him, he probably would have spent the entire duration of the rest of their marriage away, with her chasing him always. God, she was a *fool*. An overemotional fool who attached herself too easily to hope.

A tear fell down her cheek and onto his pec.

Her mother had been right. It was a farce of a marriage.

She inhaled, taking a deep breath of his scent, committing it to memory before pulling away, physically and mentally. She needed to stop chasing. She needed to leave, to regroup, to undo the mess she'd made of both their lives.

This had been a mistake. A well-intended, lovelorn mistake, but an error nonetheless.

She took a step away and felt his eye on her for a long minute, his thumb tracing the tear on her cheek.

"What just happened?" he asked softly, and she avoided looking at him, straightening her clothes.

"I have to go," she told him, breaking his grip and heading for the door, needing space from him.

His hand on her arm stopped her. "What just happened?" he asked again, and she took another deep breath in, not knowing how to answer him. So she didn't. Their communication sucked anyway. She pulled out of his loose grip and opened the door.

Victor was standing guard outside, keeping anyone from coming their way.

"Can you hand me your jacket, please?" she asked her bodyguard, feeling dirty and miserable, and truly degraded for the first time in her life.

Victor wordlessly shrugged out of his jacket and handed it to her, his eyes averted to the man she could feel at her back. She could feel his singular gaze piercing her, and she ignored it. Wrapping the jacket around herself as Victor handed her the bag she'd left on the chair, she stepped away. She took the bag and kept her head down, walking out of the warehouse and into the dark parking lot. Her breaths shook. She got in the car, and Victor got in to drive. "Home?" he asked, starting the ignition, and no, she didn't want to go home because it didn't feel like her home. She didn't feel like she belonged, not in a place she'd thrown her heart again and again, only for it to be rebuffed.

"I'd like to go to my sister's apartment, please."

She saw Victor's eyes in the rearview mirror, but he held his tongue and drove into the night. Zephyr stared out the window, leaning her head against the glass, trying to sieve her thoughts and understand what she was feeling, the overwrought jumble of emotions inside her confusing. A part of her still wanted to return and fight for them, the part that had been fascinated by him at ten, fallen in love with him at eighteen, and found him again now. That part wanted to jump into his arms like she had that first night at the fight, and that part wanted her to stay in the hope that she could maybe make him love her too.

But another part, a darker part, mocked the girl with the love and taunted the hope. It told her she was a fool for thinking it could be possible, an idiot for trying, and she'd done nothing but set herself up for more hurt over the last few weeks. While he might not intentionally hurt her, he had the power to break her. She remembered the feeling when he'd left her alone in Tenebrae, when he'd told his brother it wasn't a 'real marriage', when he'd taken her to his house and left her completely alone in a new place.

One step forward, ten steps back. And she was just ... done.

The car came to a stop in front of her old apartment building, and she got out, dragging herself to the door. She entered the code and turned to Victor who'd escorted her to the point.

"I'll be staying with my sister," she told him, still clutching his jacket. "I don't have work tomorrow, so you don't have to be here. I'll get your jacket cleaned and return it."

Victor gave her a concerned look. "Send me a text if you need me."

She gave him a small smile and entered the building, closing the door behind her. By memory, she ended up in front of her old apartment and rang the bell. It was a late weekend night, and usually Zen stayed up on those, binging on some crime show.

The door swung open to reveal her surprised sister, who took one look at her and pulled her in. "Oh, Zee."

Zephyr burst out crying.

CHAPTER 21

ZEPHYR, TEN YEARS AGO

The parking lot of the old school where they met would be creepy if not for the lover's lane around the corner where all the kids sneaked to meet.

Zephyr waited near the boundary fence, in the shadowed space behind the building, hearing the sounds of a school party somewhere in the field as she waited. It wasn't her school, nor her neighborhood, her home two miles away from the location. But it was the closest private spot for them, away from her world and away from his. He never wanted her to come close to his neighborhood, and she couldn't have him in hers without her parents finding out, and her mother would never accept it.

Zephyr looked down at the watch on her wrist, a gift he'd given her for her eighteenth birthday a few months ago, her face flushing at the memory of what else he'd given her that night. He'd pushed her against the very fence she was leaning on and eaten her out. She wanted more. She wanted him.

A noise from her right made her look up, a smile splitting her cheeks as she saw him jogging toward her, in a black t-shirt and jeans, his dark hair messy and wet from a shower. He came right into her personal space and held her face in his large hands, slanting his lips over hers, kissing her thoroughly.

"I want to eat your smile, sunshine," he said against her mouth. "Swallow it whole and light up my insides with it."

She smiled wider, letting him kiss her as much as he wanted, pushing her fingers through his damp strands. Meeting him had been fateful. Though she'd kept her eye on him over the years, thanks to one of her friends who lived in his neighborhood, she'd never spoken to him until two months ago. Her friend had taken her to see him fight, but ditched her for her boyfriend. Zephyr, alone and scared, had been going back home when he'd seen her. He walked her home since he didn't have a car, and for five miles, they'd talked and talked and talked. She'd confessed to seeing him a few years ago, meeting his mother, and keeping an eye on him over the years from a distance. And he'd wanted to see her again after dropping her outside her house.

And it had only gotten deeper, more intense since. She knew they were going to be together forever, their love fated like her parents and grandparents. She'd always had a connection to him because they were meant to be.

He suddenly winced against her mouth and she pulled back, looking up to see why. The side of his lips was slightly bruised.

"Did you just come from a fight?" She touched the bruise lightly. His intense amber eyes, almost light as liquid gold, watched her. She knew he enjoyed it when she fussed over him, even though she didn't like the fighting.

"You should see the other guy." He gave a dark chuckle. Though he was just a few years older than her, his life experiences had hardened him, matured him beyond his age. He tried not to let that seep into their limited time together. He pressed her against the fence, peppering kisses on her neck, where it met her shoulder.

"One day soon," he told her between little bites. "I'll get a car and pick you up from home, so you won't have to walk here. A Jeep." His nose inhaled her scent, and she was glad she'd put on his favorite perfume. "And I'll take you for a long drive away from the city. Would you like that?"

She smiled, looking up at the stars. "Mmmhmm."

"And one day, I'll get out of this shithole. Get rich. Build you a house. Get dogs. You like dogs, right?"

In theory, she did. "I think so."

He huffed a laugh against her neck. "And one day, when I have money, I'm going to buy you the prettiest ring, sunshine. Would you take that?"

She pulled back, her hands cupping his shaven cheeks. "I would love nothing more."

He dropped a kiss to her lips. "My sunshine. Lighting me up from the insides."

Zephyr melted against him, her eyes burning as he continued speaking.

"You make me want to be a better man for you."

Oh god, he was going to make her cry.

The sound of his phone ringing pulled him away. He took the call, softly playing with her hair as he listened to someone speaking on the other end. "Okay, give me two minutes." Zephyr looked up at him with silent questions.

He gave her a wicked smile, suddenly looking boyishly handsome. "I have a surprise for you."

Her heart fluttered in her chest. "What?"

He shook his head, walking backward, pointing at her with a grin. "Stay there. Don't move. I'll be back."

Zephyr laughed. "Okay. What if a boy comes to flirt with me while you're not here?"

His eyes darkened. "Tell him you're mine. He'd get away if he knows what's good for him."

Zephyr chuckled as he pushed his hair back from his forehead, running around the corner, and disappeared from view.

She kept her eye on the corner, waiting, a smile on her face.

Ten minutes.

The smile dimmed.

Fifteen minutes.

A weight settled in her stomach.

Thirty.

She called him. *"The number you're trying to reach is unavailable."*

Forty-five.

She began to pace, her eyes going to the corner.

One hour.

Lead settled in. She walked around the corner, over to the road. Empty.

Two hours.

She called again. *"The number you're trying to reach is unavailable."* And again. *"The number you're trying to reach is unavailable."*

And again. *"The number you're dialing is incorrect. Please check the number and try again later."*

She waited on the side of the road, panicking, but certain something had just held him up, that he would come back and apologize for scaring her.

He didn't.

Dawn came, but he didn't.

CHAPTER 22

ALPHA, PRESENT DAY

Something was wrong.

Alpha stood on his deck, looking down at the view, something hollow in his chest. He'd just returned from his run with the dogs, and he couldn't place his finger on what was off, but something was.

He didn't know if it was the fact that Dante had called him two days ago with the news that he had heard an update from his undercover guy, Vin. Or whether it was the fact that one of his feelers about the missing girls had also come back with some information about the three untraced girls, and they needed to meet to give him the info. Or the fact that the murders in the city had suddenly stopped in the last few weeks, and Alpha knew in his gut it was the calm before the storm.

Maybe it was none of those things. Maybe it was just the fact that his house, for the first time since he'd lived in it, felt empty.

Everything felt empty. And quiet. Too quiet. There was no sound of laughter, no feminine banter, no pop music on loudspeakers that he didn't enjoy one bit. Just him and his solitude, just like he'd wanted before. He didn't want it now.

She's just gone to her sister, he told himself. He knew they were close and she missed her sibling. It wasn't a big deal.

But something inside him disagreed. It knew he'd fucked up. It knew this was big. It reminded him of the way she'd withdrawn into herself after he'd stepped back, and god, he felt like the biggest bastard on the planet. Maybe, he was. She'd avoided looking at him in the locker room, and she *never* did that. She stared at him constantly, always finding new reasons to check him out, and he loved that. He loved the way her eyes appreciated his damaged form, openly and honestly. He loved how she lit up when he looked at her. He loved how her eyes followed him around even when she thought he wasn't aware of them.

And he'd missed it. For the entire time he'd been away, he'd missed her.

"You forgot me."

She'd meant something when she'd said that. He didn't know what, but it kept bugging him. It had been clear from the beginning that she'd known things about him, that she'd been hiding something. And suddenly he wondered if it had something to do with a part of his life he couldn't recall. He needed to talk to her.

"Ah, I hope Zee is finally sleeping upstairs," Leah commented as she brought him his coffee. Alpha took it, frowning. "Thank you. What do you mean?"

"She was sleeping on the couch when you were gone." Leah shook her head. "I think being around the dogs made her feel better. Being all alone in the house must have been scary for a city girl like her."

Fuck, he was such a dick. He'd not even spared a thought to how

THE FINISHER

she'd be in his absence. Whenever he left the city, she spent the night at her parent's house, only coming back when he returned. How had he not thought about that?

Bear whined from his corner on the deck, his soulful eyes sad. He'd gotten attached to her the most, and he'd been sulking without her. Even Bandit had been going to her room, probably to get her scent and steal another item of clothing. Baron didn't give a shit.

He gave the dogs a pat with one hand, sipping the coffee and looking out at the view.

He'd make it up to her when she came back.

It'd be fine.

It wasn't fine.

His wife had disappeared.

For three days, he waited for her to come home. She didn't. Her room, her things, the places he'd fucked her, her yellow bra that Bandit had become obsessed with, all mocked him. He gave her some space, knowing he'd done something to mess up.

On day four, he called her.

She never picked up.

Something tight lodged in his gut.

He drove by her work, and they told him she'd taken the entire week off. He even stooped to asking Victor to reach out about his jacket, which he hated that she had, and Victor's message went unread.

And now, for the first time, he was worried that it was something else. Had it been the fact that she'd seen him, truly seen him in his monstrous form, slicing a man's neck and covering her in blood like a primitive beast that had spooked her? Had she realized that she didn't want a part of him and his world anymore? Or had it been something else?

"You forgot me."

The words rang like an accusation in his head. The way she'd said the words, it haunted his mind, the distance giving him sudden sharp clarity to look at the last months in retrospect. She'd not asked for anything from him, not even his reciprocation for her affection. And yet, he felt like he'd made a huge, huge mistake by withdrawing, by being wary of her.

Alpha sat outside her apartment building, pondering over all the possibilities, and wondered when this farce of a marriage had become so important to him.

"Are you going in?" Hector asked from the front, knowing there was something going on between him and his wife, but not prying.

The phantom pain in his right eye socket made the skin under his patch itch. The memory of her soft lips kissing him where he was the ugliest made the weight in his chest heavier, so heavy he had to drag a breath in. Fuck, how bad had he messed up?

Gritting his teeth, he stepped out of the car and went to the door, pressing the button for the apartment.

The buzz cut off as Zenith's voice came from the speaker. "Who is it?"

"Alpha," he said into the little machine and heard silence over the line. He hoped she didn't lock him out. Given how close the sisters were, he didn't think Zenith had a high opinion of him at the moment. He'd break the fucking door if he had to, but he wanted to avoid it. No sense in making things unnecessarily hard.

Thankfully, the door buzzed open and he went in, dread pooling in the pit of his stomach for the first time in a long time, at the possibility that Zephyr might not want to go back with him. It made him halt in his tracks, the epiphany that he didn't want to lose her, not yet, sinking over him. He hadn't had enough of her light. There was so much more to be had between them, so much that he'd been denying them both deliberately. She'd snuck in, whether he'd wanted to or not, and now he didn't want her gone. It was a realization that he had something to lose, for the first time since his mother died.

He rubbed at his chest, a low rumble escaping him at the thought of her telling him she'd never come back.

No. He'd find out what went wrong, and he'd fix it.

What if he couldn't?

The door to the apartment opened before he could complete the thought, his younger sister-in-law considering him with a seriousness that belied her age. She stepped out of the apartment and shut the door behind herself, crossing her arms over her chest, steadily watching him, no sign of the nervous girl he'd encountered weeks ago.

"I am not Zephyr's sister by blood," she began, her tone somber. "Our parents adopted me when I was young. I don't remember much of my childhood before them, but I do remember when I came to this family, I was alone and I was scared."

Alpha took her words in, trying to understand where she was going, slightly annoyed that she was keeping him from his wife.

"Zee took one look at me and decided she loved me," Zenith recalled, her voice shaking with emotion. "She didn't know me, but she didn't care. And since that day, she's loved me. She snuck in my bed at night because she knew I was scared of sleeping alone. She talked to me for hours because she knew it made me feel good. She gave me all of her love even when I couldn't love her back, and she saved me in more ways than she knows. I love our parents, but the only reason I am who I am today is because of my sister and her unconditional, endless love for me. That's just who she is. That's how she loves. And anyone she loves is the luckiest person on this earth."

Alpha felt the rock get heavier on his chest with each word, the gravity of every word pulling on his insides. His respect for Zenith went up a notch. Anyone who protected someone so fiercely was admirable. ~~That she was~~ protecting her sister was even more so.

"She loves you," Zenith said quietly in the space between them, tilting his world askew. "And she'll kill me for telling you this, but she's loved you for a very long time."

"You forgot me."

Fuck.

She'd been a part of his life. Had he loved her once too? Had his dead heart felt something for her at a time he couldn't remember?

Zenith went on, unaware or uncaring of his turmoil, "How and when is her story to tell. The only reason she cooked up the entire scheme to marry you was so she could love you freely, as her heart desires, and maybe, just maybe, you would learn to love her in return."

"My agenda was to make you love me."

She'd told him that and he'd not believed her.

Something moved inside him. He rubbed at his chest again, trying to dislodge the weight Zenith's words got on him. The fact that Zephyr had gone to the drastic length to marry him just to love him was unfathomable. No one did anything without an ulterior motive. But if Zenith was to be believed, his wife had.

"She's withering." Zenith's voice trembled, her eyes moistening with anger as she looked at him. "She's been withering every day that you've pulled back from her. And I don't know what you did, but she just tipped over the edge."

What had he done? Alpha recalled the locker room for the hundredth time, trying to pinpoint where it all went wrong, and he still didn't know. Had it been when he'd smeared her with the blood? When he'd finished coming on her? When he'd told her she shouldn't have been there? He'd replayed it all in his mind a hundred times and he still didn't understand what exactly set her spiraling.

Zenith wasn't finished. "She's been in bed, depressed, and while she has her occasional mood swings, this one ... it hurts me to see her like this. If you enter that door, do it only if you can make her feel better. You have one chance." She took a step closer, pointing a finger at his face. "Because let's get one thing clear, brother-in-law. I don't care who you are. If you break her again, I will end you or die trying."

He really fucking liked his sister-in-law. And at that moment, he was really glad Zephyr had someone like her in her corner. He didn't think she could end him, but he appreciated the sentiment of violence. But he'd spent enough time lingering outside. It was time to find her.

"Where is she?" he asked her, pointedly looking at the door.

"Don't let the best thing that's happened to you slip away." Zenith took a step back and opened the door, giving him a small glare. "She's in the bedroom. Right door."

Alpha braced himself, and entered, going straight to the door she indicated, not knowing what he'd find behind, but ready to battle for it.

CHAPTER 23

ZEPHYR

There was nothing like cocooning under a blanket, lying down on soft pillows and clean sheets, and letting time pass by while hiding from the world.

Zephyr didn't know how much time had passed since the moment she'd come to the apartment, and she didn't care. She'd cried, showered and washed everything away, and dyed her hair blue like her heart. Nothing said change like hair color. She'd cried some more, taken a week off work, and slept. And when she'd woken up, she'd stayed in bed, never wanting to get out of it. She knew she was having one of her depressive episodes, the ones she'd been having since her hormonal imbalance years ago, but she wasn't bothered. She felt what she felt and it was valid, and if it was a depressive void, well, she was going to drown in it. She'd either emerge on the other side, or she wouldn't. It didn't matter. Nothing mattered.

At least, staying in bed, she'd come to the decision to just let it all go, let him and the memories of him go. Once she felt better, she would contact a lawyer and get the divorce paperwork done. She would send Victor a message and ask him to arrange to have her stuff boxed and sent back. And she would record a message for Alpha, telling him it wasn't working, wish him the best, and set him free to live his life without any baggage.

And just the thought of doing that made her eyes wet, but she would do it. She would let him go. Maybe someday, she'd be happy with someone again.

You'll never be enough.

You love, and love, and love, and still lose it all.

No one loves you back.

The ugly voice whispered, and Zephyr stayed under her cocoon, hiding from it.

It was just an episode. It would pass, and she'd go back to being her jovial self on the outside at least. She hoped it was soon because her sister was worried about her and she didn't want that. If she took too long, her family would get involved, and that would just do more harm than good. She'd be put on medication that made her slightly numb, and eventually, it would get better.

You're worthless, you fool. You trust too much. It'll never matter.

Maybe the numbing medication wasn't such a bad idea. Anything that could push back the black sludge spreading inside her, eclipsing the light she loved, slowly taking over her mind, one ugly thought at a time.

She heard her door open, and stayed under the blankets in the darkened room, knowing it was just Zen checking up on her.

She'd be fine.

Fine, but not loved. Never loved.

She inhaled a breath through her mouth, keeping her eyes closed, letting it pass. It would pass. No matter how bad it got, everything passed.

The door clicked shut, and she stayed the way she was, hoping for sleep and sweet, sweet oblivion from the eclipse.

The bed dipped near her hip, and she really hoped Zen would just check her pulse and let her be for a while. Her sister, thanks to all her work with the survivors that she did, was really good at understanding what someone needed at a certain time. She'd always been like that, emphatic despite being quiet. And Zephyr needed space to let the ugly be without it touching anyone else.

The blanket lifted up, and a body settled down behind her.

Strong, muscular arms wrapped around her waist, pulling her back into a large, hard body, the scent of wilderness and musk she instinctively recognized pooling her senses.

She froze, completely stiffened, trying to process this development.

In all her projections of the future, and she'd had many owing to her overactive imagination, there hadn't been one possibility where he came to find her. She'd always just assumed that he'd say good riddance, let her be, and simply live on as he always had.

This was unexpected, and she didn't know how to feel. Was she happy he was there? Sad? Angry? Resentful? Bitter? Loving? What was she feeling?

She wished emotions were like flowers, pretty and color-coded so she could pick and choose which ones she wanted at what time. For some, maybe they were. Not for her. Her flowers had thorns, and they made her bleed.

And it didn't escape her notice that it was the first time he was holding her in his embrace like that, his solid heat and strength wrapped around her, better than her blankets; she had to admit. Yet, she couldn't relax into him. Her heart, bruised as it was, recognized him as both its tormentor and its healer, and she let it fight the internal battle, too tired to be bothered. He wanted to hold her now, of all times? She'd let him, keeping in mind each time he hadn't, each time he'd rebuffed her or walked away when she'd needed the affection.

His arm tightened around her waist, giving her a soft squeeze, his lips kissing her skin under her neck. The other arm he settled under her head, plastering her body to himself. He inhaled the spot where her neck and her shoulder met. He rubbed her stomach softly with his large palm. He gave her little squeezes in between.

And she hated the way her traitorous heart fluttered at his tender petting.

"I miss you, rainbow."

His gruff words in that deep voice made her clench her eyes shut. No. No. No.

He wasn't doing that. Nope.

This was not her plan. He was spoiling her plan. The plan was that she was going to wallow and then send him a recorded explanation and divorce papers. He wasn't supposed to say he missed her, not now. He wasn't supposed to call her rainbow, not now. And he definitely wasn't supposed to hold her like she mattered to him, not now.

She stayed stiff, pursing her lips.

"Talk to me, please."

No.

She had nothing to say.

His hand went down her arm, taking a hold of her hand, twisting the ring that she had on her finger, the ring she'd taken with such hope. He intertwined their fingers together, his hand rough and large, and so, so tender with hers.

Her nose stung.

He wasn't supposed to do this.

"I'm sorry," he whispered into her neck.

He needed to stop.

And what was he sorry for? For leaving her when she'd been eighteen? For not remembering her? For not even trying with them now? For not accepting her love and not trusting her and keeping his distance? For leading a life that had hardened him to the point she'd bled on the barbed wires around his heart? None of it was his fault. He didn't do that on purpose. He was just who he was, and she was who she was, and maybe, just maybe, they weren't meant to be.

"Talk to me, rainbow," he murmured against her ear. "Please."

No.

He needed to go and not make this harder for them.

She swallowed, keeping her eyes closed, memorizing him again with all her senses.

"I don't know how I lost my eye," he began quietly. "My memory around that time ... it's blank. I don't remember if it was an accident or someone trying to kill me. It could have been either. I don't remember a lot from that part."

Zephyr stilled, unsure at why he was sharing it now. She'd begged him for crumbs of himself, and he'd rejected her over and over. And though the girl in her felt for him, the woman was mad.

She stayed silent.

"You were a part of my memories, weren't you?" he asked softly, making something inside her tremble. Screw him for making her feel like this.

"Yeah." She hated the way her voice cracked.

She felt his relief at her response. "Were we together?"

She nodded mutely.

"Did we break up?"

No. They hadn't.

"You left me," she told him, keeping her eyes closed. "You'd told me to wait, that you had something to show me, and you never came back. I didn't know why, not until I saw you at the fight. Now, I know something must have happened, whatever took your eye. For ten years, I didn't know. I wondered if you'd died, if you'd abandoned me, or if you'd simply lost interest."

His hand rubbed over her belly. "I don't remember."

"I know," she croaked. "It's okay."

God, she hated confrontations, but it was the best they hashed it all out now.

"I—" she began, swallowed, began again. "I didn't tell you because I wanted us to have a clean slate, to see if you could fall for me again. But I also didn't want to remind you of whatever your brain was hiding and risk triggering some trauma again."

God, this was hard.

"But we've both changed. You're a different man, and I'm a different woman, and while my heart still loves you—"

"Zephyr—"

"—I think this was the closure I needed. I tried, and it didn't work, and I'm okay with that. Really, I am. But I need to let you go now. Move on. Maybe find someone else, have the family I always wanted. Put you in my memories and—"

She was suddenly on her back, a very large, very intense Alpha looming over her, caging her in with his arms. "Say that again," he dared her, his voice the dangerous edge of a blade.

Zephyr blinked, confused.

He leaned closer, brushing her blue locks with his fingers. "I cut the hand of a man who touched your hair, Zephyr. What do you think I'm going to do to the one you *move on* with?" Her breath caught.

She hadn't anticipated this.

"I might not remember you," he whispered, his lips almost at hers. "But you're my wife now. Mine. And I'd bathe this whole city in blood before I let you change that."

He was being intense, too intense, and she didn't know how to deal with it.

"It was only for six months." She threw his own words back in his face.

He pressed a silent kiss to her neck in reply.

"We signed a contract," she reminded him, hating the way her heart thudded against her ribs. He pressed a kiss to her nose. "I'm not done with you, little rainbow. Come home."

"And when you're done with me?" She turned her head to the side. "Go back, Alpha," she called him by that name, knowing he didn't like it when she did. "I'm tired. It's best for both of us if we move on."

"Not happening," he stated firmly, settling beside her, pulling her into his arms.

She tried to get away. He kept her close.

And it was maddening. He hadn't cared one bit when she'd been clinging to him, needy for whatever he threw her way, no shame in the way she'd given her love. He hadn't even spared her a touch when she'd been at her most vulnerable.

Her sadness and pain and rage all merged together. She wanted to claw at his chest, make him hurt even an iota of the little ways he'd hurt her, over and over and over again.

No. She'd give him the truth, and she'd let him go.

Zephyr stared at his tattoo peeking from under the shirt.

"Your mother told me about the alfajores."

She felt him still at that.

She ignored his response, quietly telling him about her meeting with his mother, the two days she'd spent befriending her and how she'd talked about Alpha. She didn't tell him that she saw him at the hospital breaking down, didn't want him to know that she'd been witness to something too private for him.

He stayed silent for a long time, processing everything.

"How did you find me?" he asked after a long time, and she sighed.

"I had a friend in school who lived in your area. She told me about you. I'd go to see her and occasionally catch a glimpse of you. It went on for a while."

"So you stalked me?"

Technically, yes. But her intent had never been anything beyond curiosity. She'd never even thought she'd talk to him, and definitely hadn't been threatening to his peace of mind like stalkers were.

She stayed silent.

He pressed a soft kiss to her head, rubbing her back, tucking her into his large form. He was gentling her, and it was working. She could feel her insides softening. But a part of her, the part that had given and given and spiraled, that part still held back.

You're doomed. Admit it.

She possibly was.

"We should get a divorce," she mumbled into his chest, trying for the last time to get him to leave. "I've told you whatever I knew. It's done. You have no more curiosity to handle. This . . . this is never going to work. I was a fool to believe that and to go after it like I did. Let's just not waste any more time, okay?"

"I'm not letting you go, Zephyr." His hand simply traced her hip, his words tender in the space between them.

Her heartbeats escalated. "But—"

"You know how a rainbow is made?"

Zephyr frowned. "When sunlight passes through a raindrop."

"My life has been nothing but gray for as long as I remember," he told her softly.

"Rainstorms and thunder clouds that never went away. You filtered through that, all bright colors and exuberance and *life*. And the clouds are still there, but my eyes can't leave the rainbow long enough to see them. You changed things. And I'm not letting that go, Zephyr. I'm not letting *you* go. Get that out of your head right now."

Her eyes burned.

That was beautiful. The way he saw her was beautiful. And though she was still mad at him, she hugged him tightly, sobbing into his arms, not even knowing why, and for the first time in her recent memory, he held her.

PART 3

THE CORE

"You cannot save people, you can only love them."

-Anais Nin

CHAPTER 24

ZEPHYR

She didn't go back with him that night.

But he stayed the night. He stayed the night, just holding her, letting her cry, letting her hit him, but not letting her away from himself. She fell into an exhausted sleep and woke to his fingers gently stroking her back, her cheek on his chest as he lay awake, lost in some thought. And something shifted in their dynamic since that morning. Zephyr didn't know if it was the fact that she'd begun to hold back, or the fact that he'd begun to give more, but things didn't remain the same.

She stayed with her sister that night too, and he stayed with them, not leaving her side while she was awake, knowing she was vulnerable and letting her be. She emerged from her room with him in tow, to see Zen watching *Criminal Minds*, and plopped down beside her. Alpha took a seat on the other side of the couch, a silent conversation happening between her sister and him, and the three of them just watched one episode after another. When she fell asleep, he took her back to the bedroom and only left afterward.

The next morning, he was back not just with breakfast, but also the dogs, all leashed in one hand.

Bear, her special boy, saw her and his tail began to wag incessantly. The moment they were free, he attacked her with his love, pushing her on the floor and licking her hands as she hugged him.

"He was whining at home," Alpha said wryly as he took a seat on the stool beside the kitchen counter. The other two dogs went around the apartment, investigating the new scents, Baron sniffing Zenith as she watched with amusement, Bandit giving her a customary lick.

Hector entered from the open door, checking Zen out before nodding at her.

"Yo, Zee. You doing good?"

She gave him a smile, petting Bear who put his head on her lap and began to make happy sounds like a rumbling motor.

"This was sneaky," she told Alpha, hugging the dog. "You brought them to tempt me to come back."

The unscarred side of his mouth twitched, his eye patch dashing in the morning sun.

Zen laughed from the side. "Well, as romantic as this is, I have to go." She put on her silk scarf around her neck. "By the way, Mama and Papa want to talk to you. You better call them." She looked at Alpha. "Brother-in-law."

Alpha gave her a nod. "Sister-in-law."

That was cute.

Zen left the apartment, and Hector followed, leaving them alone with the dogs.

"You should invite your parents for dinner," Alpha suggested, a wicked gleam in his golden eye.

"You're only saying that so I'll come back."

He didn't reply, but he was right. She still didn't feel ready though, so she stayed away.

He persisted. Earlier, she'd been the one to visit him at work in the evenings, but now, he waited for her outside the salon when she finished, driving her from there to the apartment, leaving her at the door with a hard kiss. Every day was the same—their new routine. He brought her breakfast and the dogs, dropped her at work, picked her up, and repeat. Each day he tried to get her to go home with him, and each time she refused, he didn't give up.

It was odd, this Alpha who doggedly refused to let her go, one who slowly let her into this new heart of his. Day after day, to the point Zen told her to give him another chance. So she went home. It was the same, but it felt different. Maybe she felt different.

Leah was happy to see her, saying the house was too empty without her now. Nala was happy to see her, saying nobody appreciated her food as she did. And Alpha, he was happy to see her there, saying nothing but taking her bag to the master bedroom.

She called her parents and invited them for dinner over the weekend. She called Amara and gave her some updates. And then she went to her old room, and lay down in bed.

That was the thing about a depressive episode. She bounced back usually, but sometimes, she didn't. Sometimes, it changed her just enough for her to notice. Sometimes, she just wanted to stare at the wall and let everything pass by, no matter how good things seemed to be going. A weight settled on the bed with her.

Bear.

He whined softly, and lay by her side, and Zephyr smiled, petting his soft fur.

"You think we'll be okay?" she asked him quietly.

He pressed his head to her stomach.

"I don't know where I'll go from here."

Arms slid under her knees and neck, picking her up easily.

"For now, you're going in our bedroom," her husband declared gruffly, carrying her through the adjoining door and dropping her on the bed.

Zephyr bounced once before settling, watching him shut the doors and take off the loose vest he wore at home, watching his muscles ripple as he stripped and prowled to the bed. She backed up instinctively, never having seen this side of him, her eyes taking in his scars, his tattoos, his muscles, his everything.

He put his hands beside her head, his single eye focused on her. "You sleep here now." Zephyr swallowed. "You're only doing this to lure me back in."

"Damn right I am."

Zephyr held his gaze, and then slumped down. She was tired. Turning on her side, she looked out the tall glass doors that led to the balcony, listened to the sound of the gushing waterfall and animals, and felt him slide behind her.

She slept fitfully through the night, and he held her tight, not letting her out of the circle of his arms once. For once, giving and giving and giving, while she only took and replenished herself.

It was the heat that woke her up in the morning. Zephyr felt like a furnace, sweating, caged against a very hot, literally hot, body. She groaned, turning her neck to see and actually believe she was in the master bedroom where her husband had carried her *(carried her!)* after bringing her back home.

He was asleep.

She turned as gently as she could to not wake him, taking him in the early morning light.

He slept, his leather eye patch on the bedside table, the scarred side of his face still in the permanent scowl, but the other side relaxed, eased, his brow not as severe as it was when he was awake. Zephyr leisurely clocked every detail of him, going down from his face, down his neck. The big scar extended down, over his right pec, ending just under his ribs where a larger clutter of tissue had healed together, almost as if someone had dragged a knife down and stuck it in his ribs. Tribal tattoos decorated around the scars, almost as though he'd seen them and decided to highlight them on his body. The tattoos didn't have any particular shape or writing; just designs.

Other smaller scars littered his torso. Zephyr counted them. Nine. So many scars.

She touched the one beside his light abs tenderly, softening, wondering again at how hard it must have been for him to not only survive, but survive alone while leading a tribe of his own. Even though she was mad at him, it was commendable.

"Your touch." His voice, deep and grainy from sleep, startled her. She pulled her hand back, but he snatched it with lightning-quick reflexes, placing it on the scar again. His golden eye opened drowsily, the other sealed shut by the mottled tissue, and she marveled again at the fact that he was letting her see under his skin.

"My touch?" she asked, urging him to complete the sentence.

One of his large hands came up, stroking the side of her cheek. "I didn't realize how much I missed your touch. You gave a starved man a feast every day until he forgot what hunger felt like, and then took it away."

God, he spoke like the boy she'd once known. Younger Alpha had said the most beautiful things to her, whispered them to her in private while he still remained a badass on the streets. "I'm sorry I forgot you," he told her quietly, and Zephyr soaked up the moment, his sincerity, his softness, his touch.

She patted his scar. "It's not your fault."

He leaned in, giving her a tender kiss. "We'll make this work?"

It was the first time he asked, and not told her, to be back.

"If I say I want to leave?" She nuzzled his nose.

"I'll just keep you in bed."

A bubble of laughter escaped her chest. "And what will you do?"

He didn't answer, just pulled her under him and caged her in with his massive arms, his body hulking over her as he bent his head, kissing her neck softly, going down to the juncture of her shoulder where she was extra sensitive. "I will tempt you."

Zephyr chuckled, holding his sides, tilting her neck back. "With your magic dick?"

She felt the left side of his mouth lift up.

Her phone buzzing from the side made her look over.

"It's Mama," she told him, grabbing the phone and pushing him away, even though he didn't budge.

"Zephyr." Her mama's voice came through the speaker, bright and early.

Alpha dipped his head, tugging her pajama top down with his teeth, cupping her breasts in his massive palms. What the hell was he doing?

"Good morning, Mama," Zephyr greeted her mother, her head hitting the pillow as he squeezed one breast, licking the other nipple with a flick of his tongue. His short scruff added to the sensation, rubbing against her sensitive skin. She pushed her fingers in his hair, keeping the phone in the other.

"Why did Mrs. Billie from your building call me and tell me you were with your sister this last week? Did you leave that husband of yours?" The hope in her mother's voice was truly incredible. Zephyr wondered what her mother would say if she knew that husband of hers was currently feasting on her boobs like it was his sole purpose in life.

He tugged at her nipple with his teeth, and she bit her lip, keeping the sound rising in her throat trapped as she gathered a breath to answer her mother.

"No, Mama," she breathed out, trying to sound as normal as she could. "Zen just missed me. She'd not used to living alone—ahh—so I decided to visit for a few days."

"What was that?"

That was her husband, tormenting her, biting the flesh of her breasts, sucking her nipples deep into his mouth, doing wicked, wicked things with his tongue as she lay on the bed, wanton under him. Sex had always been something they'd been good at, even when he'd been holding himself back. She wondered what it would be like now when he gave it to her.

"Nothing," she answered her mother. "Just walking the—um—dogs."

Why were his hands going down and spreading her legs?

She stopped him, only to see a gleam in his eyes as he ripped her panties right from the center.

"Good," her mother said, the sound of the microwave behind her. "At least you're getting some exercise in."

Zephyr stared up at the ceiling, her mood dampening.

"Mama, I'll call you in a bit," she disconnected, her jaw tight.

Alpha looked at her, his left eyebrow slashing in confusion.

Zephyr looked down at her thighs, thighs he held open, thighs with cellulite that her mother had very well intentionally told her to tone. Usually, she didn't let stuff like that get to her, but with the depressive, insecure episode she was rebounding from, it was easy to see the flaws and believe what everyone tried to feed her.

She tried to close her legs, only to have him hold them in place.

"Do you think I'm beautiful?" she asked him, genuinely curious about what he would say. She didn't think she was by society's standards, but she liked how she looked.

Alpha placed a kiss on her mound. "What happened?"

"You didn't answer my question."

"I think"—he settled in comfortably, tilting her hips and opening her up, watching her with that golden stare—"you're both my rainbow and my treasure at the end of it. And nothing"—*bite*—"will"—*lick*—"ever"—*suck*—"compare."

He won.

"You're the twisted beauty, and I'm the beast, remember?" His hot breath blew over her. "Now let this beast eat you up."

Alpha spread her wide, licking her from top to bottom, his tongue sinful as he lashed it against her flesh.

Zephyr lay on her back, her hands gripping his head, letting him make her feel like the most beautiful woman in the world.

CHAPTER 25

ZEPHYR

There had been another murder, and this time, Alpha's hair had been found at the crime scene.

Zephyr stared in stunned surprise as she looked toward her husband in the car, getting updated about what she'd missed since she'd stopped going to his office.

They were on their way to one of Alpha's clubs in the city, her old request to meet some of his girls something he was finally fulfilling.

She didn't know if her withdrawal had truly affected him so much, or if he'd genuinely missed her, or if it was just the fact that she'd become a convenient companion. Whatever it was, he was trying. Physically, emotionally, he was trying, and that meant everything to her. He still wasn't the most talkative, but he'd spent their last few days truly wanting to connect with her. He'd quizzed her about their pasts, told him about the aftermath of his injury and consequent recovery, let her see him the way he hadn't before, and she appreciated that. Eating meals with her, watching shows before taking her to bed, and eating her out had become some of his favorite things. She knew he was taking time away from his busy schedule to give her those moments, and that more than anything made her feel cherished.

Some nights, he used his fingers or her toy and brought her pleasure she couldn't even grapple with. Some nights, it was his tongue and teeth. But he pleasured her and then held her until they slept, not trying to find his own release with her. She didn't know if it was because she'd left after the last time he had done that, or if it was something else, but he was trying to let her in, and she saw that. Still, she remained a bit wary, her heart still not entirely healed from being rebuffed over and over again.

And she missed having him inside her, but he kept himself completely away. She didn't know why. But she loved the other parts that had come with Alpha 3.0, as she was referring to this new phase of him. Earlier, she'd talked and he'd listened, occasionally responding. Now, she talked, he engaged a bit, encouraged her to talk more. He still stayed in his grumpy mode around people, but privately, he began to ease off, letting her see another side of him he'd been holding on to before.

"First semen, now hair," Hector said from up front where he was driving, Victor on the passenger's side. "This has gone overboard."

Zephyr watched her husband looking out the window, lost in thought, and she bit her lip, fear invading the happy bubble she'd made for herself in the last week. A serial killer in the city framed her husband in ways that were severely implicating—and the fact that they were clueless about him. Was it someone wanting Alpha's power or someone from his past? And if it was someone from his past, did Alpha even remember him? Oh god. Her eyes flew to the scar on his face.

"Your scar," she said out loud. He turned his face to the side to see her, moving his neck entirely since she sat in the periphery of his eye patch and out of his line of sight.

"What?" he asked, the left side of his face serious.

"Could this killer ..." She trailed off and shut her mouth, realizing that the brothers upfront might not know about the fact that he didn't remember anything. She swallowed. "Later."

He considered her, before giving her a brief nod.

"We're here," Victor announced, and she looked out, focusing on the present.

They were in the industrial district. More precisely, they were in the same parking lot where she'd come to see him fight weeks ago in the larger arena.

Alpha got out of the car and came to her side, picking her up by the hips and putting her down, even though she wore jeans and not a dress. She realized he enjoyed doing that, helping her out and in the car with his strength, making her feel smaller and safer next to him.

"Thanks." She gave him a smile and saw the way his eye lingered on her dimple.

Putting his large hand on the small of her waist, he led her to the warehouse where the fight had been. That night, with her nerves and emotional turmoil, she'd not noticed the building beside the warehouse. There was nothing indicating it was anything but a random building, nothing except a neon sign on the door that read *Club 69*.

How original.

Zephyr rolled her eyes at the sign and entered behind Hector who led from the front, Victor following them at the back, gasping as the interior came into view.

Whatever she had imagined an underworld club must have looked like, it definitely had been nothing remotely close to this. The entire warehouse had been converted into a classy nightclub straight out of some 80s mafia movie. The open area had wooden flooring, the long bar at the end was polished and stacked, comfortable seating areas lined both sides of the central dance floor. A set of stairs led to what she assumed was the glass-ensconced VIP area on both sides. The whole space was done in classy browns and reds, and she shouldn't have been surprised. From what she'd seen of her husband's interior design tastes, he enjoyed extravagant surroundings.

During the day, it was mostly empty, with a few women sitting at the bar, talking.

Zephyr recognized Jasmine right off the bat.

The other girl turned to look at them and gave Zephyr a smile. "Well, look who it is. Mr. and Mrs. Villanova in the house!"

She wasn't going to lie; it gave her the best thrill to hear that.

The other ladies sitting with Jasmine—two of them—turned to look at her curiously. Another girl sat off to one side, and Zephyr watched as Hector made his way to her.

"Taking a tour?" Jasmine asked, her pretty face tattooed with beautiful roses over her jaw. Zephyr nodded. "I wanted to meet ... the girls."

Jasmine's eyebrow hit her hairline before she shook her head. "They're not all here. That's Irina and Katelin. Come, I'll introduce you."

Zephyr followed the other woman as Alpha went to talk to another guy behind the bar, maybe the manager.

The two seated women, maybe a little older than her, studied her inquisitively.

"You're not what we expected," Katelin stated, looking her up and down, but not in a mean way. "You're ... small."

Zephyr laughed. "I am. I'm Zee."

"Nice to meet you, Zee," Irina said with a heavy accent. "I must say, it is unusual for you to meet us."

Zephyr shrugged. "I just wanted to learn about this place, and about AV from you ladies. Understand the business better since I'm an outsider, you know."

If they found her weird, they were polite enough not to let it on. She spent the next few minutes talking to the women, understanding the inner workings of her husband's empire, getting most of their stories, and realizing how glad they were to work under AV's security. Jasmine, she learned, had been pimped by her father since she'd been twelve for almost a decade until she tried to leave, and he beat her to the brink of death. Alpha found her and sent her to SLF, and made her his eyes on the streets afterward for pay.

Irina had been a freelancer and had been raped by two men who'd taken her in a car. She had jumped out of the moving vehicle when she'd realized she needed protection, but didn't want a pimp. So she'd come to AV.

Katelin had been with The Syndicate, working as a human slave since she was eight up until a wealthy gentleman bought her. She killed the man, changed her name, and escaped to AV. Zephyr also realized while talking to them that not all sex workers worked the same. Katelin, for example, had one man she spent her time with for the money, and then she was free to enjoy life as she pleased. Irina, on the other hand, came to the club twice a week to pick up clients. Jasmine didn't work sexually at all.

"On fight nights," Irina told her, sipping iced water, "it's especially good for business. The arena is just next door. After the fight, people want to drink, to talk, spend more money. It's a full house during that time."

Damn.

Zephyr wondered if all people in the industry had such horrific backstories, if they were all survivors of immense trauma that they masked with the business of sex. It made her realize how lucky she had been in her life, how privileged to have been born to good parents who had taken care of her, to have a sister who loved her, and then to find a man who liked her well enough to miss her when she was gone.

The extent of what Alpha had done for them hit her then. He had given these women a choice, but more importantly, he'd given people who'd constantly looked over their shoulders safety and hope. And she couldn't even fathom what that must feel like, of being able to sleep at night without worrying about physical safety, of knowing there was an exit if they wanted it.

She was lucky and sitting in the company of women who hadn't been, and that made her want to do something for them. But she didn't know what she could do. She had no skills except hairstyling, and to an extent, baking. What could she do for them that would give them a little joy, a little happy memory? She didn't know.

A muscular hand slid around her waist, the height of the stool putting her on an almost similar level as her husband.

"Are you done?" he asked, his voice deep and dark.

She nodded, giving the ladies a small smile. "Thank you for talking to me."

They gave her nods and waves as Alpha picked her up by her hips again, putting her on her feet, and led her outside.

"Satisfied?" They exited into the parking lot, a lot more crowded with people on the other side now. Zephyr watched curiously.

"What's happening?"

"It's a fight night," Hector piped from the side, joining them. "They're finishing up the semifinals before there's a final showdown."

Wait, it was like a tournament? "Is it for a title or something?" Zephyr had never really watched sports on TV, so she didn't know how this worked.

Hector chuckled. "It's for survival. Most guys who fight aren't there willingly."

Wait, what? She looked up at Alpha, his eye on the entry to the arena. "What does Hector mean?"

Alpha sighed. "The fighters are owned by ... people. They train them and then bets are placed at each fight. Since there aren't any rules, death is usually how it ends."

Her stomach sank.

She watched the men outside the entrance, trying to see if she could see any of that dynamic. She recognized the guy they'd called the Ravager the other night, the one who'd snapped a boy's neck in a few seconds. He stood to the side in boxer shorts and vest, his ice-blond hair out of place in the tropical city, his eyes on something in the distance. Another fighter in shorts stood next to two men in a suit, looking subservient.

"That boy wants death," Hector pointed to the quiet fighter. "The Ravager is one of the most brutal killing machines in the circuit. And with the way the boy is standing, he knows it too." The well was deep. She hadn't known, hadn't thought there was an entire industry flourishing on the business of death.

"So why do you still fight?" She looked to Alpha, trying to understand why he would risk himself like that every time when he wasn't forced by someone to do it.

He shrugged a broad shoulder. "I got my reputation with street fights growing up. And occasionally, I have to step in the ring to send a message." He gave her a heavy look with one eye. "Not to fuck with me or what's mine."

If he was trying to distract her, it was working.

She shook off the last line and the meaning behind it, keeping track of the conversation.

"That's why you were in the ring the other nights? Or were you avoiding me and fighting?" From the way his back tensed, she knew it was the latter.

(245)

She sighed. "At least you won't have to go back to the death ring again."

His pause made her heart skip a beat and not in a good way. "What?"

"I have to go into the ring. One more time for the tournament."

Lead infused her veins. "What? Why?"

"Because I've already fought and won." Alpha chucked her chin lightly, talking as casually about going to fight to the death as she talked about her hair. "Throwing the towel in will send the wrong message now."

"But—"

His grip on her chin tightened. "That's the way my world works, Zephyr. The message you send is the man you are. I might be your husband in here, but out there? I am the Alpha. So, I'm going to fight in that ring, and you, my dear wife, are going to sit in the front like last time and cheer for me, and show everyone that you may be small, but you're not weak." Zephyr stared up at him, her heart pounding, and looked away to find the Ravager watching them. If what Alpha said was true, he'd be fighting the killing machine soon, and she'd have to watch it all.

CHAPTER 26

ALPHA

Hearing from his sister-in-law during the day was a surprise.

Alpha wiped his face with the towel, sweat pouring down his chest as the ringing of his phone interrupted him mid-training. With the fight coming up, knowing his opponent would be the Ravager, Alpha was preparing for the first time in a long time.

He picked up his phone, putting it to his ear, his scarred eye itching with the phantom sensation because of the sweat.

"Sister-in-law," he greeted, curious as to why she would call him and not Zephyr for something. The only thing he could think of was SLF.

"Brother-in-law," Zenith greeted back, her serious tone immediately making him focus.

"What is it?" he demanded, a tightening in his chest at the thought of something happening to his wife. That could be the only reason she would sound so somber.

"I just got home and found an envelope," she informed him. "It's addressed to you."

Fuck.

Why the hell would he send a note to Alpha through Zenith, of all people? Jasmine, he could understand. Zephyr too. But leaving a note for Zenith, at her home, made no sense.

Alpha looked around the training center, the one he had for fighters in the industrial district near the arena. It was about fifteen minutes from where she lived.

"Can you please bring it to me?" he requested. "It might be urgent."

Zenith agreed and he told her the address, hanging up and going to the locker room to change, his mind whirring with questions.

His phone rang again, his wife calling this time.

"Rainbow." He put her on speaker, tugging on his jeans. "I take it your sister called you?"

"Oh god, is it the same black envelope thing?" her voice, sweet and feminine, rushed out.

"Do you think he knows something about your DNA at the last scene? Will you meet him? I don't want the cops trying to arrest you for something you didn't even do so—"

"Breathe," he commanded, a sliver of amusement curling inside him despite the grim development.

He heard her catch her breath, blowing another out, and felt the movement in his lips at her compliance. She did that a lot, did things naturally that made something inside him lighten up, though he didn't know if she knew that. Since he'd brought her back, she'd been a bit more reserved, held herself back just a tad bit enough for him to feel it, and fuck if it didn't make him feel like shit. But it also lit up a fire inside him—to make her love him again, as openly, as completely as she had, and banish all doubts from her mind. He was the one with the trust issues between them, not her.

"Ask Zen to read the note when she gets there," his wife suggested after she'd calmed down a bit.

He tensed instinctively. He didn't like anyone knowing about his inability to read small words. He didn't know why it was the way it was, but he could make out billboard signs and large posters well enough to understand what they read, but trying to focus on smaller fonts just made his head ache. And it wasn't his vision, because he saw both near and far with clarity with his one eye. It was just another peculiarity related to his missing eye he didn't comprehend anymore.

Why he'd told her he couldn't read, when his sentinels were the only other people who knew about it, he didn't know. Maybe his instincts had known deep down that she was worthy of his confidence, maybe he'd been too bull-headed to listen to it.

He fucking hated trusting people.

But he had begun to trust Zephyr, and she trusted her sister implicitly. And it wasn't like he had a choice anyway. Hector was out of town so one of his other guys had been driving him, and he sure as hell wasn't going to give him the note to read. No, Zenith was a better bet. "Okay," he told her, hanging up, then realized maybe he shouldn't have been so abrupt with her. That was just the way he was with everyone.

Sighing, he pocketed his phone and went out into the parking lot in the falling dusk, darkness encroaching on one end of the horizon, chasing the day away.

Someone exited the training building behind him, coming to stand at his side.

The Ravager.

Alpha had known him once, fought with him as a younger man

on the streets. The hate-filled boy had channeled it and grown into a weapon that made the industry a shitload of money.

"Adrik," Alpha greeted him by his real name, wondering how someone could have such natural white hair.

"Alpha," the dangerous man said from his side, cracking his knuckles. "You shouldn't have entered the tournament this time, not with me in the ring."

Alpha had definitely avoided that. Adrik was probably the only man who could seize his advantage over Alpha in the ring, even though he was leaner and a few inches shorter. He was another boy of the streets, much harsher streets in his homeland, and he'd grown up as a force to be reckoned with when he got in the ring.

Alpha stayed silent.

Adrik twisted the ring on his left hand, keeping his eyes forward. "I don't want to kill you, Villanova. And I'm not ready to die. There are things I need to do. Debts I must ... settle." Alpha's focus sharpened on the man. He'd have to get more research done on the man. The file he had was old—he had files on everyone he considered important enough in the underworld—and clearly, there had been some changes from then to now.

Alpha kept his tone deliberately light. "My wife wouldn't like it if I let you touch me. She's possessive."

Adrik chuckled, bringing up his bottle of water to his mouth. "You're lucky. Mine would slice me open the first chance she could."

Interesting. Very interesting.

"So neither of us is dying," Adrik declared. "Think about how we do that without throwing our names in the mud. Think about it."

With that, he went back to the building, leaving Alpha mulling over his words. He was right. There had to be some way they could throw the fight without throwing their reputations.

As he thought, a silver cab pulled into the parking lot, his sister-in-law emerging from the back. He was truly surprised at how the sisters had gone living in the city without any personal mode of transportation. Zephyr, he knew, just didn't know how to drive, mainly because she'd not shut up about how much she feared driving one night when Hector had almost hit a car from the side. Zenith, he didn't know about.

The beautiful young woman came to him, her face serious as she rummaged in her bag, taking the envelope out.

"Read it for me, please," he requested, saw her dark eyes go to his eye patch before understanding dawned. Smart girl.

She ripped the flap of the envelope and took the notecard out, exactly like the ones he'd been getting.

"It's time we meet," Zenith read out loud verbatim from the note. "Consider this a courtesy. If you want the truth, midnight at Old Town Pier. Come alone. I won't contact you again."

Alpha knew exactly which location this was. Right next to the river, old, abandoned, a place no one went to since a small flood had destroyed it years ago.

It could be a trap. For all he knew, the killer was the one sending him the notes, wanting to lure him to the location. But his gut told him something else. His gut knew it was the one man he'd never been able to get a file on, because the man was a myth, and he existed in the very shadows he was named after.

Taking the note from Zenith, knowing he couldn't drive himself but couldn't take his men, he looked at his sister-in-law. "Can you drive?"

Zenith blinked in surprise, taken aback by his request. "Um. Yes."

He nodded. "Good. I'll need you to drive me to the location."

She looked at her wristwatch. "It'll take two hours with the traffic to get there. It's on the other end of the city."

Then he'd have a while to scope out the place. "Come to the compound. We'll leave after dinner."

He had his substitute driver take them to the compound, too many things going on in his head, questions he'd been putting off coming up. Yesterday, he'd had a visit from the homicide department at Trident, interrogating him about the whereabouts he'd been at the time of the murders and why someone would want to frame him. His alibis had been solid for most of them and the cops had been on his payroll, but it definitely irked him that some asshole was running about in his city, not only targeting and hunting the very people he protected, but also framing him systematically for it.

Zephyr greeted them on the deck, giving her wide-eyed sister a tour of the place, while he showered and set the table for their meal, the dogs sitting around the kitchen—Baron ignoring everyone as he always did; Bear, like the sucker he'd become, looking at Zephyr like she hung the moon; and Bandit chewing on a new bra he'd stolen from her closet, this one a blue that matched her new hair.

He'd always liked her hair, wavy and long enough for him to wrap his hand around twice in his fist, little fringes at her forehead that made her look adorable when she smiled, which was almost all the time. But he'd noticed her smiles weren't all the same. Sometimes, she smiled at people out of politeness even when she didn't want to because she was sweet like that, completely unlike him who had forgotten what a smile felt like until she poked the beast inside him. Sometimes, she smiled when she cried, and she cried a fucking lot, much to his consternation, and those smiles always made her mouth quiver in ways he wanted to steady it with his lips. Sometimes, her smile was wicked and naughty, the green in her eyes popping more than the brown, the dimple in her cheek deep, and getting that smile made him want to turn her and smack her ass.

And then she smiled the soft smile, the one that was his favorite, the one that knocked him in his chest because of how tender it was. Gentleness was not something Alpha had been familiar with in a very long time. His life had been brutal and ugly and monstrous, all rough edges and bleeding wounds and selfish interests, and Zephyr? She was all softness and light and generosity. Her very existence was proof enough that there was good in the world, that beyond the pain and the hurt and the darkness, joy existed in the form of a small woman. Even though he didn't like that she'd changed her hair to a 'sad' blue, as she'd called it. He hoped she changed it again because seeing the strands just made him remember how he'd almost lost her to his stubbornness.

They wrapped up dinner, Zephyr and Zenith mostly chatting, telling him about their childhood and various antics from their younger age. For the first time, sitting with the two women as they argued in jest, surrounded by good food and his bois, Alpha felt a sense of family wash over him. He'd wanted it for such a long time deep down and eventually began to believe he would never have it. In the beginning, it had been the fact that he didn't have to eat alone, that he could share a meal with someone. It had been sitting on his big couch with her presence by his side and watching some show with her, warmth pressed against him. It had been just coming back home and being greeted not just by his bois, but by her genuine joy at seeing him. Little by little, she'd shifted things in his life, minuscule bit by minuscule bit, in a way he'd not even been aware of it happening until it had stopped. And now she was a part of his lifeblood, vital to his functioning.

He never wanted to tell her, but the best thing she could have done for them and their relationship had been to leave. It had shaken him up enough to make him open his eye and realize a life with her was something he wanted, a future with her was something he craved. It was extraordinary—the little things she kept adding to his life.

The only issue now, on his end at least, was physical.

She was an amazing lover, aware of what she wanted and vocal about asking for it, completely abandoned in the way she accepted him and her pleasure. And fuck if he didn't love pleasuring her, hearing those little noises and loud demands, seeing her body shake and writhe as she came and drenched him, feeling her full tits in his hands and tasting her over and over. He loved it.

But he wanted more, and he didn't know how to have it. He couldn't go back to the way they'd been in the beginning. He'd held back in so many ways, and it had given him the control he'd needed.

Now though, he wanted to bend her over the table and pull her hair and fuck her until the legs of the table cracked with the pressure. He wanted to finish inside her and push any cum that escaped back inside, making sure it stayed there, marking her from the inside out. The force of his desire scared him, enough to realize that he could lose control and severely hurt her, and he couldn't live with himself if he did that. She was so much smaller than him, tight enough that pushing his cock in her always made him realize he could tear her if he went hard. He wasn't detached anymore.

"I think Mama is accepting him." Zenith pointed to him as they cleared the dishes. "She told me she wanted to organize a proper wedding for the two of you. She's forgetting the toad."

Zephyr sighed. "Do we even want a wedding?"

That pissed him off. "You're not leaving." His voice came out more like a growl.

She gave him a look, one he'd become used to recently, one that said she wasn't sure if they shouldn't *move on*. As if he'd let her. She'd know the real meaning of stalking if she tried. He had a plan ready just in case. He'd simply show up everywhere and kill anyone she wanted to *move on* with. Fucking hated that term. She'd given him everything, and he'd be damned if he let her do it again with someone else. It was all his. She was all his.

Alpha ignored the look, addressing Zenith, "We should go."

Zenith hitched her bag on her shoulder, ready to leave.

Alpha bent down, tilting his wife's adorable face up with his fingers, putting his thumb in the little dent, loving how his digit fit like the groove had been made for it. He pressed a hard kiss to her plump mouth, telling her very clearly what he thought about her even entertaining the idea of an alternative, and pulled away.

She looked up at him, her pupils blown and eyes slightly dazed. "Be safe."

He gave her a chuck under the chin and left.

Zenith was a careful driver.

She drove slowly but steadily to the location, mostly keeping to herself and focusing on the road. The two hours flew by, with Alpha lost in his thoughts and Zenith in hers, the silence comfortable.

The pier came into view, moonlight glistening over the dark river waters, just an old boathouse in sight that remained intact. A few decades ago, it had been a trade route crowded with shipments and such with cities that followed the river. After the flood, a better, newer, more sustainable dockyard had been made on the other side of the city, and this one had been abandoned. Alpha had never been there before, but as he looked around, an ominous sense of déjà-vu washed over him, like he had been in this place.

"Stay in the car. Lock the doors. If I don't come back in fifteen minutes, drive back," he instructed the younger girl, arming himself with his trusted knife in his left boot, and a backup gun at his waist, even though he wasn't someone who liked guns. With his vision, shooting a moving target accurately almost never happened, but at close range, it worked well enough.

Zenith looked around the abandoned area and gave a reluctant nod. "Be careful."

He exited, making sure she locked the doors behind him, a little at ease since the entire vehicle was bulletproof. Once locked, it would be impossible to break in.

It was time to meet the man who'd left him the black envelopes.

There was no one that he could see in the area as he walked to the boathouse, and leaned against it, keeping an eye on the car, while keeping his ears open for any sound besides the usual. The sound of the river, of some animal in the forest beyond, of the engine of the car, those were the only ones around him.

Standing at the abandoned pier in one of the worst areas of the city at midnight was not his idea of a meeting. But the fucker was careful, to say the least, if he was who Alpha suspected. Alpha leaned against the wooden wall of what had once been a boathouse, watching the moonlit river that went into the forest and disappeared. He almost wished he smoked, just for something to do as he waited. He'd tried as a teen with a chip on his shoulder, but just never got into it.

Taking his knife out, he began to twirl it between his fingers, like a student would a pen. But it was a training trick he'd learned after his injury when the scar on his right hand had pulled at his muscle. The twirling helped keep the muscle mobile and nimble. It also helped him feel more at ease, knowing the knife he'd had since he was seventeen was still with him.

Suddenly, the hair on the back of his neck prickled.

Someone was there.

Alpha didn't look around, instead, focused on his other senses, trying to narrow down where the presence was.

Animal? No. Human. Eyes.
To the right? No.
Left.

Close?

No, a few feet away.

"Mr. Villanova," the quiet voice from a few feet to his left confirmed his suspicion. He looked to the side casually, seeing nothing but the dark umbra of a shadow at the edge of the boathouse.

"Shadow Man," he greeted, keeping his voice level. The myth. The only one he knew of that everyone in the underworld stayed far away from. They said if the Shadow Man came calling, you'd never be heard from again. He sure fucking hoped that wasn't true in his case.

"The note said to come alone," the voice, with a slight accent he couldn't place, said without inflection.

Alpha shrugged. "Can't drive with the bad eye. You wanted to meet?"

There was silence for a long minute, a long minute that Alpha stared at the river, keeping his ears open. A slight rustle before the voice came back. "The killer wants to frame you."

Alpha huffed. "That's obvious."

"He's made a deal with The Syndicate."

What?

Alpha looked to the side, just able to make out a tall silhouette. "What kind of deal?"

"He's to deliver them something, and they would help him take you down."

Interesting. He'd not heard of the organization making deals with rogue killers.

"Why tell me about it?" Alpha asked, the itch in his eye getting worse.

A lighter flicked on, showing the flesh on a gloved hand, before flicking off again.

"You leading the city suits my purpose in the grand scheme of things."

He had a purpose? Alpha didn't voice the question. He knew nothing about this man, and that made him a wild card he didn't know how to deal with.

"So the killer works for The Syndicate?" Alpha verified.

"He kills because he enjoys it," the man clarified. "The organization is simply a means to an end ... your place in the narrative."

"You talk like there's a bigger picture."

A dry chuckle. "There always is."

The chat was interesting, to say the least. "Do you know who the killer is?"

"Yes."

Alpha waited for him to fill in the blank, but he didn't. "And you won't tell?"

The man waited for a beat. "Call your brother in Tenebrae. His undercover dog has information that will help you."

Alpha tensed, the knife stilling in his hand. His connection with Dante was not common knowledge, neither was the fact that Dante had sent one of his guys, Vin, undercover in the organization a few months ago. Who the hell was this guy?

"Was that all?" Alpha tried to keep the anger contained, seriously pissed at the cryptic replies. He wasn't there to play whatever mind games this guy came with. "That's the truth you wanted to tell me?"

A small pause. "You don't remember, but this killer is the same man one who took your eye years ago."

Lead filled his veins. Alpha straightened to his full height, taking a step closer to the silhouette that didn't move. "How the fuck do you know? Who is he?"

The man didn't reply.

What the hell? This was personal. This man knew that he didn't remember, knew who the killer was, and knew that he'd been the same person to destroy Alpha. And he still said nothing.

Seriously irritated, Alpha advanced toward him, ready to beat him to a pulp if that was what it took to get some answers.

"I wouldn't do that if I were you."

It was the tone that gave him pause—calm, clear, lethal. Any man who spoke a threat with that eerie calm with a man like Alpha coming to him meant business.

Alpha stayed at the edge of the shadows, able to make out the silhouette putting his hands in some kind of jacket pockets.

"I'm going to find out who you are, Shadow Man." Alpha meant it. He was going to make a whole fucking file on this guy and distribute it to every underworld boss he knew.

The voice came again, this time with amusement, one chilling word before he was gone.

"Try."

CHAPTER 27

ZEPHYR

The fact that the killer was the same man as the one who'd given her husband partial blindness and a wicked scar chilled Zephyr more than she let on. It meant whoever it was, he'd been holding a vendetta against Alpha for long enough to try to kill him, and when that had failed, to kill others and frame him for it.

Alpha didn't talk much about this Shadow Man character, and Zen hadn't even known someone had been there even though she'd been watching the entire time. But if he were to be believed, shit was hitting the fan.

Alpha had been on the edge since the meeting, darker, quieter, with a cloud hanging over his head that she didn't really fault him for. Up until that moment, he'd had the hope that his injuries had been the cause of some freak accident. But now knowing that it wasn't, that it was deliberate, knowing that someone else knew about it while he didn't remember—it was eating him alive, and she felt for him.

Even her mother had noticed and been concerned that he'd been off when they'd come for dinner, and her mother didn't like him at all.

Zephyr watched at him as he lay on the bed, the netting partially covering his shirtless form, phone on the speaker at his side, his eye staring off into space.

"Well, Vin did find something," Dante's smooth voice said through the speaker. In the background, she could hear a baby's gurgles. He must be talking with Tempest around him. That was cute.

"Listen," Dante said after a little pause. "I was thinking of flying down there on the weekend. Discuss this in person. Especially with the Shadow Man involved. We don't know how he knows what he knows, and it's best to be careful, especially since we don't know what game he's playing. It's not a coincidence that he's been in touch with Morana, and now he's coming at you with helpful but selective information. I don't trust him."

Alpha nodded, curling a hand behind his head, his bicep bulging with the move. "I agree. I have a fight this Friday," he informed Dante, his eye coming to her to see her reaction. She kept her face neutral, her stomach in knots over his upcoming fight.

"Cool," Dante quipped. "I'd like to attend it."

"Sure," Alpha agreed, and Zephyr was happy listening in, realizing that though tentative, the brothers were working around each other to find some common ground without being obvious about it. *Men.*

"Morana has been hounding Tristan about visiting your place, by the way." Dante chuckled.

"She's been obsessed with honeymoon resorts lately, and Tristan told her your place looked like one."

Alpha grunted, "It's not a fucking honeymoon resort."

It kind of was. Not that there was a lot of honeymoon part happening. Mooning, yes. Honeymooning, no.

Tempest blabbered some nonsense in baby talk and Dante blew

her kisses before coming back to the line, the grin in his voice evident. "That was my polite way of telling you she won't let Tristan come on his own this time. I'll also bring"—Dante spoke in a baby voice, clearly to his daughter, and Zephyr *melted*—"my adorable little princess. I have separation anxiety these days. That means my baby mama"—Dante yelled in the distance, clearly to Amara—"my wife will also be coming with us."

"You're whipped." Alpha huffed a laugh.

"Happily too," Dante agreed, no shame in his voice whatsoever. "So two couples, two kids, and five security guys. We'll land Friday afternoon."

"I'll arrange the pickup," Alpha confirmed.

"Okay. Give my love to Zephyr." And now he was blowing raspberries.

Alpha looked at her. "I'll give her your greeting."

"I said, my love."

"Fuck off."

Her husband hung up with Dante chuckling.

Zephyr grinned, climbing into bed and adjusting the netting as Alpha turned the remote-controlled lights off.

He was still on the edge, his face a dark cloud of apprehension, his mind preoccupied with too many things he did and did not remember.

She climbed on top of him.

She had felt herself open up to him again, bit by bit, her reservations going down with everything he'd been dealing with over the days, and still reassuring her that she wasn't going anywhere. She didn't want to. And she wanted it to be one less thing he worried about. Since she'd come back, things between them had evolved. With him knowing the truth about their past, even limited as it was, and her accepting and becoming completely okay with the fact that he would never remember it, things had become better. Though he tried to pry and ask about their brief but powerful relationship from a decade ago, Zephyr made him understand that maybe it was best left behind, especially since his mind had deliberately forgotten certain things, most probably due to trauma. She'd told him to trust her on that, and though he had trust issues, she could feel him trying to let it go.

She brushed his hair away from his face, straddling him, taking the eye patch off, exposing the scarred tissue underneath. She loved that he let her see him like that, at what he felt was his ugliest. Idiot man. His ugly was her beautiful.

As she did each night, she pressed little kisses on his scar, starting from his hairline, going over his eye, down his cheek, to the corner of his mouth. Usually, he turned and took over her lips at that point, but Zephyr had had enough of him trying to keep their lovemaking contained. She wanted him, as he was, brutal and raw, and she would have him.

Bypassing his lips, she lowered herself, following the scar with her lips, going down the side of his neck, lower, over his muscular, sparsely-haired chest, right to the end where someone had twisted the knife in his side. She kissed it, giving it all the love and attention it deserved, wishing she could've been with him when he'd had to heal. Her tongue flicked over his nipple and she heard his breath catch, his boxer shorts tenting slightly.

Smiling, Zephyr went lower, following the line of his abs, muscles he'd worked his body into acquiring over the years, both with fighting and training. She licked down the line, making sure her hair trailed over his torso with her motion, adding sensation for him. His hand wrapped it once in a loose fit, not stopping her, but letting her know he could.

She felt his hard length against her boobs, and shook them, letting him feel them move around his cock.

"Fuck," he grit out, his hand tightening a bit around her hair, and she smiled, repeating the action. Her hands pulled his shorts down, her tongue trailing down his prominent oblique, down where he jutted up, long and thick and hard, a vein prominent on the underside.

Zephyr squeezed him between her ample breasts, knowing he loved the visual, and his hips moved automatically, sliding in the space she'd created. On one of his upward movements, she kissed his head, letting her boobs go, and gave the vein on his shaft a long lick, her mouth salivating to taste him as his other hand came to her hair, flexing as he let her set the pace.

She took a hold of him, taking the head into her mouth, licking the slit where he was already dripping, tasting his essence for the first time. And then she took him down her throat.

He groaned, and she looked up, seeing his neck cording as his head dug into the pillow.

It was a heady sensation, seeing this beast of a man come undone by her lips.

She closed her eyes and began giving him the blow job of his life, adding hands to the up and down motion, alternating between twisting and swallowing, sucking and licking, giving him the most sensation she could, driven on by his hands in her hair and the rumbling noises leaving his throat.

One of his hands left her scalp, and she opened her eyes, watching him as he touched her ass, his fingers finding her folds where she was already wet. She'd wondered what it had been about giving head that aroused her so much. Was it the feeling of power or a simple biological response, mental or physical? Zen had told her there was a nerve that went straight from the roof of a woman's mouth to her vagina, and maybe it was just extra sensitive in her case because giving her husband a blow job had her clenching.

Suddenly, he pulled her with the strength of a single arm, and before she could blink, she was straddling his face, his cock in her mouth, his hands spreading her over him.

It was *hot*.

She'd never been in this position before. *69*, that's what they called it.

He tugged her down over his skilled mouth, his facial hair rubbing the insides of her thigh in the most delicious friction, his tongue slurping over her with a loud, obscene noise that made her moan around him. It was odd but incredible, feeling him do something to her, reacting to it, and feeling him react to that by doing something else, like an endless loop of sensation, ending where she began and ending where he did. A sexual yin and yang.

He spread her cheeks, his thumb stroking her rosebud as he ate her out, making her clench hard around him.

"Has anyone been here before?" he asked into her thigh, biting the inside of it as she pulled up for air.

"No," she panted.

He went back to devouring her, fucking her with his tongue and rubbing her clit alternatively, making her mewl and moan around his cock, the vibrations of her throat pushing his arousal higher.

She didn't know how long it went on, how long they stayed like that, connected by their body and minds, reacting to each other's responses, stimulating and being stimulated simultaneously. But after a while, he pushed his thumb in her ass while sucking on her clit, and she came, feeling full and invaded and owned, the sensation strange and taboo, her nerve endings on fire all over her body. She pulled her head away from his flesh, screaming at her orgasm, her nails digging into his solid thigh muscles, her own muscles jerking and squeezing around his head as she slowly came down from the high.

He pulled away, giving her butt a smack, making her yelp.

"Turn around," he instructed her, and Zephyr, boneless, somehow managed to turn and face him. He pulled her legs on each side of his hip, giving her an intense stare. "Take me in." Her heart began to pound again, realizing that for the first time, he would let her be face-to-face with him. Before, it had all been from the back, all without truly connecting as intimately as this. He was letting her in.

Silently, she angled him and slid down, feeling the stretch in her pussy, panting as she went down inch by inch. She'd forgotten how huge he'd felt inside her, how he split her open by the time he bottomed out.

"Jesus," he cursed, his hands gripping her hips, her head falling back as the pleasurable burn ensconced her again. Finally, he was completely in, pushing so deep she felt his pulsing match in her chest.

"Rainbow," he called, and she looked down, locking gazes with his again, seeing the expanse of him laid out before her, scars and muscle and tattoos and man, all hers.

"Ride me."

She placed her hands on his chest and complied, rotating her hips experimentally to see how it felt, grinding her clit on him.

So good.

She bit her lips, feeling sexy, feeling horny, feeling like a goddess as she rode him slowly, gradually increasing pace, trying different movements, understanding which brought them the most pleasure. He held her breasts, tugged her nipples, played with them. Slapped them, pulled them, twisted them, each action making her cry out and clench like a vise around him. After a point, when she got tired, he twisted positions and put her legs over his shoulders, never once separating, stretching her hamstrings until she felt taut, but the angle made her see stars.

She came again.

He got her on hands and knees, pulling her hair back and hammering into her, his pace increasing, his stamina consistent, and she realized he'd never unleashed the full force of it on her.

"Harder," she pleaded as she did before, and this time, he answered, "I'll hurt you."

"You won't," she argued, turning her neck to see him. "I'm not fragile. Now fuck me like you mean it."

He tugged her head back, almost tilting it upside down, and kissed her, his hips picking up the pace just mildly. It wouldn't do.

"Think of me *moving on*." She deliberately used the term he hated. "Look at me now, on my hands and knees for you, exactly how you love it, and take me. Take me like I'm yours."

"You are mine," he growled, biting the side of her neck in a move that made her grapple for the sheets.

"Then show me. I don't feel it."

He *snapped*.

He pushed her down into the bed, completely immobilizing her, and leaned into her ear. "Don't hate me tomorrow when you're too sore to sit."

And Zephyr realized the extent to which he'd been holding himself back.

She couldn't move, she couldn't react, she couldn't do a thing except lie there with her hips in the air and take it, the force of his thrusts making the bed creak, the power behind each snap making her fist the sheets, the angle of each hit making her delirious as the edge of discomfort spiraled with pleasure that made her teeth chatter and body shake and mind blank. She was nothing but sensation, hanging on as he rode her, hard enough that she didn't even recognize the sounds she made anymore.

She came again. And again. And again. Endlessly, her body jerking and blacks expanding behind her lids, her mind going completely numb to anything but the reactions in her body, her heart thundering inside her chest, her lust frantic, her love infinite, her life his.

She probably passed out, because the next few minutes were blank.

She came to, lying on her stomach, him at her side, his chest heaving as he looked at her with that singular golden gaze, his fingers pushing his seed back inside her body.

Damn.

"Don't leave me again, rainbow," he spoke quietly in the space between them. "I don't know if I'll ever remember anything. I don't know if what I feel is love. I don't know what the future holds. But I know I want you by my side. I know I don't want to forget you now."

Zephyr melted, her heart softening. She pressed a soft kiss to his lips. "I'm not going anywhere, handsome. I've loved you as a boy, and I love you as a beast. All of you has always been loved by me."

They shared the air for a long moment. "Remember when I told you my heart was a dead scar tissue?"

"Hmm."

"I feel it pumping again with you. My lifeblood. My little rainbow."

And he was hers. With his words warming her to the bone, Zephyr slept with her husband by her side.

CHAPTER 28

ZEPHYR

Three days later and she was still sore.

And her husband? He was *pleased*.

She frequently caught a self-satisfied look on his face, and now that his fear of breaking her had passed, she had to shove him away to let her pussy heal. With his stamina, he'd done a number on her.

She walked out to the deck, wincing slightly at the soreness, feeling exactly where and how deep and how hard he'd been with each step. The dogs—all except Baron who she was convinced just hated her—followed on her heels, trying to sniff her extra since the night, possibly because they smelled Alpha all over her.

Or maybe because she was nervous.

She was nervous because Dante and the party were on their way from the airport, and she wanted to give them a good impression unlike last time when she'd been lost and adrift. She was also extra nervous because her husband was going into the death ring to fight that evening, and even though he was cool and collected and completely relaxed about it, she wasn't. She was terrified that he would die or get severely hurt and she didn't want either of those options. Fuck reputations, her husband was more important. But he was also the leader in a pit full of snakes, and sending the right message was important, not just for his reputation, but for the safety of everyone associated with him. If there was one thing she'd learned about this world from observation, it was that weaknesses were sniffed out and exploited until there weren't any left. And she hated that, but it was what it was and she had to make peace with it too.

She was also nervous because the serial killer who'd been framing Alpha had been silent since the Shadow Man meeting, and her husband believed it was the calm before a storm. Her gut agreed, and that made her nervous, nervous enough to consider bringing her family to the compound for safety even though they'd hate it. Well, except Zen. Her sister had fallen in love with the place. Maybe she could talk to Alpha and have her move into the guesthouse.

Later.

Pasting a smile on her face, she ignored the twinge and looked down at the stairs where the weekend guests were climbing up. After living at the compound for months, the vista and the forest had become home to her, and watching her guests' faces and the awe on them, she was reminded of her first day climbing those very steps.

Hector led the group, after being back from whatever mission Alpha had sent him on, and she was glad. She'd missed him and his brand of humor, especially the ease with which he pulled Alpha's leg.

Speaking of, her husband stepped beside her, his hands coming to her hips in a move that was pure proprietary, and waited to greet them.

Dante, as handsome and suave as she remembered, stepped onto the deck with a smile, little Tempest who wasn't so little anymore in his arms, dressed in a bright yellow jumpsuit that was absolutely adorable, little yellow bow on her head.

"Thanks for having us, brother." Dante nodded at Alpha, and pressed a platonic but affectionate kiss of greeting to her cheek. "Beautiful as always, Zephyr."

Oh, he was a charmer to boot, but damn if he didn't make a woman feel good.

His wife Amara, the goddess of a woman Zephyr still didn't know could exist, greeted both Alpha and her with a warm, sweet-scented hug. "Thank you so much for having us. We needed the break. Your home is stunning," she complimented in a raspy voice, and Zephyr felt pride fill her. It was such a contrast to the last time she'd met her, when she'd been unsure about her marriage with Alpha, insecure in both herself and their relationship. Standing there, she realized she had changed too, become more certain of herself and her relationship, her insecurities still present but taking more of a backseat with the reassurance of her love. God, she loved him, this him. Not just for who he was now, but who he let her be.

She liked this version of herself, the woman who could be strong, be vulnerable, love openly and lust shamelessly, and know it was all okay, that she wouldn't be judged for it, or would never be told she had to change certain aspects to conform better in his life.

She loved that.

"Of course," she answered Amara. "We're family. You're always welcome here."

Amara gave her hands a squeeze and Zephyr saw a scar on her wrist. But she didn't say anything, turning to the other couple in the back, one she'd seen at the wedding but hadn't been introduced to. The intense man and the spectacled woman, and with them the young boy who'd talked to her at the wedding, the boy who was currently kneeling and petting the dogs.

"Oh, hey!" She waved at him. "You remember me, right?"

The boy didn't look up, just scratched Bear. "You cry a lot. Yes."

"Xander!" the spectacled woman admonished, giving her a slightly embarrassed smile. "Hi. Sorry. That's Xander. I'm Morana. This big guy is Tristan."

Tristan gave her a nod, but kept his distance, aloof. Yikes. There was no warmth to the man. She would've thought him a robot except for the way he looked at Morana and checked Xander with his eyes, occasionally looking over at Tempest and Amara. Interesting.

"Let's get you settled." Zephyr clapped her hands and led them all inside, giving them a tour of the place, guiding a few of their guys to set up their stuff in the guest house. Nala and some of her helpers worked in the kitchen to prepare everything for them, Leah coming over to help with the kids, which was useless because Tempest didn't want to leave her father's arms, and Xander had found himself a comfortable spot on the rugs with the dogs.

It felt different from the time her parents had come for dinner. This time, she felt like the woman of the house, like an equal hostess rather than a daughter trying to prove everything was perfect. They sat and talked casually, keeping it light mostly because the kids were awake and members of the staff were around. Out of the couples, she realized Morana and her were the talkers, although the other woman was a genius and she was not. Amara piped in but listened, maybe owing to her profession as a therapist, which Zephyr thought was really cool. It made her wonder though what her contribution to the group was. She was a hairstylist, and she loved her job, but in present company, it reminded her of the questions she'd had when she'd met the ladies at the club, about what she could do for them.

Tristan and Alpha were the quietest of the bunch, Dante the most easy-going, Alpha talking when he had to, and Tristan not talking at all. But he did sit with his arm around Morana, his fingers touching her neck and the romantic in her slightly swooned at that.

Soon, Alpha left to warm up before the fight with Hector. Leah took over babysitting duties, and the rest of them got into a Rover, Victor driving them to the arena where *The Finisher* would fight.

The crowd was much larger than the last time she'd been there. Zephyr sat in the exact same seat she'd been in, Morana on one side, Amara on the other, their respective partners covering their corners, Victor and one of Dante's guys behind them, giving them all the cover.

More men in suits and women in dresses sat in the upper sections of the arena, getting a bird's eye view of the ring in the center. Other rowdier crowd stood all around the huge warehouse, behind a single row of chairs on each side just a few feet from the fighting ring. People were betting, scores were being kept, both the classy and the ugly in the underworld gracing the fight.

Zephyr sat with her heart in her throat as the announcer jumped up, clapping his hands for silence.

"What a fantastic tournament it has been, ladies and gentlemen." His voice boomed again. "We're at the final fight, and oh, what a fight it will be."

She didn't know how, but she needed Alpha to make it out.

"Ladies and gentleman, he trains the best fighters in his homeland, his name instills fear in the ring. Please welcome our Russian killing machine, The Ravager!"

A cheer went up in the crowd as the man with the icy hair and icy eyes walked from what must've been the locker room to the ring, not giving the crowd a look, just jumping in the fighting ring.

"He looks scary," Morana whispered from her side, and Zephyr nodded, remembering when he'd dropped the boy in five seconds.

"And now," the announcer yelled. "From the host city, the legend who doesn't start a fight he cannot finish, the one-eyed beast, The Finisher!"

Another roar went through the crowd, the noise so loud Zephyr felt it reverberating through her body. She looked to the side to see her husband, no, *The Finisher*, walk out in his black fighter's shorts out of the same locker room, wrapping his tape around his hands, going straight to the ring, jumping up beside the Ravager.

Alpha turned his head and looked at her, just to make sure she was there, and turned back.

"How the hell is he going to fight with one eye?" Amara whispered from her other side.

Zephyr didn't know, even though she'd seen him training and fighting and killing. She didn't know, but she prayed he did.

The men exchanged a look, bumping their fists.

The announcer dropped down and rang the bell.

The fight began.

Zephyr gripped the arms of her chair, not daring to blink, not daring to breathe as the Ravager got behind Alpha, her husband immediately pivoting and coming at him from the side, to which the Ravager ducked and moved away, both men circling each other.

A hush fell over the crowd as they studied each other, adrenaline filling her veins as she rooted for the man she loved to come out the victor, no matter what the cost.

"He needs to go from the right," Dante muttered under his breath, leaning forward in his seat and observing the fight as closely as he could.

"He's blind on the right," Tristan commented to Dante from the other side. "It'd make him weak."

The commentary on technique kept on, as did the fight, much longer than any of the previous ones had lasted.

Zephyr looked at the announcer to see him looking agitated, realizing the fight had gone on for over ten minutes, with both men just fighting and ducking and dancing around each other.

"What is he doing?" she mused out loud and felt Amara give her leg a squeeze.

Suddenly, the sounds of fireworks penetrated the air.

A collective gasp went up in the warehouse. People began screaming, and Zephyr looked around in confusion, her heart threatening to burst out of her chest as Dante covered Amara and Tristan covered Morana, pushing them both to the floor. She saw Alpha looking at one corner of the warehouse before jumping over the ring, abandoning the fight to come to her. He picked her up in his arms, on the move toward the locker room.

"Find the shooter," he ordered Victor, who was already running to the other side of the warehouse.

Dante and Tristan followed them to the back exit, the Ravager surprisingly opening the door to let them out near the back of the parking lot, now filled with people running away.

"I owe you, Adrik." Alpha nodded to the Ravager, who gave a solemn nod in return.

"What just happened?" Zephyr asked, still shaken from the adrenaline pumping through her blood. Had she just been at a shooting? An actual shooting? One that sounded like fireworks?

"It was a shooting." Alpha's grim tone confirmed.

They reached the vehicle and put her down, looking back at the warehouse.

"Did anyone get hurt?" Amara asked, checking everyone.

"I think someone died inside," Morana surmised, slumping against the car. "Behind me. The bullet was close. But were they the target or were we?"

Tristan pulled her into his body.

Zephyr leaned against Alpha, trying to wrap her mind around the shooting, the shooting at an underground death fight where someone might have died. His arm came around her, holding her close as they all watched and waited in the aftermath.

After a few minutes, Victor came out with his brother and Dante's man, a gun in his hand.

"Found this at the back, boss."

Alpha took the gun in his right hand, checking it out. "This model isn't made here."

Morana opened her phone, furiously typing on the screen. "It was manufactured in Svoski. There's no name of registration or license number."

That was fast.

Hector looked at Alpha, a silent conversation happening between the two.

"Victor, take the girls home," he told the younger man.

Dante gave his man a nod to go with them, and gave Amara a kiss.

Tristan pulled Morana by the neck and they had a silent conversation as well.

Alpha turned Zephyr's face up by her chin, giving her a hard kiss. "Be good, rainbow."

"Whatever you say, sexy," she whispered, even though her voice shook, her mind processing the rapidness with which the night had gone to shit.

Zephyr did what she always did when something eventful happened to her—she called her sister.

After returning home with Morana and Amara, both women going to the guest house to freshen up before joining her, Zephyr decided to take the time alone to tell her sister about the shooting, her only company Bear, the other two dogs missing somewhere in the house.

"Are you okay?" Zen exclaimed in her ear. "Wait, I need to see you. Switch to video right now."

Zephyr shook her head and switched, showing her sister herself on the camera. "I'm perfectly fine. See?"

"Oh god, Zee," Zen groaned. "Mentally? Are you okay?"

Zephyr told her sister honestly that she didn't know. She was still processing it, and it was probably going to take a while before she accepted that. It also made her realize, given her reaction, how much of an outsider she was to this world. None of the others had reacted to the shooting in a surprising way, which made her understand that they'd obviously had previous experience dealing with similar violence. She'd had none of it, and she didn't know if it was good or bad. It just was, and she had to learn if she wanted to stay a part of Alpha's world, which she definitely did.

"Please tell me you have some wine." Morana entered from the back deck with Amara, both dressed in pajamas, Morana in a t-shirt and shorts, Amara in a silky robe. Zephyr had simply stolen one of Alpha's t-shirts and put them on with leggings that she'd take off once they went to bed.

Still on the call, Zephyr pointed to the wine cabinet and turned the phone, introducing the girls to each other. Morana waved at Zen, Amara smiled, and they chatted for a few minutes before she disconnected, promising to call again. Wine glasses in hand, all three of them went to the sunken living room with the interior garden, sitting around on different couches, Bear slumping down drowsily at Zephyr's feet.

"He's like my cat Lulu." Amara pointed with a delicate finger to the canine at her feet.

"Lulu is adorable," Morana gushed. "I've been trying to convince Tristan to get a cat."

"And failing." Amara laughed.

Zephyr couldn't help but grin. "What about a dog? I didn't ever want one and now I have three of them. I can't imagine life without them now, even the one I'm sure hates me."

Morana sighed. "A dog seems more plausible, honestly. I'm sure Tristan noticed the way Xander responded to your dogs. He doesn't respond outwardly to stuff easily, so we'll talk to his therapist about it."

Zephyr didn't ask, but the question must have been on her face.

"He's high-functioning autistic," Morana clarified. "We had him tested recently and the counselor suggested getting an emotional support pet. Xander hasn't really shown any outward interest in Lulu, not like he showed your dogs, though he's met her enough times."

Wow.

"Is he yours?" Zephyr asked. Morana looked too young to be a mother to a child his age.

"No, but we might adopt him soon."

Over the next hour, the girls brought her up to speed with their lives and their loves, grilled her about how she, a personality completely in contrast to Alpha, became his wife. While Zephyr had never had any dearth of friends or female companionship, not with her best friend being her sister, she got the feeling the two women hadn't been as lucky, so she tried to bond with them and let them know that she was there if they needed another friend.

The guys returned soon after, crashing down beside them, something dark hanging over their heads.

"Did you find anything?" Zephyr asked, curious and needing to know if they had found any answers. She snuggled into Alpha's side, letting his familiar weight settle around her and his scent comfort her.

Dante shook his head in answer. "No. But now that we can talk in privacy." He turned to Zephyr. "Do you remember anything about your encounter with the Shadow Man at my wedding?"

Zephyr bit her lip, trying to recall. "He was tall, wore a black sweatshirt, kept his face out of my line of sight."

Morana nodded. "Sounds like my airport man."

"Not yours," Tristan corrected from her side, and she rolled her eyes behind her glasses. "We need to figure out what he's doing. First, he contacts me about the missing girls, and then he's at your wedding sending cryptic messages, and then he's meeting Alpha about serial murders? What's his agenda?"

Zephyr wished she could help. And in a way, maybe she could. Maybe her outside perspective could glean a new light.

"What if . . ." She hesitated, felt Alpha give her a squeeze, and began again, "What if you guys are too close to it to see the bigger picture? What is the one thing that connects all of you? Forget familial connections. Why would a girl from Shadow Port work with a man from Tenebrae? Why did the king of Outfit come to the king of the south? What is the underlying thread here?"

Dante tilted his head to the side, his eyes going to Tristan before settling on Alpha. "The Syndicate?"

Zephyr encouraged. "That's as good a start as any. Maybe the Shadow Man is helping you because he's got beef with the organization too."

"But how the hell does he know what he does?" Dante shook his head, frustration evident on his face.

"Could he be a part of The Syndicate?" Morana mused out loud, tapping her phone on her thigh. "They're giant, which obviously means they have resources. It could make sense."

"Then why lead us to them?" Amara asked, her husky voice quiet. "If secrecy is their thing, and it's his thing, why leave breadcrumbs for us?"

There was silence for a beat as they all considered the questions.

"Did you find anything about my sister?" Tristan spoke for the first time, and Zephyr realized he had a nice voice, though quite intense.

Her own intense grump replied, "We tracked down the girls in the shipment, all but three."

"Were you able to track me?" Morana asked, and Zephyr felt her eyes widen. She'd been a missing girl?

She felt Alpha tense beside her. "No. That makes it two missing girls."

"What happened to the rest?" Amara locked her fingers with Dante's, her green eyes on Alpha.

"Most died," her husband answered, remorse in his deep voice.

Zephyr watched Morana put her hand on Tristan's thigh as he looked away, the muscles in his neck working.

After another beat of silence, Dante spoke up, "One of my guys, who's been undercover in the organization for months, found something."

Alpha listened intently and Zephyr sipped her wine, invested.

"The last contact Vin had with me a few months ago, he mentioned the handlers give the kids numbers for identity. They also keep track of the kids in the organization as long as they are alive. He found a file for one of the girls in the batch from Tenebrae twenty years ago leading to Los Fortis." Dante paused. "5057. The file had a seal on it. He opened it and found that someone had bought her and the transaction was to take place next week. If we can find when and where in the city—"

"We can find a girl," Alpha completed, looking toward Tristan.

It went unsaid that if they found a girl, chances of her being his sister were high. They sat in silence, with endless questions, elusive answers, a small, tentative hope that maybe, there would be dawn to the night.

CHAPTER 29

ZEPHYR

Something bad was going to happen.

Zephyr woke up the next morning with the feeling, and the lead weight sat heavy in her stomach. She didn't know if it was an aftermath of the shooting, or because of all the talk of gloom and death over the night with everyone, or a response to the dark, heavy clouds that had taken over the skies.

She didn't know, and since she wasn't someone who got ugly feelings like this frequently, she didn't know what to do with it.

"Don't go to SLF if it's bugging you," Alpha suggested while trimming his beard in a towel as she stood to his side, brushing her teeth while wearing his t-shirt, their domesticity at its peak.

"I always go," she talked over the brush in her mouth, the toothpaste messing her words, the amusement in his eye contrary to the heaviness in hers.

He put his trimmer down on the counter and stepped behind her, standing a head taller in the reflection. He put his hands on her waist and leaned down to the spot at the juncture of her neck and shoulder blade. "Or you can stay, and we can spend the day in bed. How does that sound, hmm?"

Zephyr spit and rinsed her mouth, before locking eyes with his reflection. "Sore. My vajajay needs time to adapt to your beast mode." One side of his lip twitched. "Besides, Zen would want to see me after I told her about the shooting. Which reminds me, I was thinking if I could talk to her about moving here . . . in the guest house if that's okay with you?"

Alpha shrugged. "I wouldn't mind. She's a good kid."

That went smoother than she'd expected. She was half ready to bribe him.

They took a shower together and went down to meet the guests, Nala and Leah getting the breakfast ready. Between all the guests and kids and dogs and staff, it was a madhouse of sounds and scents and just senses.

And even in the midst of all the joviality, the lead in her stomach remained.

Morana wanted to see the city, Amara wanted to relax in the pool. In the end, they decided that Morana would accompany Zephyr to SLF while she volunteered and met her sister, and then she'd take her on a tour of the city.

The two of them gave their men kisses and left with Victor driving them. Zephyr pointed out different tourist attractions to Morana on the way, enjoying showing her lively hometown to someone who didn't live here. On the edge of the rainforest, with a river going around it, Los Fortis was a bustling hub of culture, people, and food, a thriving business center with over five million residents and counting, a mix of tropical paradise and corporate skyscrapers. It was also an underbelly of dark industries she'd not known about before she stepped into Alpha's world, now her world too.

They exited at the SLF building, and Zephyr explained to Morana how things worked at the organization and what the non-profit did, introducing her to different people as they made their way to the back where Zen usually was. Weekends usually have heavier foot traffic with volunteers and staff coming in, making the building a loud space.

Zen was in the corner office surrounded by paperwork that she handled. Her sister looked up as she entered. "Oh, Zee." She came to give her a tight hug, looking her all over. "Are you okay?" She was still worried about the shooting and its effect on her.

"I'm trying not to think about it," she told her sister honestly, turning to properly introduce her to the other woman. "Zen, you remember Morana. She wanted to see the city so we came out."

Silence from Morana made Zephyr turn to find her at her side, her head tilted to the side, scrutinizing Zen.

Her sister frowned, exchanging a look with Zephyr. "Is everything okay?"

Morana seemed to shake herself out of a stupor. "Yes, of course. I apologize! I just get lost in my head sometimes."

Zen chuckled. "That is Zee's favorite habit. Come, I'll show you around. Zee, there's a sixteen-year-old wanting a makeover in the common room."

As the girls departed on the tour, Zephyr went to the common room and met the girl, chatting with her as she gave her a makeover, her eyes going to Morana to find her and Zen looking at the laptop, talking, chuckling, talking again. A sense of foreboding sat like an unwanted rock in her stomach.

Zephyr rarely got such gut feelings, but as she stood there, the feeling crawled over her skin like scorpions, stinging in its wake. The clouds rolled heavily in the sky outside the window, matching her insides, heavy and full and about to burst.

Somehow, the day passed, and her anxiety got worse with each passing hour, to the point she decided not to take Morana on a tour at all, but simply return home and ride it out.

"You've been a bit off today," Zen mentioned as the three women walked out of the building. "Is it because of the shooting?"

Zephyr shook her head, looking around to see where Victor had parked the car. "I don't know. It's just . . . something feels off."

Morana pushed her glasses up her nose. "You should trust your gut, you know. If there's one thing the last few months have taught me, it's definitely that."

That was all great, but where the hell was Victor? It was getting late, the night was setting in, and she just knew she had to get back home.

Zephyr looked around, trying to understand why her bodyguard who never strayed from his location, was not in his usual spot.

Suddenly, a dark van with tinted windows came screeching into the parking lot.

Zephyr froze as the doors opened and four men with balaclavas on their faces got out, heading straight for them.

"Run, Zee!"

The shout spurred her into motion. She saw Morana and Zen running back toward the building and she sprinted after them, her heart beating out of her chest as the men chased. She had no idea who they were, but the entire setup, hell the entire day didn't bode well.

Gunshots rang out, and she saw Morana fall, screaming as she held her shoulder, blood tinting the white of her top.

Zephyr stopped, kneeling down to help her up while Morana yelled in pain, "Go. Go, get help!"

Before Zephyr could get up, two muscled arms grabbed her. A dark cloth covered her face and she was bound and carried to the van, her last sight of one of the men chasing her sister, leaving Morana on the cemented parking lot.

Fear, true unadulterated fear, consumed her. She didn't know who these guys were, but they pushed her into the van. Another body collided with her, Zen's lavender body mist giving it away.

"Zen?" she asked, needing to be sure she was okay.

Zen's response came from her side, muffled by some cloth. She'd been gagged.

Zephyr tried to struggle against her bindings, trying to get out, all in vain. The zip ties dug into her wrists, cutting her circulation off.

The doors to the van shut and then it was in motion. They were taking her and Zen? And Morana was being left behind? She was shot! She needed help before she bled out. God, she hoped she got help for herself and called for rescue for them.

"Where are you taking us? Who are you?" The fact that she couldn't see a thing scared her even more.

Her demands went unanswered.

She didn't know how long they were in transit for, but she heard Zen stop struggling to get free. She stayed silent, knowing the kidnappers were there listening. She had to try to figure some way out of this mess. Soon, the vehicles stopped and someone picked her up. She felt someone pick up her sister as well. The one carrying her put her in a chair, retying her wrists to the arms of the wood with the zip cuffs.

The cover was removed from her face, and she blinked, trying to focus on the sudden sight before her. Zen was similarly strapped to a chair in front of her, quiet but awake, looking around, thankfully uninjured and unhurt, just shaken up. Zephyr couldn't get the sight of Morana from her head, blood spreading down her arm from her shoulder, her white top completely red. God, she'd lost a lot of blood, and if the bleeding didn't stop before someone got to her . . .

No.

Focus here, Zee.

She looked around, trying to gauge their location. It looked like a small wooden shack, old and unused. The sound of water nearby alerted her of their closeness to either the river or a waterfall. The men who'd abducted them left the shack, leaving the two sisters alone.

What the hell was this abduction for? Was it The Syndicate? The killer? Someone else? Did they want her or Alpha? Had Morana's gunshot been an accident or was she the target? She didn't know, but she knew they had to get out somehow.

"No," Zen's broken whisper brought her eyes up to see her sister looking behind her, horror on her face.

Zephyr tried to turn to see what it was, but the chair held her in place.

She heard footsteps behind her, a man's footsteps, and her heart began to thunder as she waited to see who it was.

His bald head gleaming in the light from the bulb, he came into the view, smiling at her, a knife in his hand. "Yo, Zee."

Hector. Alpha's most trusted man. It was him.

Looking at the sinister smile on his face, seeing his true form, Zephyr knew he was the killer they've been looking for, he was the man who had tortured and blinded her husband. Hector.

CHAPTER 30

ZEPHYR

Hector had to have gone off the deep end.

There was nothing that explained what she was seeing, nothing that made sense of the man she'd become friends with to the monster in front of her.

Zen sat still in the chair in front of her, her eyes sharp on Hector as he walked around them, the only thing giving away her anxiety being her loud breathing.

Zephyr tried to keep hers calm, knowing it would only make her sister more anxious if she panicked.

"What the hell are you doing, Hector?" Zephyr asked, as calmly as she could. They needed to get out, get help. She didn't know where Victor was, or if he, too, was involved in whatever had happened, or if help was on the way. God, could she trust any one of her people?

"This isn't personal, Zephyr." Hector gave her a small smile, the same he'd always given her, his bald head gleaming menacingly under the harsh overhead light. "It's just a deal."

"What deal?" she demanded. What the hell was going on?

Hector circled them again, coming to stand beside Zen. He took his knife out, running the blade over his thumb. "No one escapes The Syndicate. But you did, didn't you, 5057?"

5057? What the hell?

She saw Zen's breath catch, her eyes flying to Hector with true fear. It reminded her of when she'd had panic attacks as a kid.

"Zen," she called to her sister. "Breathe, Zenny. I'm right here." She wished she could get out of her bonds and go to her, take her hand and tell her it'd all be okay.

Hector continued circling them. "Your luck must have been golden. You ran away, straight to the cops, and got adopted by a normal family. You got a new name. All traces of 5057 erased from existence. Did you know what your real name was?"

Zen swallowed visibly.

"Morana Vitalio."

Morana?

Wait, Morana had been one of the missing girls. Did that mean her sister had been one of them and they'd been exchanged?

What the hell?

Zephyr watched the scene in shock, pieces falling together.

She'd never given much thought to her sister's past, or ever wondered where she came from. As a child, she'd just believed her sister was found by her parents, and that had been it. Even growing up, knowing her past sometimes affected Zen, she'd always thought she'd been orphaned by an accident. This was much, much gruesome than anything she could've imagined. And she knew, listening to all of it, that it must've been so much harder on Zen.

"How do you know this?" Zen whispered, her voice shaking, her dark eyes wide and terrified.

"Do you remember, Zenny?" Hector mocked. "You remember how you left behind your friend? Ever gave a second thought to what became of her life while you lay warm in your bed? Oh, she's quite in demand now."

Zephyr saw her sister trembling, and her protective instinct rose to the fore. She remembered when Zen had been a kid, scared like she was now, and Zephyr had always fought her demons.

"Get away from her," she told Hector, drawing his attention back to herself. "I'm not a killer, Hector, but you better hope I don't get out of these ties. I will murder you."

Hector laughed, like it was the most hilarious thing he'd heard. "Zephyr, you were always fiery. As I said, it's nothing personal."

He turned back to Zen. "So, where were we? Yes. You escaped, and it was all good. The Syndicate didn't care about one little girl running away."

"Then why now?" Zen asked, despite the visible tremor in her body.

"Because you got on the radar, sweetheart." Hector touched her sister's cheek, and she flinched. "You should've laid low, but with your bleeding heart at SLF, seeing how pretty you'd become, they wanted you back. One of them, in particular, wants you bad before he puts you to work."

Oh, hell no.

Zephyr struggled against her zip cuffs, trying futilely to escape.

"My deal was simple," Hector continued. "I deliver you to them, they help me take down Alpha."

Zephyr stilled, her mind reeling. "Alpha? You're his friend!"

"And his second," Hector pointed out. "We were born on the same streets, to the same life. He got everything, and I got the second. No."

His voice changed, the ugly finally coming out. "I want this city; I want the power. And the only way to take it? Get him out. And the only way to take him out? By people more powerful than he is. The Syndicate went through me so many times, it was easy to make a deal."

"And the murders?" Zenith asked, her eyes on the knife in his hand.

Hector chuckled. "Just for fun. There is nothing better than seeing the hope strangle in their eyes. Fucking whores, thinking they're better than this life we're born into. They're not."

Another circle.

"I went to them with Alpha's name, telling them he would help them out since they wanted to leave, and like faithful idiots, they followed me, trusting his name and his word."

He circled them again.

"I took them to an alley, held them down, raped them. Told them it was the price for freedom, and oh, they let me. For freedom, they did."

He laughed, and Zephyr felt the ugliness in his soul creep out of every pore, nausea filling her stomach as he recounted each horrific detail with such glee.

"And then, I slipped my knife into them right here," he whispered, putting his hand to her side, making the vomit rise up.

"There's nothing like fucking them as they gasp for life. Makes them so tight."

"You're sick," she gagged, breathing through her nostrils.

"I am." He grinned, getting in her face. "But when they die, I am their *god*. I am inside them, outside them, leading them from this life to the next."

She was going to throw up.

He pulled back. "But it was nothing like the feeling of knocking out the Finisher and carving him open while he lay there, helpless and drugged, unable to remember a thing that happened to him."

Zephyr emptied the contents of her stomach to the side, shaking with the rage that filled her body. This monster had destroyed Alpha, her, and countless other women. She'd met the women he called whores, spent time with them, befriended them. Alpha's mother had been one of them. They were *people* and he'd slaughtered them like they were worthless.

She swallowed, focusing on her sister. Okay, they had to find a way out. She knew no one might be looking for her for a while, not with Morana injured, unless she somehow managed to get help. Even if they were looking, they might not find them soon enough. They had to rely on themselves.

"But before I hand you over, Zenny." Hector licked the edge of his blade. "I need to have a taste, after waiting so long." He took the knife to Zen's top, ripping one side off her shoulder. She gasped, and Zephyr struggled.

"Get the fuck away from her, or I swear to god—"

Her threats went unheard.

He untied Zenith, pushing her down on the floor, and her sister was paralyzed, like a deer in the headlights.

Zephyr held her stare, sobbing but keeping it together for her sake. "Fight him, Zen. He's weak. He's a fucking coward. You're stronger than this. Fight him, baby."

Her words broke whatever daze her sister had been in. It triggered something in her. Zephyr saw her look change, determination filling her face as she began to push back, catching Hector off-guard. Seems he wasn't used to women fighting back, especially not if he blackmailed them with their freedom.

Zen somehow wriggled out from under Hector's grip and ran to the chair she'd been tied to. Picking it up, she smashed it over his head.

He went down.

Breathing heavily, she took the knife from his side and ran to Zephyr, slicing through the zip ties with trembling hands. Free of her bonds, Zephyr jumped up and hugged her, feeling Zen's arms tight around her, both their bodies shaking.

"Let's get out of here before he wakes up."

She tugged her sister out.

They both ran through the shack, out onto the abandoned pier, trying to figure out where to go. There were no lights, no boats in the area, no sign of life.

"That way," Zen pointed to the road. "This is where Alpha came to meet the guy. There's a road there. We might find help."

They both started to run toward the road, both panting, Zephyr's muscles sore and aching, and she doubted her sister was in any better shape. Chests heaving, both breathing hard, they kept going. Almost at the turn, a shot rang out.

Flinching, Zephyr increased her speed, only to feel her sister's hand slip out of hers.

She stopped running to see what had held her back.

And everything inside her *froze*.

Zen stood at a spot, looking down at the blood on her hands, a large dark patch forming over her stomach. She looked up at Zephyr, her eyes wide, her beautiful face pale and scrunched in pain, before her legs crumpled.

"No."

Everything stilled.

Zephyr fell down on her knees at her side, pulling her sister into her arms. "No, no, no, no, no! Zen. Look at me, just breathe with me, you'll be okay, it's nothing. Shhhh—"

Sobs wracked her as she felt her sister trembling, similar tears on her face.

"It's ... it's so cold, Zee." Her sister's teeth chattered, her body shivering violently.

Zephyr gathered her tighter into her arms. "I'm here, baby." She hiccupped, tears endlessly pouring down her face and dropping on her sister's slackening body. "You'll be okay. Everything will be okay. Help is on the way."

Zen gave a quivering smile, her eyes going slightly hazy. "Liar. I love you, Zee. You're ... the best ... sister ... I could've ... hoped ... for."

Zephyr shook her head, her hands finding the blood coming out of her sister's stomach. "Don't you say goodbye! Zen. Please. Stay here."

Zen's hand came to her face, bloody and shaking, her eyes fluttering close.

Zephyr shook her, voice breaking. "Zen. Zenny. Hang in there. Stay with me, please. We'll get out of here."

They wouldn't. The place was abandoned, there were no cars on the street and no way to contact anybody. Helpless, in pain, Zephyr screamed, holding her sister to her chest, not knowing what to do.

Zen was just unconscious from the blood loss. That was it. Somehow, they'd get to a hospital and everything would be okay. Someway, she'd find a way.

Something moved in the periphery of her vision. Zephyr looked to see a man emerging from the shadows, his face hidden under his hood as he bent down next to them.

"Where did he go?"

She recognized his voice, the same man who'd given her the envelope in Tenebrae.

Hope blossomed in her heart.

"Please help her," she begged him, her voice a mess with her tears. "Please. I'm begging you. Please. Please. Help my sister."

She saw a gloved hand reach for her sister's neck, checking her pulse.

Of course, it would be there. Slow, but there.

"I'm sorry."

No.

No.

No.

No.

She shook her head. "No."

Shaking her sister, Zephyr checked her pulse. Nothing.

"Zen, baby, c'mon, answer me. Zen. *Zen!*"

Agony, nothing like she'd ever known before, stabbed her heart, splintering it, scarring it, a piece forever gone with the sister she'd loved more than life. Zephyr wailed in her pain, sobbing and sobbing and sobbing, until everything went black.

CHAPTER 31

ALPHA

Hector had gone missing.

It was a good thing or Alpha would have sliced him up and strung his insides around the city. The rage he felt simmered inside him, tempered only by the pang of loss as he looked down at Zenith's body in the morgue. Though he'd known her briefly, his sister-in-law had been a light, and he could feel the loss left by her absence.

"It's her," he identified her for official purposes, his voice gruff, and walked out of the room. His eye burned, the itch behind his eye patch intensifying. He fisted his hands and inhaled deeply.

He fucking hated hospitals. They brought back ugly, ugly memories of his childhood, of the time he'd spent trying to save his mother. But he couldn't be anywhere else at the moment, not with Zephyr inside sedated, not with Morana in trauma recovery from blood loss, not with Zenith, beautiful Zenith, gray in a freezer.

In a single day, his world had tilted upside down. His closest friend had been his biggest enemy, his family had gone missing, and this loss . . .

Morana had somehow, even injured and losing blood, managed to call Tristan long enough to tell him what had happened while on her way to the hospital. Alpha had seen the usually aloof man completely go feral on his way to the hospital, while he himself had turned the city upside down trying to find his wife and her sister. And then he'd gotten a call from an unknown number, an accented voice telling him they were at the hospital too.

One day she'd been at the hospital, and he'd killed more of his men in that duration than he had in years. Anyone who'd been found associated with Hector's crimes had been eradicated. Victor had been found knocked out in his car, completely oblivious to what his brother had done. He was perhaps the only one more enraged than Alpha was.

A car screeched to a stop. Alpha breathed out through his nose, watching as his in-laws rushed out of the vehicle he'd sent for them, both their faces confused and horrified and disbelieving of the storm that had swept their lives.

"What the police said . . ." Zephyr's father swallowed. "Is it true?"

He wished he didn't have to do this. Alpha nodded.

A palm struck his face, the slap heating his cheek. Her mother. He took it quietly.

"It's all because of you." She slapped him again, crying. "You destroyed our lives. I'll never forgive you. All because of you!"

Zephyr's father held her mother back, and she turned to him, sobbing uncontrollably.

Alpha couldn't even imagine the pain she must have been going through, losing a child she'd loved so much, the other in the hospital. It was one of the reasons he stayed silent and didn't tell her that The

Syndicate would've come for Zenith, with or without him. She had been marked from the moment she escaped them. It was still hard for him to wrap his head around the fact that she had been one of the missing girls, had been the real daughter of Gabriel Vitalio.

Fuck, it was a mess.

His in-laws went upstairs to where Zephyr was being kept, and he leaned against the wall outside, looking up at the stars, trying to understand where everything had gone wrong. Was her mother right? Could Zenith have been alive had she not come under Hector's radar due to his proximity or would he have found her regardless through SLF? How many other people were hiding through the organization that he didn't know about? Was running it worth the cost of innocent life?

"Hector has gone underground." The voice from his side startled him slightly.

Shadow Man.

Fucking moved like a shadow. But Alpha owed him now. "Thanks for bringing my wife back."

There was a pause. "Will she live?"

"Yeah."

"I'm sorry I couldn't help her sister."

"Me too."

Another pause. "You should've sought me out sooner. I would've led you to him."

Something in his tone made Alpha's eye twitch. "Why were you following him in the first place? What's your interest?"

A lighter flickered, showing just the line of the hand holding it. He didn't think the guy would answer.

"He broke my toy."

Vague.

"Go to your wife, Finisher," the man said. "And brace yourself. It's just begun."

With that ominous warning, before Alpha could say anything else, the presence from his side was gone.

Rubbing his chest, Alpha went inside to the private room corridor.

Zephyr was in one of the rooms, and since her parents were visiting, he stayed outside in the corridor. Dante sat there too, on one of the hospital chairs, leaning forward, his elbows on his knees, his face somber. Amara was at the compound with the kids, not wanting to leave them alone for too long in a new place or bring them to the hospital. Tristan stood against another room's door, his eyes never straying from the glass that let him look at Morana inside.

Alpha had seen her, strung up with tubes going into her body, not looking good. But the doctor had reassured them that she'd make a recovery.

His wife, on the other hand, would never recover. He had seen firsthand how close the two sisters had been, and just remembering Zenith's warmth made his throat tighten with emotion. The world was a darker place without her.

"You okay?" Dante asked him. Alpha didn't know. He was still in a rage, juggling with both betrayal and loss, and knowing he'd have to push it all aside to be there for Zephyr when she woke up.

He shrugged, folding his arms across his chest, looking at Tristan. "I'm sorry Morana got hurt in my city."

He saw the other man's jaw clench, but he didn't say anything, just stared inside where the girl lay.

Zephyr's parents came out of the other room. Her mother looked at him with such hatred he felt it in her bones, and he didn't blame her for it. Her father stopped at his side. "Send Zephyr home with us to recover. We have one daughter left, and we don't want to lose her too."

Alpha tamped down the urge to refuse immediately. He didn't want her to leave. He never wanted her to leave. Tasting the fear of the last day, tasting what a life without her could be like . . . she gave him meaning. She was his lifeblood.

"If she wants to come to you, I will bring her. You have my word." It cost him to say that, but he did, not knowing what she would need, if she, too, would blame him for the loss.

Her father gave a nod, his face moving with emotions, and took her mother with him.

Dante slapped him on the shoulder, his eyes serious. "Men in our world don't find love, brother. Don't let it go. Whatever you need, I'm here."

It moved him, Dante offering that. And he would need help, with his second gone.

He inhaled deeply and entered his wife's room. She was asleep on the bed, after having been sedated, her face tensed even in her unconscious state.

Alpha sat down beside her, taking her small, soft hand in his, and felt his eye burning, wetness sliding down his face into his beard.

He let everything crash down on him, everything that had been building and building in the last day, last month, last decade, being in the hospital and the memories it brought—losing his friend to betrayal, realizing he had been the one to blind him, forgetting Zephyr and still not getting those memories, losing Zenith and almost losing his wife. Everything crashed on him, and there, holding her hand while she slept, he cried in a hospital after twenty years.

PRE-EPILOGUE

ZEPHYR

She woke up in the hospital, her first memory that of Zen throwing a pillow at her, laughing with a wide smile that lit up her eyes, telling her not to get herself killed. The next memory crashed in, Zen on the ground in her arms, a trembling smile on her lips, the light leaving her eyes.

Zephyr stared up at the ceiling, blinking, tears falling down the side of her face, unable to give thought to the hole in her heart. Sometimes, grief was like that—thoughtless, wordless, soundless. Sometimes, it was inexplicable, being pumped out by a cracked heart, infusing in the blood that went to every part of the body, mixing with the cells until it became as regular as breathing.

She looked to her side, to see her husband looking at her with quietness, the loss she felt in her bones reflected in his single eye. She clutched his hand, holding tightly, and he gave her his strength, letting her take whatever she needed.

After a few moments of letting herself grieve, she croaked out, "Is she ..."

The look on his face was answer enough.

Tears slid down her face. "Was she ... did she escape The Syndicate?"

"Yeah."

Oh god, what had she endured? Her baby sister.

"Do my parents ...?"

He gave her a nod.

Zephyr felt her nose twinge, her lips quivering. He got up from the chair and came to her side, pulling her up into his arms, and the floodgates opened again. She sobbed into his chest and wept, her wails leaving her body in the remembered pain of holding her sister's body, seeing her last breath, and he held her through it all, his strength a rock against the storm within her.

They had the funeral after a week.

Her baby sister was laid in the ground, Zen's family and friends and colleagues and all the lives she'd touched with her light, attending the event. Morana sat on the side, her arm in a sling, with Tristan at her side, and seeing the other woman just made her question so many things about her sister. Morana probably knew, because there was a pain in her eyes every time they looked at each other.

Her parents clung to her, but barely spared a glance at her husband. She knew they blamed him, but knowing what she knew, it wasn't his burden to carry. Zenith had escaped something evil, built a good life for herself, and it had caught up to her. Alpha couldn't have seen it coming. No one could have, except possibly Zenith herself.

Her sister was gone, and her secrets with her. They'd never know what she'd run from and what she'd left behind.

The funeral had taxed her, in more ways than she'd ever been. It felt like her lungs weren't getting enough air, and no matter how much she tried, they felt tight and heavy and short of breath. The only time she felt she could catch a breath was when she let herself fall into her husband's arms, and he held her, letting her borrow all his strength.

Taking a sip of her wine, Zephyr sat on the deck, looking out at the forest laid out beyond her, all three dogs around her chair. Since she'd come back home, they'd sensed her grief, and all of them, even Baron, had been near her with their compassion since.

She heard everyone's voices inside, talking about The Syndicate and how to proceed, and she was torn. One part of her wanted to know everything, wanted to know what her sister had run from, and get her vendetta against the assholes who had hunted her down. For the first time in her life, Zephyr felt capable of taking another life. They had told her Hector had escaped, and she knew if she saw him again, she would kill him.

Another part, the larger part, didn't want to know anything. It wanted to remember Zen as she'd been, with her big heart and beautiful soul and selfless way of loving. She didn't want to know if her sister had done something bad to escape whatever hell she'd been in. It didn't want to know why someone had hunted her down the way they had. Her baby sister had been the first person she'd loved unconditionally, and she always wanted to remember her as that.

But she also wanted the truth. As much as she wanted to hide, this was her world now, and it had taken her sister, and she wanted to know the facts.

Pushing to her feet, she padded in, the dogs on her heels.

Dante and Amara sat on one couch, Tristan and Morana on another, and her husband sat alone in the armchair. His golden, powerful gaze came to her as she entered, and he held out his hand, calling her to him. She quietly walked to his side, settling as he pulled her on his lap.

"Where are the kids?" she asked, looking around and seeing the absence of chaos.

"Upstairs, sleeping," Amara answered in her soft, husky voice. "Leah is staying with them."

Zephyr nodded, a seed in her doubting if Leah was trustworthy. If any of them except her husband were trustworthy. She didn't know if she could trust anyone anymore.

Alpha rubbed her back, soothing her tumultuous thoughts.

"She was Gabriel's daughter." Morana swallowed, her eyes visibly misting, coming to lock on Zephyr's. "She was the real me. And I always wondered what happened to her, you know? If she was okay. And even though she'd gone, I just want you to know I'm really glad she had a good life, that she had you. She was loved, and she knew that."

Zephyr felt her throat tighten, her grip flexing around her wine glass that she carried with her. Alpha's arms squeezed her softly, reminding her she wasn't alone.

"That day, when you were staring at her ..." Zephyr trailed off, remembering that day so vividly.

"She seemed familiar," Morana completed, leaning into Tristan's side. The man hadn't left her alone since she'd been discharged from the hospital.

"The Shadow Man," Zephyr shared. "He was there that night. He came after ... I don't remember, but I think he dropped us at the hospital."

Her husband nodded. "He was following Hector for his own reasons. That's how he knew about the murders, I think."

Dante quipped from the other couch, "I've put Vin on Hector. We'll know who he made the deal with soon."

"His brother is already looking for him," Alpha mentioned. Victor, she'd been told, had raged after finding out what his brother had done. He had gone hunting him down. Hector was a dead man.

"Is Vin trustworthy?" she asked.

"Very," Amara replied, surprisingly.

"The Shadow Man warned me this was just the beginning," her husband informed them all. She heard Morana's breath catch, Amara swallowing at the ominous words.

Silence fell over them, all of them consumed by their own thoughts.

Restless, Zephyr stood up, going back to the deck, the dogs again at her heels, not leaving her alone.

She looked out at the view, everything looking dark and bleak, and wondered what the future would bring them.

A presence came behind her, before strong arms wrapped around her. Zephyr sunk back into the embrace of her one-eyed beast, the only solid, real thing in her topsy-turvy world right now. Through the days, he'd been her mountain, solid, impenetrable, immovable. She had raged upon him, knowing he wouldn't be shaken by an avalanche of emotions.

"We'll be okay, won't we, handsome?" she whispered softly, almost fearful to hope for better.

His arms tightened around her, and he dropped a kiss on her head. "The gray won't be forever, rainbow."

No, it wouldn't be.

Hector was in the wind, The Syndicate was only beginning, The Shadow Man was unknown, and the future was uncertain.

But in the arms of the man she'd loved for years, would love for years, Zephyr felt herself being able to breathe.

The gray won't be forever.

I hope you enjoyed the journey in the Dark Verse with Alpha and Zephyr. They have another bigger epilogue that falls after the timeline of the last book in the series. As a continuous series, this is their happily-for-now. You will see them and the rest of the characters in the final book.

Turn the page for a glimpse at Book 5.

BONUS

HIM

He sat in the shadows watching her.

The strobing lights in the auction club went over the stage, three women in translucent robes standing in the center. He didn't look at the ones on the sides, his heterochromatic eyes on the one in the middle. He studied her, the way she blinked at her feet, her face dead to the world. The only sign of her life remained her hair, hair that had grabbed his attention since that first time.

He pretended to sip on his drink, wondering who there was going to die by his hands tonight. They all knew never to bid on her, a trail of bodies of her suitors sending a loud message. Yet, someone always did. Someone always tempted their fates. And someone always died. Last time, it had been a sniper bullet through the brain, the poor shit's blood splattering across her pale skin. This time, he'd make it more personal. Maybe douse them in gasoline while she watched.

As though feeling his gaze, she looked up. Her eyes swept the crowd of well-dressed men, going straight to the shadowed corners, knowing that's where he stayed. He liked that.

He saw the moment she saw his silhouette, a mix of hatred and betrayal etched on her face for everyone to see. Her hands fisted at her sides. His obsession deepened.

A man from the front bid on her and won. Her flame hair whipped behind her as she left the stage.

He followed, knowing who he would kill tonight.

She was his toy to play with, after all.

The Annihilator - A Dark Obsession Romance, the final book in the Dark Verse series.

ACKNOWLEDGMENTS

This book was tough for me, not to write but to edit. As the second last book of this series, I had a hard time deciding what to keep in this one and save for the next, which made what had been a long rough draft a shorter book. It was a journey, especially with Zephyr because she experiences things so vulnerably, and it's not easy to open your heart like that and get hurt.

I want to thank a few people for making this book and my writing journey what it is.

To my readers, the ones who've been with me since the beginning, on the Dark Verse train with Tristan and Morana, you're my OGs. It's incredible how you've been on the ride with this series even after two years. To my new readers who've just hopped on, your excitement is infectious! Thank you for giving me such joy and strength to persevere, especially with my debut series. This will always have the most special place in my heart.

Second, to my parents – thank you for always having my back and believing in me even when the chips are down. I am grateful to be yours every single day. Thank you.

The book community that has showered me with such love and kindness. To all the bloggers and bookstragrammers, artists, editors, photographers, friends I've made, thank you. Your love and your generosity means the world to me. You talk about my babies, and your word of mouth has been the most incredible experience for me to witness. Thank you so much for everything!

And to Nelly. You're my hero. There will never be enough words in my heart to thank you for lending your talent and vision to my stories. Thank you for giving my words the perfect visuals and for tolerating my bizarre requests. I love you.

To Rachel, thank you for dusting off the cobwebs when I got squinty. I appreciate you!

To Zainab, for being such a fantastic set of eyes on this, and for helping me out absolutely last minute. I appreciate you!

To Emily, for being a rockstar of a PA and keeping everything organized for me!

To my friends. I don't reply to messages for days, and I'm zoned out most times, and you still love me. Thank you for putting up with me.

All of you make my world a better place.

Most importantly, I want to thank you, the one reading this, for picking up my book and choosing to read me. If you've made it this far, I'm eternally grateful to you. I hope you enjoyed it but even if you didn't, thank you for choosing it. I appreciate you taking the time so much. Please consider leaving a review before jumping into your next bookish world.

Thank you so much!

CONNECT WITH RUNYX

Newsletter: https://runyx.kit.com/newsletter

Reader Group: https://www.facebook.com/groups/runyx/

Facebook: https://www.facebook.com/authorrunyx

Instagram: https://www.instagram.com/authorrunyx/

Website: https://runyxwrites.com/

Turn the page for an exclusive extract of ENIGMA ...

DEATH SMILES...

Unknown Girl, Mortimer University

The girl stood on the edge of the cliff.

There was no moonlight for anyone to witness her demise, not a concerned soul around to make her question herself, not a sound beyond the sea and the whispers of her own moral decay.

Oh, she was of sound mind and judgment. Yet, she stood on the cliff on that moonless night, walking to her own destruction, an invisible gun of her own making to her head.

Maybe, things would have been different, could have been different, if she just had the courage. The world thought she was brave. They would remember her as such. There was nothing to indicate otherwise. Would this be a murder or a suicide or an accident? Would she become the girl on the news pushed by invisible hands, or a girl who jumped of her own free will? Or maybe, they would speculate a tragic fall of a girl who wandered too close to the edge. Literally, metaphorically, who knew?

The wind whistled around her, blowing her dress up and whipping her hair over her face. To anyone watching, she would have painted an ethereal, haunting picture.

Picture. Photographs. Memories.

She had so many of them.

She didn't want to stand on that cliff.

But she had to. There was no other choice, not for her.

Not when they were watching.

And they were always watching.

Even as she stood weighing her decision, her choices, her mortality.

Even as she stepped closer to the edge, her body shaking, resisting the directives of her mind.

Even as she closed her eyes and took the plunge, the wind rushing in her ears, the silence shattered by her scream piercing for a split second before cutting off abruptly.

They were watching as she lay on the dark sand on a dark night, and died.

DISCOVER THE MOST LOVED MAFIA ROMANCE SERIES

evermore

Love, spice and sleepless nights.

The hottest new romance publisher at Penguin Random House UK.

Prepare for excessive swooning, devouring love stories and dangerously high standards for your own happily-ever-afters.

Proceed with caution... and an open heart.

FOLLOW US ON SOCIALS:

 @evermorebooksuk

On a station platform, with nothing to read,
and a four-hour train journey stretching ahead of him...

That's where the story began for Penguin founder Allen Lane.
With only 'shabby reprints of shoddy novels' on offer,
he resolved to make better books for readers everywhere.

By the time his train pulled into London, the idea was formed.
He would bring the best writing, in stylish and affordable
formats, to everyone. His books would be sold in bookstores,
stationers and tobacconists, for no more than the price
of a ten-pack of cigarettes.

And on every book would be a Penguin, a bird with a certain
'dignified flippancy', and a friendly invitation to anyone who
wished to spend their time reading.

In 1935, the first ten Penguin paperbacks were published.
Just a year later, three million Penguins had made their
way onto our shelves.

Reading was changed forever.

—

A lot has changed since 1935, including Penguin, but in the
most important ways we're still the same. We still believe that
books and reading are for everyone. And we still believe that
whether you're seeking an afternoon's escape, a vigorous debate
or a soothing bedtime story, all possibilities open with a book.

Whoever you are, whatever you're looking for,
you can find it with Penguin.